Slave Girl

Slave Girl

JACKIE FRENCH

HarperTrophyCanada™
An imprint of HarperCollinsPublishersLtd

Published by Harper*Trophy*Canada™, an imprint of HarperCollins Publishers Ltd.

First published in Australia as *Rover* by Angus & Robertson, an imprint of HarperCollins Publishers: 2005
First published in Canada as *Rover* by Harper*Trophy*Canada™, an imprint of HarperCollins Publishers Ltd, in a hardcover edition: 2007.
This trade paperback edition: 2008

HarperTrophyCanada™ is a trademark of HarperCollins Publishers.

HarperCollins books may be purchased for educational, business, or sales promotional use through our Special Markets Department.

HarperCollins Publishers Ltd
2 Bloor Street East, 20th Floor
Toronto, Ontario, Canada
M4W 1A8

www.harpercollins.ca

Library and Archives Canada Cataloguing in Publication

French, Jackie
Slave girl / Jackie French.

Previously published under title: Rover.
ISBN 978-1-55468-093-1

1. Freydís Eiríksdottir, fl. 1014—Juvenile fiction. 2. Vikings—Juvenile fiction. 3. America—Discovery and exploration—Norse—Juvenile fiction. I. Title.

PZ7.F866R68 2008   J823'.914   C2007-906401-9

HC 9 8 7 6 5 4 3 2 1

Printed and bound in the United States

To Lily,
a dog of total loyalty
and perfect manners

ICELAND

NORWAY

SWEDEN

ENGLAND

ATLANTIC OCEAN

GREENLAND

Bratthalid

NEW FOUNDLAND

NORTH AMERICA

- - - - possible route taken by Freydis to Vinland

·········· route from Denmark to Bratthalid, in which Hekja was captured

x x x x x Hekja and Hikki's run

Chapter 1

THE NAMING

When a witch gives you a True Name, it sticks.

The witch was called Tikka, and she lived at the foot of the tallest mountain on the island. It was Tikka you'd go to for spider webs to staunch a cut or crushed black snails to cure a spider bite.

The witch had come to the chief's hut that day because the chief's youngest son had cut his foot on a clamshell. Even the witch came when the chief ordered.

He wasn't much of a chief, just lord of a cluster of stone huts that stood by the bay. Nor was his hut much either. It was round, like the other huts in the village, dug deep down into the rocky soil, so the lower half walls were dirt and the upper parts were rocks all fitted together, with a cowhide across the doorway and a smoke hole above the fireplace.

The chief had sent his oldest son, Bran, to fetch the witch, and the witch had hobbled down from her hut and had bound up the boy's foot with a scrap of soft leather dipped in crushed shell and her own urine, muttering all the time so that the chief and his wife would think that she was wise.

Once the wound was bound and the boy had stopped snivelling, the witch accepted a horn of ale and a barley cake with cheese and looked around the hut.

A witch doesn't ask for a fee. People give what they like, but if you don't give her what she wants a storm will blow up next time your man is out fishing and the sea will have his bones. Or that was what the witch hoped you would think.

There wasn't much to see inside the hut – just the peat fire glowing and the iron pot simmering with stew for the evening, the fish hung up from the rafters to dry, and the chief's fine hunting dog[1] with all her little puppies crawling round her lying in the corner by the hearth.

"Would you name the puppies for us, Tikka?" asked the chief's wife.

Old Tikka laughed and picked up one of the puppies. It growled, and tried to lick her nose. "I'll call this one Courage," she said.

"That's the dog for me then," said Bran boastfully. He was the tallest boy in the village, and the strongest, with thick brown plaits to his waist. His father had promised him the pick of the litter.

The witch picked up another puppy and held her up so she could see her in the light from the open doorway. "Ah, a fine bitch this," she said approvingly. "I'll call her Faithful Long Legs. May she always…"

That's when it happened.

It was the smallest pup of all, the one with the fattest stomach and the longest ears, feet the size of barley cakes and a nose that looked like it had been stubbed on the

---

[1] Please see notes on page 280

floor. He'd been suckling his mother long after the others finished, and there was milk dribbled all down his front.

He toddled a step or two, just far enough so he didn't widdle in the bed, then crouched and let fly.

The witch let out a yell and lifted up her foot, all wet and dripping.

Bran chuckled and so did the chief, though he stopped when Tikka glared at him. Even the chief wouldn't cross a hag. His wife raced up with some soft cowhide and mopped Tikka's foot. The witch put the bitch down, and picked up the other pup by the scruff of his neck.

"Arf arf arf," he barked, sending a spray of milk all over the witch's face.

Tikka stared at the puppy thoughtfully. "As for you," she said, "I'll call you..." She grinned, showing her long white teeth. "I'll call you Riki Snarfari," she decided. And with that she put him down.

Bran let out a yell. "*Riki Snarfari?*[2] That pup will never be a mighty rover! He's the laziest pup of the litter!"

The witch held his eye. "Are you arguing with me, boy?"

Bran subsided. "No, Tikka," he muttered.

Riki Snarfari, the Mighty Rover, crawled back to his mother's side and tried to hide his head under her warmth. He peered out at the witch, who was filling up her second cup of ale and accepting the best of the barley cakes.

The witch saw him peering at her and laughed.

Chapter 2

HEKJA

Hekja sat on the rock by the shore and let her eyes follow the clouds as they floated on the far horizon. Pa had once sung a song about a land of cloud, where fish swam through the air and jewels grew on the trees.

Hekja wasn't sure what jewels were – a type of cheese, perhaps – for Pa had died before she could ask him. But every time the clouds hung on the horizon, Hekja dreamt that they were the island Pa had told her about. *One day*, she thought, *when I am married, I'll ask my husband to sail his boat out to the horizon. We'll step out onto the cloud land and pick the jewels...*

Hekja smiled to herself, and picked up her cockle[3] stick again. At this rate the tide would be in before she had her basket half full.

Then she saw the puppy.

He was the smallest dog Hekja had ever seen. He had the fattest belly too. It almost dragged along the pebbles as the puppy stumbled from the chief's hut down to the shore.

Hekja put down her bag of shellfish and watched the pup toddle across the salty, damp stones, sniffing as he went. And then he found it. A dead seal pup, half buried in a drift of seaweed, with the waves lapping just below.

None of the village folk ate seals – too many of their families, they said, were descended from seal ancestors. Which meant that rich and meaty as this seal was, no one had come to eat it.

Hekja watched as the puppy nuzzled at the seal, trying to find a way in to the good meat. But the furry sealskin was too tough for his small jaws and tiny milk teeth. He was almost ready to give up when he found a soft patch, where the skin had rotted through…

"Craaaarrrrk!"

The pup paid no attention.

"Carwwkkk!" The seagull was closer now, and angry. It wanted that seal for itself.

"Grrr," snarled the puppy warningly, lifting up his tiny nose.

"Keeerk!" shrieked the bird. It flew at the pup and pecked his eye.

The puppy screamed. The bird pecked again, this time at the pup's leg and rounded stomach, and then once more at his eyes. The pup tried to stumble away. He couldn't run, for one leg dragged behind. Nor could he see because of the blood.

Hekja grabbed a stone and threw it as hard as she could. "Get away from him!" The bird gave a startled squawk and flapped away. The puppy cowered, whimpering, by the drifts of seaweed.

Hekja ran towards him, her shellfish forgotten, and picked him up carefully. Blood welled from above his eye and his torn leg dangled limply. The puppy yelped with pain.

"Let me see!" It was the chief. He grabbed the pup by the scruff of the neck. The puppy yelped louder as the chief's hand pulled at his injured leg.

"He's lamed and blinded. Stupid animal, he's good for nothing now." The chief's voice was angry. The pup had been worth a good calf, or more. "He's not worth feeding. There's only one thing for him… " said the chief as his hands closed around the puppy's throat.

"No!" Hekja's voice was high and fierce. "You can't kill him!"

The chief stared at her. "He's mine. I can do what I like with him."

"I'll look after him! Please! I'll make him better!"

"Pa?" It was Bran. He must have been watching from the hut. "Let Hekja have the pup if she wants it. It's no good to us."

The chief paused, then dumped the puppy in Hekja's arms.

The pup had stopped whimpering now and was limp and still. Was he dead already?

The chief shrugged. "Keep him then. He's done for anyway." He turned and stamped off up the shore.

Chapter 3

THE RESCUE

Hekja ran along the shore to the hut she shared with her mother. Once there had been five of them in the hut. But Hekja's brothers had been drowned when a storm raged across the islands, and Pa's back had been broken when he'd fallen from the cliff when the men were collecting eggs. So now there was just Hekja and her ma.

Ma sat in the doorway, grinding the barley flour for their meal. She stared at the bloody bundle in Hekja's arms. "What in all the islands is that?!" she exclaimed.

"It's a puppy! He's hurt. Ma, please! Please let me keep him!"

Her ma stood and peered at the puppy, then shook her head. "He's hurt too bad, love."

"I'll look after him! I'll make him well!"

Her ma picked up the quern⁴ of barley flour and began to mix it with water to be baked on the hearthstone for their dinner. "He'll die and break your heart," she said softly. "And even if he lives, what would we feed him? Barley bread and fish heads? There is little enough for ourselves."

Hekja stroked the puppy silently. Her ma gazed at her without speaking. Finally she said, "You know what it was like with your pa, after his accident. It's not easy, love, tending someone you love, watching them die."

"I know," whispered Hekja. "But I can't just leave him. I have to try to make him well."

Hekja's ma bit her lip. Then she nodded. "Alright. You can try."

"Could you fetch Tikka for him? Please, Ma!"

The woman's voice was firm now. "Tikka would need rewarding. I'll not be asking her to come all this way, just for a pup that won't last the night."

"Then I'll take him to her myself!"

"Hekja, love… " pleaded her ma. Then she bit her lip. "If you will."

It was cold outside. Hekja hugged the puppy close to keep him warm and began to run.

Hekja was good at running. She'd had a lot of practice, chasing the cow as it nosed after pasture, and running down to the fishing boats to beg the scraps from other families who still had strong men to fish for them. Sometimes she ran along the pebbles of the bay when there was no one else to see, feeling the foam lap at her toes, just for the joy of running, to pretend that if she ran fast enough she could catch the sunset.

But this run was different. There was no time to enjoy the wind in her face today. The scent of the sea changed to cattle smells and heather. The puppy whimpered in her arms and then was still.

Tikka's hut sat by the burn[5] that bubbled down from the snow-melt great mountain. The witch lived by herself as long as Hekja could remember, picking her herbs by moonlight when their magic was the strongest, muttering her curses if the men forgot to bring her share of fish, or if the chief was late bringing his bull to her cow. Today the witch's cow was grazing across the burn, near to calving. It stared at Hekja then bent its head to the grass.

Hekja paused by the cowhide door. She'd have just called and gone in to any other hut. But no one entered Tikka's uninvited. Hekja caught her breath then called as politely as she could, "Tikka, please, it's Hekja. I have a puppy. He's hurt."

The tattered cowhide moved and the witch's face emerged. She looked at the pup and grinned. No other woman the witch's age had all her teeth, but Tikka's were long and white. The other girls said Tikka had charmed them from a wolf, up on the great mountain.

"Ah, that one is it?" said Tikka, the toothy grin pushing the wrinkles on her face into new patterns. "Riki Snarfari, the Mighty Rover. I knew that he'd be trouble."

"Riki Snarfari?" Hekja glanced at the pup doubtfully. He didn't look like a mighty anything.

"Named him myself. It's a True Name too." The witch stepped out of her hut, bringing with her the scent of fish oil and old herbs, and just a breath of barley beer. She lifted the pup's nose then twisted his leg. The puppy howled in pain.

"Will he die?" whispered Hekja.

"Yes," said Tikka. And then she cackled, just like a witch should, and the smell of herbs and beer became stronger. "But not for many years yet! Bring him inside, girl, and let's see to him."

Hekja hesitated. "I have nothing for you."

"You have your legs, girl," said Tikka. "You can take my cow with your mother's up the mountain in summer. Now bring him in here."

It was dark in the hut, with the hide across the doorway blocking out the spring sunlight. A pot bubbled on the smouldering turf fire underneath the smoke hole. Hekja blinked at it. "Those look like… snails…"

The witch peered at her then cackled again. "Most girls would scream at a pot of snails. Nothing wrong with snails, girl. Cook them with their shells and mush the lot and eat them once a week and you'll have teeth as good as mine, no matter how many babies your husband gives you."

"The girls said you have wolf teeth." Hekja could have grabbed the words back, but the witch just grinned, her white teeth glowing in the dimness. "I'm happy they think so, so don't go telling them otherwise. But they're my own, every one of them. How'd I get wolf teeth to stay in? Now, let's see this pup. How did you end up with him?"

"I rescued him. The chief said I could have him."

"Generous. Bet he'll wish he hadn't when the pup gets bigger."

Hekja felt her heart pound louder than the bubbling burn. "Then he'll recover?"

Tikka nodded. She laid the puppy on the stone bench and he whimpered with the cold and the pain of being moved. "The eye's bad," she muttered. "Nothing we can do about that except help it heal." She bent down and sniffed Snarf's blood-stained stomach. "Can't smell guts, so nothing's punctured. That's how you can tell how bad a wound is, girl. If you can smell guts then there's no hope."

"Will he be able to walk?" said Hekja anxiously.

"He might limp a bit. But his bones are still soft because he's young, so they should heal. Aye, he'll recover, if you care for him enough."

"I will," promised Hekja.

The witch stirred up the turf fire. She poured the boiled snails into a wood jar and refilled the pot with water from the bucket by the door. Next, she selected herbs from the long lines drying from the roof and threw them into the water to heat.

"See? You'll have to do this too." She thrust the herbs at Hekja's nose. "Smell! Think you can find those again?"

Hekja nodded. "Yes. That's wild garlic and that—"

"I know what they are, girl! As long as you do too. Now, cook them for as long as it takes to sing two verses of the 'Fisherman's Lament'. Wait for the potion to cool and wash him with it. Then mix the herbs with honey to cover up the wounds. You've got honey at home?"

Hekja shook her head. The witch sighed. "There's a pot of it behind the door. Take it. But this autumn you look out a hive, mind, and pay me back."

"I will," promised Hekja.

"Mind you don't burn him – the herbs should be hot. And you bandage him like this, just firm enough to hold the herbs. Change the dressing twice a day," instructed Tikka, "until the wounds start to scab, then leave them clear."

"What about the magic?" asked Hekja timidly. "Don't I have to say words over him or something?"

Tikka laughed. It was a real laugh, not her witch's cackle. "The power's in the herbs, not me. Magic is good to trick the foolish into doing what they should have done if they'd had sense in the first place. Though sometimes…" The witch paused suddenly, and frowned. "Hekja…"

"Yes, Tikka?"

"Tell your ma this dog will be useful. He'll be worth the feeding. Tell her you'll be needing him."

"To help watch the cows?"

"For that too," said the witch cryptically. "Now be off with you."

Hekja nodded. She lifted the pup carefully and kissed his nose. "Come on, Riki Snarfari, my little Snarf. You're going to get better now. We're going home." She carried Snarf out into the fresh, cold air and ran back to the hut by the shore.

Chapter 4

THE PROBLEM OF FOOD

That night Hekja slept on her bracken bed with Snarf beside her. She kept him warm with her cowhide cover, and when the pup whimpered she held him closer until he forgot about the pain.

The next morning she changed the bandages. The pup whined, especially when she pulled the herbs off and then put on more. But when she had finished he snuggled close, as though grateful for her warmth.

Her ma peered through the door. She'd been dragging the wood plough through the rocky soil outside the hut so they could plant the spring kale and barley seed. Normally Hekja would have helped, but today she was staying close to Snarf.

"How is he?"

"I think he's stronger," said Hekja hopefully. "Aren't you, Snarf?"

"Arf arf!" said the puppy weakly. Hekja laughed. "He knows his name!"

Her ma smiled. "Riki Snarfari! What a name for a pup like that! You should call him Cuddles, or Wimperwail."

Hekja shook her head stubbornly. "Tikka says his name is Riki Snarfari. She says it's a True Name and that he'll be useful."

Her ma opened her mouth to speak, then saw the happiness on Hekja's face and shut it again. Happiness came too rarely to the hut on the shore since their men had died. So she said instead, "You need to feed him something."

Hekja nodded. She put the puppy on her lap and held a handful of warm barley mash up to his nose. Snarf whined and held his nose away.

"He won't eat," said Hekja despairingly.

"He's too small, perhaps," said her ma. "He's forgotten how to lap, if he ever knew it. Here." She lifted Snarf's chin with one hand and gently edged the tips of two fingers in his mouth. A trickle of the barley mash was down his throat before he realised. "My gran showed me that for a poorly calf," said Hekja's ma. "You try it."

Snarf swallowed a few mouthfuls, then seemed to realise what was happening. He shut his jaws and tried to squirm away.

Hekja's ma shook her head. "Dogs like meat," she said quietly.

Hekja said nothing. The hut had no smoked legs of meat hanging from its rafters. Even fish was precious.

Then a shadow darkened the door.

"How is the pup doing?" It was the voice of the chief's son, Bran.

Hekja had caught him looking at her lately, when he thought she wasn't looking. Sometimes she looked at him as well. Nothing could ever come of it, she knew, even if she had been old enough to think of marriage. A chief's son should marry another chief's daughter, who could bring a herd of cattle and a year's worth of cheeses to her husband.

"He won't eat," said Hekja worriedly. "And we don't have any meat to give him."

Bran shrugged. "Too bad," he said carelessly. Then the light came through the door again and he was gone.

Snarf slept after that, with Hekja's hands stroking him, and her lap to keep him warm, while her ma went back to dig the barley field. Hekja was just trying to get the pup to take the barley sludge again when Bran reappeared. He thrust something through the door.

"Here. See if he'll eat that," he said. He was gone before Hekja could thank him.

Hekja looked at what he'd brought. It was a badger, limp and bloody.

Suddenly the pup lifted up his head. "Arf!" he announced weakly.

Hekja laughed. "You like the smell of badger meat, do you! Thank you!" she called to Bran. But there was no reply.

Hekja's ma cooked the badger with the barley, to make the meat go further. Hekja trickled the mush into Snarf's mouth, as she had done before. The pup ate reluctantly at first, and then began to gobble, as though he had realised he was hungry. Afterwards Hekja held him on her knee and scratched behind his ear, but carefully, so as not to disturb his wounds. And while she scratched she sang.

It was a song her father had taught her, and that his father had sung too, mending the fishing nets or at the summer feast. The villagers had said Pa's voice was so beautiful, even the seals came to shore to hear it. This was the first time Hekja had sung since he died.

Wind on the river,
Wind on the sea,
There the wind rests,
and my love rests with me.

Her ma smiled as she ground the barley in the quern for the night's barley cake. Then suddenly Snarf lifted up his nose.

"Hoooooooooowwwwwwwl!!!!!"

Hekja's ma laughed. "He's saying, 'No, this is how you sing properly!'"

Hekja looked down at the pup. He was so small and so earnest. She bent down to rub her nose on his. But by now the pup was nearly asleep.

Bran brought meat every few days after that. Hekja knew he must spend all his nights up on the great mountain, setting his snares for her, as well as going fishing with the men each day. But he just handed the bloody lumps to her through the door, as though the gift was nothing, and mumbled something, then was gone. One day there was hare and then a squirrel, and sometimes a puffin or a cod head or even scraps of venison from the chief's table.

Snarf grew stronger day by day. He ate barley cake now too, with cheese and sour butter and smoked fish, the same food that Hekja and her mother ate.

Before long he was well enough to limp after Hekja as she collected shellfish or seaweed, his fat belly almost dragging on the ground; nosing at the fish guts by the barrels that were dug into the pebbly shore and used to smoke the fish; bouncing at the waves; or digging in the village compost heap, stinking of rotten kale stems and dung.

When Hekja and her ma scratched the stony soil with their driftwood plough Snarf barked to keep the birds from the barley seed, or bounded round them while they dug the peat and spread it out to dry so it would burn.

And day by day Snarf's leg got better, so he hardly limped at all except when he was tired.

Sometimes Hekja felt the chief's eyes upon her as she threw driftwood for Snarf to chase on the stony shore. Snarf might limp, and his face was scarred, but he was still a valuable dog, worth three sacks of barley at least, or a cow.

But Snarf was Hekja's now.

The days grew longer. The men went after gulls' eggs, and this time no one fell from the cliffs as Hekja's father had, to lie crippled till he died. There were eggs enough for everyone, even for the hut on the shore. For weeks the whole village smelt of egg farts, and Snarf's belly looked round as an egg itself.

And then it was summer, the longer days eating up the night, the midges biting every bit of skin they could find. Above the village the great mountain turned from white to brown and then to green.

It was time to take the cattle up to pasture.

Chapter 5

✤

UP THE GREAT MOUNTAIN

Taking the cattle to pasture was a task for the girls of the village. The men and boys fished or hunted, or mended the fishing nets, and cut the turf for burning. The women dried the fish in long flapping lines outside the round stone huts, or smoked them; they planted the barley and the kale in the rocky soil, then ground the grain to flour for the barley cakes, made the barley beer[6] and collected shellfish and driftwood along the shore.

Every summer the village girls took the shaggy high-horned cattle up the mountain to get fat on fresh new grass. The girls milked the cows and made the butter and the cheese, while the bull calves got fat enough to be butchered at the end of summer, so their meat could be salted to eat through winter. The cows had calved two moons before and been put to the bull again, so they would calve next year too, but the bull stayed in the chief's enclosure, so it was just the cows and calves who were to climb the great mountain.

Twice each moon the women made the journey up the mountain to bring the girls fish and barley cakes and check the goings on, and to collect the soft new cheese and carry it back down to the village to press it, and bury the butter in the cold, wet soil by the stream, so it would still be fresh to eat in winter when the cows no longer gave their milk.

Not all the village girls went a-milking. Some were too young, and a couple of the girls that had gone last year were married now, with barley fields of their own to tend – one even had a baby on her hip. This was the first year that Hekja was to go. She had twelve summers now, and would be the youngest of them all.

The whole village gathered to see them off, the chief and all the men and boys, including Bran, staring at Hekja then pretending that he wasn't. The cows were all garlanded with wild flowers, though the calves kept chewing off the flowers.

The cows mooed, to keep the calves in line. They could smell the new grass up the mountain side, and remembered the taste of it from the year before. They'd been eating dry grass, kale stems and seaweed through the winter. Their calves had caught their excitement and were lowing too, with Snarf leaping round them all and snapping at their heels, as though he knew he was the only dog going up the mountain, while the chief's dogs stayed behind.

No other girl in the village had a dog. Dogs were for men.

The women carried the wooden pails for the milk, the butter paddles and the cheese cloths. The girls carried their bundles, barley cakes and dried fish and cowhide blankets to keep them warm, for even summer nights were cold up on the mountain. There were Raina and Reena, the chief's two daughters and the oldest of the girls, Janna from the hut beyond the bay, Banna, Hekja's best friend who lived in a hut nearby, and Hekja.

Hekja's ma had only one cow, with its calf at foot, while the chief had ten, but the village would share the cheese and butter out, a certain amount for each cow you owned, with extra for the families of the girls who'd looked after the cows up on the mountain. This year Hekja's ma would share her extra portion with Tikka, to repay her for looking after Snarf.

The clouds scattered across the sky, and out at sea the rain squalls sped across the islands as the procession headed up the great mountain with Snarf bounding ahead of them all. He was half grown now, with the long legs of his mother, and a coat as shaggy as a cow's.

The cows were slow and the calves kept trying to suckle their mothers, but the air was sweet with summer so no one was in any hurry. Finally they reached the mountain meadows and the sheiling[7] where the girls would sleep and keep the milk cool. It was no bigger than the huts down by the shore; of stone with a dirt floor, but no fireplace, as there was no wood to burn up here on the mountain.

While the girls laid down their bundles, the women set up the buckets and the butter paddles, then cut turfs to mend the holes in the roof. Then the girls began to gather bracken for their beds and the watercress that grew in the spring by the sheiling for their lunch.

Once they had finished they sat on the grass and ate the barley bread and cheese with watercress, and the chief's wife and daughters ate smoked beef too. Some of the women were tearful – it was the first time their daughters would be away. But the girls were exultant. After four summers of milking you were judged a woman and could marry, with some of the cheeses you made up on the mountain for your dowry.

Snarf sat on Hekja's ma's lap – or as much of him as he could fit – and ate some of her barley bread, spitting out the watercress and licking away the tears that she was trying to hide.

Then it was time for the women to go.

The girls hugged their mothers. Hekja hugged her ma extra hard and watched her till she was well down the mountain. The other women had husbands and other family to go back to, but Hekja's ma had no one else. Even her cow was on the mountain.

"Take care," whispered Hekja's ma.

Hekja nodded. "I will. You take care too."

Her mother smiled. "What can happen to me down in the village?" But her look was one of longing as she gazed at Hekja, and touched her cheek for one last time. "Take care of her, Riki Snarfari," she instructed Snarf.

"Arf," said Snarf, sitting on Hekja's foot and panting. He'd already rolled in fresh cow dung and looked proud of his new smell.

"See?" said Hekja. "He understands!" But her ma just smiled and bit her lip, then followed the other women down the path.

Hekja stood watching her, till the path twisted and she was out of sight. Then she turned back to the sheiling.

The other girls were already inside, setting out their bedding. Raina and Reena took charge, as the chief's daughters. Reena pointed to the back of the hut, furthest from the draught of the door. "We'll sleep there," she said.

"And you'll sleep there," Raina said to Hekja, pointing to the windy spot by the entrance. The chief's daughters weren't fond of Hekja, for their brother liked her far too much and her dress was ragged hide, not woven wool like theirs.

"And the dog can sleep outside," said Reena. "What's he doing here anyway?"

Hekja said nothing, just set her chin in the stubborn way her ma said was just like her father when he meant to do something but didn't care to argue about it. She was quite happy to sleep by the door, and when the girls were asleep Snarf could slip in beside her, just as he did at home.

The cows wandered around, remembering the meadow from the year before and showing their calves the best spots to graze. The rocky mountain slope gleamed in the last of the sunlight and the clouds raced across the sky like they were chasing hares.

Hekja smiled in spite of the chief's daughters. You could see the whole world from up here, she thought, the islands scattered across the sea and the line where the waves met the sky. And she had Snarf too. What did it matter what Raina and Reena said?

It was time for milking. The cows were rounded up, tired after their walk. There was not much milk tonight, as the calves had been drinking when they felt like it. Tomorrow the girls would keep the calves away from the cows during the day, so they'd eat the soft new grass instead of sucking at their mothers, and the milk supply would be better.

The girls put the buckets of milk in the hut for the

cream to rise, but kept one bucketful for their dinner. It was rich milk tonight too, with all the cream still in it.

They sat on the cool grass as the last of the sunlight drained away across the sea. The chief's daughters drank first, then passed the bucket around, each girl drinking her fill. Hekja was the last, then she passed the bucket to Snarf. He'd just got his tongue into the milk when someone snatched the bucket away.

It was Reena. "The milk is not for dogs!"

"I'll wash the bucket clean over in the spring," said Hekja mildly. "Snarf can have half my share."

"Why should we share the milk with your dog?" said Janna angrily. "If the chief's daughters don't have a dog, why should you?"

Janna, too, had been casting glances at Bran, down in the village.

"He stinks," said Raina.

"It's a good smell! It's a dog smell!" said Hekja hotly. She grabbed Snarf and hugged him close to her. Snarf licked her face happily and grinned at the girls, his long tongue hanging out.

"He stinks of cow shush," said Raina.

"And fish guts," said Reena.

Hekja said nothing. It was true. Snarf had been nosing in the compost heap just that morning.

"Arf!" said Snarf, looking at the girls with whiskery friendliness and licking his milk moustache.

It didn't work. "Let him hunt his own food," said Reena.

"But he's lame!" pleaded Hekja. "And he's still too young to hunt!" It hadn't occurred to her that the girls on the mountain wouldn't share with Snarf as she and her mother had done.

Reena shrugged. "Then he's not worth his keep," she said.

Hekja looked at Banna, her friend, hoping for support. But Banna just looked at the grass. She liked Hekja but she didn't want to annoy the others either.

Hekja bit her lip, then fumbled in her bundle for her barley bread and cheese. "Here boy," she whispered.

Snarf gulped the bread and cheese in two large bites, then looked for more. Hekja shook her head and tried to ignore the hunger clawing at her stomach.

The starlight lit the mountain cliffs with silver as they went to bed. Hekja listened to the talk slowly cease and the girls' breathing soften.

"Snarf!" she whispered.

He had been just around the corner, sitting puzzled in the dark. He stretched out beside her, and licked her face, scratched his ear twice where a grass seed was prickling, then laid his paws on his nose.

Hekja lay awake. It was strange to lie in a new place, the familiar sound of waves lapping on the pebbles replaced with the noises of the other girls sleeping, and the cows mooing in the night.

How could Snarf learn to hunt, with no one to show him how, and one lame leg? He wasn't even fully grown.

Perhaps she could sneak him some of the milk tomorrow. If he was just a little hungry he might decide to hunt himself. But if he ate nothing he'd be too weak to hunt…

Hekja woke as soon as the light brightened about the mountain. Snarf was awake already, sniffing around the cow meadow to find the smelliest cow pat to roll in.

Hekja tiptoed out then whistled softly. Snarf bounded up to her, licking her face and pulling at the sleeve of her dress. Hekja pulled it back. "Snarf! No! No time for tug games now! You have to go find some breakfast!"

Snarf sat back and cocked his head at her. "Arf?" he enquired.

"You have to learn to hunt! Please, Snarf!" cried Hekja desperately.

"Arf." Snarf lost interest. He began to scratch at the grass seed again.

Hekja sighed. It was no use. Snarf did things when he wanted to. She crossed quietly over to the spring and washed her face. Snarf splashed beside her, then decided it was too cold and shook himself vigorously.

"Errk," protested Hekja, as the spray went all over her.

"Arf," said Snarf, as though to say, "Well, you wanted a wash, didn't you?"

The other girls were up now, yawning and stretching and rubbing the sleep from their eyes. The whole mountain was awake, the birds chirping louder than they ever did below, and the cows beginning to roam.

"What's he doing here?" demanded Reena predictably, as she saw Snarf at the spring.

"He has to drink too," said Hekja, standing up and tipping him off her lap.

Reena sniffed. "Dogs belong in the village with the men," she said. "We've never had a dog up here before."

The cream had risen to the top of last night's milk. The girls scooped it off into the butter pail and, like the night before, passed the pail around, drinking as much as they wanted of the cold skimmed milk. Snarf watched, looking hopeful.

Hekja gave him a bit of her barley cake, while the girls looked on and snickered. There wasn't much barley cake left – the girls only had a bite or two to go with their milk and watercress, and the dried fish and cheese was finished too. Soon they'd have fresh cheese to eat, and buttermilk, but there would be no more barley cake till the women came up again.

Hekja bit her lip. A big dog like Snarf needed food every day – lots of food, as he was still growing.

Reena dusted off the last of the crumbs and took a final drink of milk. "Now," she ordered. "Hekja, you churn the butter while we watch the cows."

Hekja said nothing. Butter making was harder work than sitting watching the cows and yelling at them when they strayed. But if she was alone at the sheiling she could give Snarf some of the cream.

Hekja sat in the sheiling's doorway on the three-legged stool the women had brought up, with the bucket between her knees, and swept the butter paddles back and forth in the cream, and waited for the cows to wander off, with the girls following.

But the cows stayed where they were. They hadn't eaten the grass by the sheiling yet, and their legs were tired from yesterday. Time enough to roam when they'd eaten the greenery here.

Hekja glanced down at Snarf, sleeping at her feet, with one eye half open to check on the cows. "Please go and hunt, Snarf. Please," she whispered.

Snarf glanced up at her. He seemed quite content to wait for breakfast, whenever Hekja would get round to getting it. After all, she had always provided for him before. He put his head back on his paws and shut his eyes.

Hekja bit her lip. If she had been a boy she'd have learnt to hunt with the men. She'd be able to teach Snarf to hunt too. Maybe I should take him back to the chief, she thought hopelessly. Maybe Bran will take him...

The day stretched out. Hekja drank some of the skimmed milk with the other girls as the sun rose in the sky, and packed the first of the summer's butter into the butter crock, with its tight-fitting lid to keep out dust and flies – and Snarf's nose.

Snarf looked hopefully from girl to girl as they drank. When the bucket was empty he whined and looked questioningly at Hekja. But she just shook her head. "I'm sorry," she whispered.

"Arf? Arf!" barked Snarf, then added, "Woof woof!" as though to remind her he was there. Then he gave up and went to get a drink from the spring.

Tomorrow, thought Hekja desperately, as she gulped the milk, *I'll take him to Bran tomorrow.*

The girls milked the cows again as the sun dropped into the sea. There was more milk this time, as they had kept the calves from suckling. Again Hekja drank from the bucket and tried not to look at Snarf's accusing eyes.

Hekja put the bucket down and looked around.

"Where's Snarf?!" she cried.

Reena shrugged. "Who cares? Go rinse the bucket out," she ordered. "It's time for bed."

Hekja stared around the meadow. Raina laughed. "At last! The dog stink has gone!"

Hekja said nothing. Where was Snarf? She didn't dare call him, in case he had decided to try to hunt for himself. But what if he thought she didn't love him any more?

What if he was headed down the mountain to Ma, and the food she'd always given him? Or worse – what if he went to the chief's hut instead? The chief would welcome him now he was a fine, big animal. He'd become the chief's dog again, not hers.

Hekja rinsed the bucket. The sun had vanished, though the summer twilight would linger for a long time yet. She placed the bucket with the rest of the milking equipment, wrapped herself in her cowhide, and lay down on her bracken bed, feeling the familiar scratchiness beneath her.

Where was Snarf? Where?

Chapter 6

A HUNTER AT LAST

Hekja tried to sleep. Over in the corner of the sheiling Reena gave a gentle snore, and Janna the faint hiccupping sound that she made when sleeping too. Outside the calves wandered over to suckle their mothers, then moved away again when they realised they'd been milked dry, and began to chomp at the grass in the dying light.

Where is Snarf? thought Hekja desperately. *Maybe he'd had an accident! Fallen down a cliff like Pa... or maybe a wolf has caught him...*

Finally the night grew truly dark. Hekja watched the stars pop through the blackness one by one. The moon rose above the ridge like a small yellow cheese.

Hekja sat up. She had to find Snarf! She had to!

Hekja crept from the hut, then called softly into the darkness, "Snarf! Riki Snarfari!"

No answer. She walked a little further and called again, "Snarf! Snarf!"

Suddenly, something bounded out of the darkness. "Arf," said Snarf softly, bulling her with his furry head. Then he leaped into the darkness again, turning his head as though to say, "Are you coming?"

Hekja followed him. The moonlight cast shadows on the grass as Snarf began to run. Hekja tied her skirts about her waist and ran too. It was hard at first avoiding the clumps of heather. But as the moon rose higher it grew easier. If she looked at the ground, Hekja discovered, and not the moonlit sky, her eyes grew used to the dimness.

Deep into the night they ran. A lone deer saw them and ran off, with Snarf following. For a moment Hekja thought Snarf might bring it down. But the deer was too fast and Snarf was too young, Hekja realised, to bring down a full-grown deer.

Hekja could feel hunger nibble at her tummy. And if she was hungry, what must Snarf feel like, she wondered. Then suddenly Snarf stopped, as still as the mountain crags about them. He sniffed then crept forward, his nose to the ground.

Hekja froze. What had Snarf found? If she moved she might scare it away.

Then Snarf pounced. He thrust his nose into a hollow in the ground among the heather. When he lifted it again a bird fluttered helplessly in his jaws. It was a ptarmigan. Snarf held it high, as though to ask, "Would you like some too?"

Hekja smiled and sat on the cold ground and watched while Snarf began his feast.

When he had finished, he trotted over to Hekja and flopped into her lap. "Arf," he said contentedly.

Hekja smelt his warm dog's breath. But this smell was different from before. She hugged him hard and picked a feather from behind his ear.

"Good dog," she said, and that was all.

"Arf arf," said Snarf happily. They ran back to the sheiling together.

So the days continued. Spring's flowers gave way to summer. The cows were growing fat.

Each morning Snarf left at dawn to hunt, returning with a fat belly and meat on his breath, and sometimes blood about his whiskers. He was a giant dog now, and only limped a little when he was tired.

But the girls still treated him as an interloper, and Hekja too. Hekja was different – different because of Snarf, because Bran liked her, because she was poor. A girl without a dowry had no right to look at the chief's son. *Maybe*, thought Hekja, *I'd be different anyway*. Did any of the other girls ever gaze at the horizon, or dream of running with the wind?

It felt strange to be so lonely, with the other girls around her. She had never known it was possible to feel as alone as this.

At least during the day she was away from the sheiling. Every day the cows ranged further. It was Hekja's job now to run after them and stop them straying over the cliffs, and to bring them in for milking at the end of each day, with Snarf nipping at their heels and barking when they didn't obey.

The other girls all stayed at the sheiling to make the butter and cheese. Even Banna avoided Hekja these days.

It was so lonely. And without Snarf it would have been more than she could bear.

Chapter 7

DANGER ON THE MOUNTAIN

The dried bracken bed crunched under her as Hekja rolled over and tried to go back to sleep. It must still be a long way from dawn she decided, for Snarf still lay beside her, with his comforting, furry warmth.

Just a few more days and Ma would be here, with the other women, she thought longingly, to take the cheese and butter back, and to bring them more rennet[8] and barley cake and cooked fish.

And for a while there'd be someone to talk to, to tell how Snarf had nearly caught an eagle, napping on a ledge, and how he'd learned to catch a dried cow pat in his teeth. Hekja missed being able to talk about Snarf's adventures most of all.

"Arf," said Snarf softly. His cold nose touched her cheek.

Hekja stroked him without opening her eyes. "Sshh. Go back to sleep," she whispered.

"Woof!" said Snarf more urgently. And then he whined.

Hekja opened her eyes.

It was a world of white. The whiteness even swirled inside the doorway, cold and damp, the noises muffled as though the white had smothered them as well.

Hekja sat up, so the bracken bed crackled, and hugged Snarf close. "Fog," she said.

Snarf whined again. It was the first fog he had ever seen, Hekja realised. Even she had never seen a fog like this.

The other girls were stretching now, yawning and rubbing the sleep from their eyes. Reena peered out the door. "Ugh, I hate fog. The cows won't go far in this," she muttered.

"They'll still need milking though," said Janna, looking nervously out into the fog.

Reena nodded at Hekja. "No need for us all to get cold and damp. You and the dog can bring the cows over here for the milking."

For a moment Hekja thought about refusing. But what was the point? And anyway, Snarf would need to go out to have a drink. No matter how strange the white world was, she was sure Snarf could smell the way back to the sheiling.

"Here boy," she said. But Snarf had already disappeared outside.

The whiteness closed about her as she followed him. Behind her she heard Raina laughing. "With a bit of luck that stupid dog will fall over a cliff."

"Do all dogs stink?" asked Janna.

"Not proper dogs," declared Raina scornfully. "Our dogs never smell."

Of course they smell, thought Hekja. *Dogs always smell of dog.* She wondered what humans smelled like to dogs. *We girls probably smell of cheese,* she decided, *and cow, and bracken from our beds.*

She stopped suddenly. Where was she? Even the sheiling had disappeared. Where was Snarf? And the cows?

"Arf," said Snarf happily, prancing up beside her, his tail pounding against her legs.

"Bring in the cows!" ordered Hekja. "Can you do that, boy? The cows!"

"Arf arf," said Snarf, as though to say, "Of course I can!" Snarf bounded off into the fog. Hekja grinned as she listened to him yipping at the cattle's heels, and the heavy beat of the cow's feet as they headed to the sheiling.

No one thanked her, or Snarf either, for bringing the cows in. Hekja sat with the others on their low wood stools, stroked a cow's teats and listened to the milk as it squirt, squirt, squirted into the buckets. Every sound seemed muffled today, as though the fog was a cowhide blanket covering everything. Even the birds were silent. How far did the fog stretch, wondered Hekja. All the way up to the sky? Was the whole world surrounded by fog, or just their mountain?

Snarf snoozed at her feet, his job done, droplets of moisture glistening on his fur.

Finally the milking was finished. The cows wandered off, though Hekja could hear them still close, munching the odd tuft of grass that they had missed before, lowing at their calves to stay nearby.

"It'll lift soon," said Reena confidently, as the girls carried the milk buckets back into the sheiling, and Hekja began to paddle yesterday's cream that had risen on the buckets overnight.

But the fog didn't lift. Hekja patted the last of the whey from the butter, while the other girls lay back on their beds and gossiped about who was the handsomest boy in the village, and who the strongest, and who had the best hand at the fishing nets.

Janna was sure that Bran was the handsomest. "And the strongest too," she added, with a glance at Hekja. But Hekja ignored her.

Raina carefully avoided looking Hekja's way. "Ma says my brother's to marry the chief's daughter from Eagle Bay. She's got a grand dowry, Ma says."

Janna looked disappointed. "Maybe Bran won't want a stranger from Eagle Bay," she said hopefully.

Hekja gave the butter a harder pat than usual and they all looked at her.

"Who do you fancy, Hekja?" asked Banna.

"No one," lied Hekja.

Reena laughed. "You must have your eye on someone! Of course as a widow's daughter you can't hope for much. There's Jan Fisherman's son. You'd soon get used to his bandy legs."

"Or maybe you won't notice them in the dark," said Raina coarsely. They all laughed except for Hekja.

Hekja refused to look up from the butter. "I'll think of that in a few years' time," she said, as calmly as she could. "And not before."

Janna shrugged. "Well, there'll be no more boys in the village to choose from then than there are now."

"Unless the Vikings call!" giggled Raina.

The Vikings were the Norse raiders, who killed and stole and enslaved wherever they landed. But the Norsemen had never landed anywhere near the village. Vikings were after better booty than stone huts and cattle skins – they wanted gold from monasteries, walrus ivory or swords and armour from a king.

Janna giggled and poked Reena in the arm. "Just what

you want for a husband! A Viking raider! At least he'd be big and strong!"

"Maybe a handsome stranger will be shipwrecked near our cove," said Banna dreamily. "We'll rescue him and he'll fall in love with one of us…"

"With you, you mean… " said Raina.

"He'll be a king's son with a palace and a golden throne, just like in the songs…"

Reena laughed. "Who'd marry a stranger, even if he has a golden throne? Imagine living with people you don't know! Besides, you've never even met a stranger in your life."

"Yes, I have," said Banna. "The monk who came, years ago, remember?"

"You were only knee-high to a herring," objected Reena. "You can't remember back that far."

"Yes, I can," said Banna. "He had a squint. And he said that…"

Something bawled outside. It was a bellow of terror, then of pain. Snarf barked, then whined and edged closer to Hekja.

"What is it?" cried Hekja.

Reena and Raina shrank back against the wall. "Wolf!" hissed Reena. "There's a wolf after the calves!"

"Everyone get back here!" ordered Raina. "A wolf won't come in here if we're altogether!"

Hekja stared. "We can't let a wolf get the calves." She ran to the door but Banna grabbed her arm.

"You can't go out there!" she cried. "Not with a wolf!"

"She's right!" Reena shook her head. "The wolf will only take a calf. If you go out there it will kill you too."

Hekja wrenched her arm free. "What if it's our calf! You have lots of calves but Ma and I have only one! Snarf! Here, boy!" But Snarf had crept back further into the sheiling on his stomach. He whined again.

Hekja bit her lip and ran out into the fog.

One step... two steps... Hekja stopped. The world had disappeared. There was nothing but whiteness all around.

She tried to orient herself. The hut was... there. And the screaming came from... Hekja ran towards the noise.

The cows had scattered in terror, all but one. It was trying to butt the wolf with its long horns. And there in the whiteness was the long black shape of the wolf, circling round to snap at the calf again, but keeping well clear of the mother's horns.

Then suddenly the wolf stopped circling and sniffed towards Hekja instead. Hekja froze. She could almost hear its thought: *here is an easier meal than a calf with a stroppy mother. Cows have horns but girls don't.*

What should she do? Suddenly helplessness washed over her. She had run out without thinking!

"Go away!" she yelled. Would sound alone frighten it? It was all she had. "Hoi hoi hoi!" she yelled. But the fog absorbed the noise. Even to her ears her voice sounded thin and scared.

Suddenly the wolf vanished in the fog. But she knew it hadn't run away. The wolf was circling, trying to get behind her in the mist.

Suddenly something leaped behind her. Hekja screamed and swirled around, expecting the sharp jaws to close upon her. But it wasn't the wolf.

It was Snarf. "Go back, boy!" shouted Hekja. Now the wolf would get him too!

Snarf growled uncertainly deep within his throat. Something else growled behind them – the wolf.

Hekja tried to grab Snarf by the scruff of the neck. Maybe if they both ran...

But it was too late. Snarf leaped! In the next instant he had the wolf by the throat. He was smaller than the wolf, and less experienced, but Snarf had taken the wolf by surprise.

Hekja darted forwards, then halted once again as the black shapes rolled and twisted in the fog.

The wolf twisted free. It sprang back, snarling, then leaped again, catching Snarf by the ear. Snarf screamed and tried to run, but the wolf had him fast.

Hekja held her breath. She had to help! But how? Behind her the cow bellowed, putting its body between the wolf and the calf.

The wolf swung back. His teeth struck Snarf a glancing blow on his shoulder. Snarf tried to bite again. But the wolf was too fast. He grabbed Snarf's leg...

The girls were screaming in the hut, but Hekja hardly heard them. And suddenly it was over. The wolf went limp, its teeth still grasping Snarf's leg. Then the great jaws fell open as the wolf rolled back.

Snarf's first blow had ripped its windpipe. The wolf was dead.

Chapter 8

A SONG FOR A HERO!

For a moment the two bodies lay on the grass, the fog sifting about them. Hekja dropped to her knees just as Snarf lifted his head, then struggled to his feet.

"Is he alright?" Banna raced from the sheiling and knelt beside her. "Is the wolf really dead?" Hekja nodded, too out of breath to speak. She ran her fingers over Snarf and he weakly licked her face.

"I don't think he's hurt much," she panted finally. "His ear is torn. But the wolf… the wolf…" Her voice choked.

"He's a hero," someone breathed. It was Reena. Hekja hadn't noticed the other girls come out of the sheiling.

"I've never known a dog fight a wolf all by itself," cried Raina.

"Come on," said Reena decisively. "Let's carry him inside. Janna, you get water to wash his wounds. Banna, we'll put him on your bed, it's warmest, and he can have my cloak. Hekja, do you think he'll eat barley bread if we sop it first in cream?"

"Yes," said Hekja simply. Beside her Snarf almost smiled.

Raina and Reena skinned the wolf carcass and hung it to dry over the rafters. The wolf skin would make a fine mat for Hekja's hearth at home. Snarf ate the wolf meat, and this time the girls didn't complain about the wolf stink on his breath, even when Janna tripped over the bones.

That night Snarf slept by the door again, but this time it was a place of pride. Snarf was the guardian, the protector from the wolves. And Hekja was the Queen of the Mountain, because he was her dog.

It was hard to tell which one was the proudest.

Snarf drank his fill of milk every morning and evening after that, and the girls competed to scratch his ears or tickle his tummy. But Snarf was still Hekja's dog and hers was the only voice that he obeyed.

He began to bring some of his catch home now and basked in the praise. "Good dog!" they called, and, "Look what he's found now!"

"He's a better hunter than any of my father's dogs," asserted Reena, and Hekja agreed.

The girls plucked the feathers from the birds he caught to keep for bedding, or skinned the hares or squirrels and hung their skins up to dry for mats or blankets or to be sewn for clothes. But they left the meat for Snarf. There was no wood up on the mountain to cook anything nor any dried peat turfs either, and it was too far for the women to cart turf up the hill. But Hekja gave her ma some of the meat every few days when she came up with barley cakes and fish.

It was in those days that Hekja began to sing again. She'd sung by herself, sometimes, as she and Snarf watched the cows. The song floated up along the cliffs until the eagles heard it, then drifted with the wind. But this was the first time she had sung when the other girls could hear it.

They were changing the cloths on the fresh cheeses. The cloths had to be washed after each new lot of cheese had been taken down the mountain, or the next lot of cheese might sour. The girls sat on the grass in the sunlight and scrubbed the cloths back and forth in the milk buckets – if they washed the cloths in the spring the water would taste of cheese for days. The eagle soared high above them and Snarf snored, and farted squirrel smells that no one now objected to.

Then Hekja began to sing.

This wasn't one of her father's songs, or one of the women's songs about grinding the barley, or bringing home the cows. This was a song that came to her with the wind, so it almost seemed she only had to open her mouth and the wind would sing the words for her.

Mist on the hillside,
Mist on the ground,
The mist hid our cattle,
And swallowed all sound.

The wolf he came sneaking,
But Snarfari he growled,
He leapt at the wolf,
In one fearsome bound.

And there lay the wolf,
By the valiant hound,
His ear torn and bloody,
The bravest around.

It was only as the song died away that she realised the girls were all staring at her.

"I've never heard that song before!" cried Janna.

"Of course not, stupid," said Reena. "It was about Snarf. How could anyone have made up a song about Snarf before!"

"Arf," said the valiant hound complacently, draped across Hekja's lap and full of pride, as though he had understood every word.

"You really made that up all by yourself?" cried Raina.

Hekja nodded.

"I've never met anyone who made up songs! Could you make up one about me?" demanded Reena. "And sing it when we go back home?"

"And one about me?" added Raina jealously.

"I'll try," said Hekja.

Every evening after that Hekja would sing a song she'd made up during the day. They were songs about the girls bringing the cattle in from the mountain or about the cheeses hanging from the rafters or the chief's daughters paddling the butter. Sometimes the girls would sing them too, though none had a voice as high and true as Hekja's. Each day Snarf grew even bigger, till his feet were the size of hearth cakes almost, and Hekja's face opened like a flower.

Mid-summer passed. The whole village trooped up the mountain to the sheiling for that – the men loaded with driftwood and burning faggots to light the fire, a whole bull calf to roast, and drinking horns and barrels of barley beer. The other dogs sniffed about, checking where Snarf had marked rocks and trees and walls, but he sat in the sheiling doorway and growled at them. This was his territory. No other dog was allowed inside the hut, not even his ma.

Hekja sang Snarf's song that night and everybody cheered. She sat with Bran by the fire, and even if the chief didn't look pleased he didn't object, for Hekja had sung a song about him too. The song was about the time he took his boat out to search for the boys from the far hut, who had gone missing during a storm, even though the waves were washing in the wind. He found them clinging to their upturned craft and nearly drowned, and brought them safely to shore.

Most people had almost forgotten the day their chief had been a hero. But now the chief would be remembered as long as Hekja's song was sung.

It was quiet after the mid-summer feast – just the girls and Snarf and the cows. But sometimes a party of hunters passed the sheiling, for now Bran made sure he took the hunt up the path to Hekja as often as he could. The chief would stop to chat to his daughters, and Bran and Hekja would talk together out by the spring, the sort of conversation that is mostly full of blushes and silences and stolen glances at one another then shy looks away.

Sometimes it seemed to Hekja that summer could never end, it was so good.

Chapter 9

RAIDERS!

It was one of those mid-summer days when sea and sky seemed to be as one, each as grey as the other, the rain gusting with the wind. Even from the sheiling the girls could see the waves crash upon the shore and the white caps across the sea.

The cows hung around the sheiling, as they usually did when the weather was bad. It was the most sheltered spot on the mountain, which was why the hut had been built there. On some of the slopes the wind could almost blow a cow away.

The girls lay on their bracken beds with Snarf flopped across Hekja and Banna – he was too big now for one lap alone – while Banna scratched his tummy and Hekja scratched behind his ears. Hekja gazed out at the rain as the wind lashed the walls and trickles of dirty water seeped through the roof. The women had been up the day before to take back the cheeses and the butter, so there was fresh barley cake to eat, and the chief's wife had even brought a giant stuffed fish head, boiled in their big iron pot.

The rain eased as the day wore on but the wind still howled, as loud as Snarf when he decided he'd sing too.

Reena and Raina shared out the fish head and gave Snarf the bones to chew, then Raina squelched out of the sheiling for a call of nature. But she had gone only a few steps when she flew back inside.

"Ships!" she yelled, her wet brown hair plastered to her face.

Her sister scrambled to her feet. "Where?"

"Out past the islands!" cried Raina.

None of the village boats should have been out in weather like this. The girls raced out the door and stared out to sea, their plaits blowing in the wind and their dresses flattened against their bodies. "Look!" ordered Raina.

Hekja stared at the grey ocean. Yes, there were ships out there, like no ships that she had ever seen. The village boats were round with a short stubby sail. These ships were long, with giant sails, and crowded with people. One even had a horse on board. Some sailors were leaping at the sails and others were bailing. The ships were making straight for the village harbour.

"Vikings!" whispered Hekja.

"How do you know?" asked Janna tremulously. "You've never seen a Viking ship!"

"Who else would they be?" demanded Hekja impatiently. "None of the island boats are as big as that!"

"But why would Vikings come here?" whispered Banna. It was as though she was trying to convince herself it wasn't true. "There's nothing here to steal."

"The storm must have blown them off course! Come on! We have to warn the village! They won't have seen them yet!"

"No!" Reena's voice held real terror. "We can't go down there!"

"We have to!"

"You fool! You know what Vikings do to people!"

"That's why we have to warn the village!" cried Hekja.

Reena suddenly sounded like a chief's daughter. "Think!" she yelled. "By the time we got there the Vikings would have landed. At least we're safe up here. Better that some of our village survives than none at all!"

"So we should wait up here in safety and let the village die?" cried Hekja.

"Better that than kill us all! And here we have the cows and shelter!"

"No! We have to try!" Hekja looked around wildly. "But you're right. There is no need to risk all our lives! I'll go!" And with that she was flying down the mountain, her face against the wind.

"Hekja!" cried Reena.

But Hekja had gone, with Snarf bounding after her.

Chapter 10

ATTACK!

The path twisted and turned as Hekja ran down the great mountain. Soon she could no longer see the ships, or the village either, just hills and the grey distance of the sky and sea, and the sea eagle peering curiously as it balanced on the wind. Behind her Snarf leaped and pranced as though he was sure it was a game.

Once Hekja slipped, but was back on her feet before Snarf had time to lick her face. Then he dislodged some rocks so they went crashing down below.

But mostly they just ran.

The path curved past the witch's hut near the stream. The witch stared as Hekja ran past.

Hekja didn't even pause. "Viking ships!" she yelled.

"Girl! Come back here!" shouted Tikka, but her words were swallowed by the wind. Hekja had gone.

Finally the path curved again. The village was below them. Hekja stopped and stared, and tried to still her breath. Beside her Snarf flopped down on to his tummy and whined at the smell of blood.

Reena had been right, Hekja realised. She was too late. No one could help the village now.

Down in the shallows the giant Viking ships bounced on the waves, fat in the middle and long at each end, while smaller boats laden with goods bobbed behind them.

But mostly Hekja saw the men.

Big men, taller than she had ever thought a man could be, with bright hair that streamed out beneath metal helmets. Bright eyes in bearded faces, and bright swords too. They strode above the bodies of the villagers. *Why do dead people look so much smaller than when they were alive?* thought Hekja numbly.

The stench of death was everywhere, a strong sweet smell, overpowering even the smells of fish and salt.

Snarf whimpered again. He had killed a wolf and hunted game. But even to him this smell seemed wrong.

Someone screamed, far away. Hekja could hear sobbing too and a faint clang, clanging that she had never heard before.

Suddenly her mind fought free of shock. She had to get to Ma! But if the Vikings saw her they'd have her too. Hekja glanced around then made for the shelter of a byre. She signalled to Snarf to follow her. He needed no urging, but clung close to her heels.

They slipped from wall to wall, from one hut to the next. They were by the chief's hut now and there was the chief's wife, lying sprawled upon the stones, and Snarf's mother too. The big dog must have tried to defend her mistress, for there was a great cut across her neck.

Hekja knelt by the chief's wife and cradled her head in her lap. The women blinked at her, as though it was hard to see. "No!" she whispered. "Don't stay here, child. Run!"

"Ma?" whispered Hekja.

The chief's wife groaned. "There is no way you can help her. Get away. Go!"

Snarf whined and bent to lick the woman's face. Hekja laid her hand on his head and whispered, "Quiet." Her hand was steady even though her voice was not. She laid the chief's wife back gently on the stones and crept back to the shelter of the wall.

They kept on going.

There was another body, Banna's ma, bloody and white, but at least she was still breathing although she didn't move. Another body, not far away – the chief – his body wet with blood. His empty eyes stared at the sea. Three of his men lay about him. They were dead. They had to be dead. No man could live with wounds like that.

Hekja kept her hand on Snarf to warn him to be quiet. But he didn't need her warning now.

The clanging sounds were coming from the other side of the hut. Hekja peered around the corner.

"Bran," she whispered. But there was too much noise for Bran to hear her.

Bran held a sword awkwardly in both his hands. It wasn't his – there was no sword in the whole village, just knives and the chief's big axe. Bran must have grabbed it from one of the Vikings.

A Viking stood before him and they banged their swords together. But even to Hekja it was clear that the Viking was playing with the youth, letting him try to hit while the Viking weaved aside and laughed.

Then all at once the Viking seemed to lose his patience. He struck a blow at Bran's head that sent him down.

Hekja's pa had sung a song once, about a warrior who died gazing in his loved one's eyes. But there was no time for Hekja to reach Bran now. He simply lay there, his blood spilling on the ground. Hekja gripped Snarf's fur so hard that her fingers hurt. But still she made no sound and neither did the dog.

There was nothing she could do for Bran now.

They crept along the wall, Hekja first and Snarf following, reluctant. Another woman's body, and another. They were nearly at Hekja's hut now and suddenly before them there was Hekja's mother, sprawled on her back on the shingle stones, and two men too.

Hekja stared, but the scene wavered in front of her, as though water had washed over it. It was impossible… impossible. How could one person do that to another? Her skin prickled with the horror. Then suddenly her vision cleared and she ran forward.

Hekja's ma was white with terror and twisted with pain too. But she saw Hekja, just a glimpse as one man moved. She screamed out, "Run!"

That was the last thing she ever said. One of the men – the largest, with a chin like a cod fish and almost no beard at all – plunged his sword into her heart then pulled it out, all bloody.

Hekja screamed. It was a scream that held all the horror of Bran's death, of the devastation of her village, of grief and pain. She ran towards her ma's body and knelt down. Her ma's eyes stared at the sky and there was a froth of blood from her mouth.

The beardless man grabbed Hekja's arm and hauled her up to her feet. He grinned. His teeth were as white as a wolf's.

"This one is mine!" he roared. The words sounded strange but his meaning was plain.

The other man laughed. He had blood upon his hands and on his face and elsewhere too, but he could still laugh. "You've had your share, Finnbogi!" he cried. He pulled Hekja away, so she stumbled against his body and half fell.

"No such thing!" the man called Finnbogi cried. For a moment the men glared, as though they were about to fight each other.

Hekja struggled, kicking and trying to bite. The man just laughed, then screamed. Snarf had leaped at him, silent as a spear, and bitten him behind the knee so deeply that his teeth met through the tendons.

The man yelled, letting Hekja go. He turned and grabbed at Snarf but Snarf had gone, leaping across the shingle. Hekja raced after him, her breath sobbing, her face smeared with tears and her ma's blood.

Snarf slowed down to let her catch up to him. Behind them the first man was examining his leg. But the man called Finnbogi gave a yell and galloped after them.

"What the—?" A woman stepped out of the chief's hut. She was a Viking, the first Viking woman Hekja had seen. She wore a dress, finer than any the village women wore, and a cap-like helmet like the men with bright red hair beneath it. In her arms she held the chief's best ale horns, carved and inlaid with bronze. They were the only good things in the hut, passed down from chief to chief. But the village had no chief now.

"Run, Finnbogi!" the woman called to the man, as though delighted by the chase.

Hekja swerved. She raced past the chief's hut then along the track that led to the sheiling. Then suddenly she veered. That path led to the girls. She couldn't lead the Vikings there! Reena had been right – the girls were safe, and Hekja had to keep them so.

The man Finnbogi was winded already. He carried his heavy sword and shield, and hadn't spent the summer racing after cows on mountain slopes like Hekja had. She could hear him gasping, but there was no time to turn to see how close he was. Through the cow field they ran, past the chief's bull, then over the stone fence. The man lumbered across the fence too then leaned against it, panting.

Hekja risked a glance. He'd given up!

Then someone yelled behind her, "You're past it, Finnbogi! Leave it to those with proper beards!"

Another called, "Let me show you how it's done, Finnbogi!"

The man Finnbogi growled. "You see if you can catch her, Leif. She must have feet like falcon's wings!"

Suddenly another man's footsteps joined the chase.

"Go to it, Leif!" It was the Viking woman, her voice high and clear above the men's.

Down to the beach they fled and along the shingle. The man Leif's leather shoes slipped on the wet rocks but Hekja and Snarf's feet were sure. Around the bay, and up the other side. It seemed to Hekja as though the world had narrowed to her feet pounding on the pebbles, breath tearing at her lungs and the speedy beat of Snarf's feet at her heels. The cliff reared up before them with its path of dirt and stones.

The man was gaining now, as he was new to the chase and they were not. Even Snarf was panting and Hekja's breath seemed torn from deep within her body.

It was impossible to go any faster up the path – any misstep might mean she slid back down into the waiting arms of the Viking. But if she had to go slowly, so did he, and she knew this path and he did not.

Up... up... For a moment Snarf's feet slipped on the loose dirt, but Hekja reached down and hauled him up.

The man was nearly on them. His sword flashed down, just behind Snarf's tail. But now the girl and dog had made the cliff top. The wind lashed at them, smelling of storm and sea and the distant tang of blood.

Back they ran, towards the village. Hekja tried to think. Which way now? There was one path that might lead them to safety, if only she could make it. It was a hunter's path from the village, up into the hills. If she and Snarf could get up there they'd be safe, hidden among the cliffs and mountain crags.

Hope gave her strength. Her feet pounded along the path, sure footed as a hare. The man was further behind now. The gap grew bigger as she neared the village. Hekja thudded down the path, towards the chief's. No time to glance at the bodies either, only time to run, to force her legs to keep on going.

Past the hut... Snarf was in the lead now, for he had four legs to Hekja's two. Suddenly something slashed across her ankles. Hekja fell forward. Her knees crashed on to the ground, jarring her. Hekja had to scream. But there was only enough breath for a gasp of horror and despair.

Hekja tried to rise. A hard foot held her down. Strong small hands grasped her wrists and tied them roughly.

Hekja struggled to see who held her. Was it the man, Finnbogi, who had killed her mother? Would she suffer the same fate, the last of her village to be slaughtered? But when Hekja turned it was a woman's face – the woman she had seen before. One hand held Hekja's hair, close to her scalp, to stop her trying to run. The other held a sword. It was this that Hekja had stumbled over, held out flat to trip her as she ran.

The man Leif was on them now. He leaned over, trying to catch his breath, then looked up and grinned. "So you have caught my fish for me, little sister," he panted to the woman. He sounded his words strangely, but they were familiar enough for Hekja to understand.

The woman laughed and let the sword dangle by her skirts. She was young, her hair the same bright colour as the man's. There were rings on her fingers and a gold band on her arm and brooches on her dress, and a necklace too, with almost enough metal to make a cooking pot.

"You're getting soft, Leif. Too much time sitting on your bum while on board the ship. Your legs have forgotten what they're for."

The man – Leif – hauled Hekja up roughly by her hair. "She's mine now, at any rate."

"She's not," said the woman coolly. "I was the one who caught her. I claim her."

Hekja gazed frantically from one to the other trying to follow their speech. How could she escape? And where was Snarf? *Please*, she thought, *please Snarf, go to Tikka or the girls. You'll be safe there. Go, or the Vikings will get you too.*

Leif stared at the woman. "Are you serious, Freydis? What do you want with another thrall?" He looked at Hekja contemptuously. "She'll be quite unskilled coming from a poor place like this."

The woman, Freydis, laughed again. "Did you see how fast she ran? She's a runner, Leif. Faster than your man Hikki."

"No one is faster than Hikki," said Leif, amused. "He was a present from the king himself."

Freydis shrugged. "We will see," she said calmly. "Will you take the girl to my ship, dear brother, or will I?"

For a moment it looked like Leif would argue. Then he dropped Hekja suddenly, so again she sprawled on the wet ground. "Take her," he said abruptly, and walked off down to the shore.

"Please," began Hekja. Surely a woman would be kinder than a man. "Please let me go…"

There was a growl behind them. Snarf leapt, as he had leaped at the man Finnbogi and the wolf. His jaws met where the woman's knees would be, underneath her skirts.

But the cloth got in the way. Snarf reared back to strike again. But the woman was swifter. She lifted her sword and struck him hard against his neck.

The dog collapsed.

"No," whispered Hekja. "No."

The woman glanced at her. "He was trying to protect you, wasn't he? That dog has courage." She gestured to one of the passing men. "Carry him to my ship." She looked around the village contemptuously. "He's worth more than anything else in this place."

"He's… not dead?" stammered Hekja.

The woman looked amused. "I used the flat of my sword on him, not the blade. Now, will you walk, or must you be carried too?"

Hekja tried to understand. But the accent was so strong. Her mind was numb with pain and exhaustion. But the word 'walk' at least was clear.

"I'll walk," said Hekja. She had no choice. Snarf had tried to save her. She couldn't abandon him.

Besides, now he was all she had.

The big ships bounced on the waves far out in the harbour, but there were smaller boats pulled up on the pebbles in the bay. One of the men shoved Hekja roughly into the nearest one. It was already piled with bags of barley, and the iron pot that Hekja recognised as the chief's.

It took two men to carry Snarf. They flung him into the bottom of the boat then pushed it out into the waves.

Hekja knelt by Snarf. She wanted to hold his head in her lap or stroke him, but her hands were bound too tight. She gazed about her. Ships, so many ships, and the shore growing more distant. Tears stung her eyes. She looked down at Snarf instead. Was he moving?

Suddenly his eyes opened. He blinked and tried to get up.

"Shh. Don't move." She was afraid that if he tried to jump out they'd hit him again. "Stay, boy. Stay."

Snarf whined. He tried to sit up, then collapsed down again. The tears were blinding her now but it didn't matter. There was nothing she wanted to see. Hekja laid her face on Snarf's fur as the boat bobbed out towards the waiting ships.

Chapter 11

THE SHIP

They spent the night on board. Driftwood fires lit the darkness back on shore. Hekja had never smelt wood fires before – wood was far too precious to burn. They sparked higher than any fire she'd ever seen, like tiny stars reaching for the sky.

She must have finally dozed from exhaustion, despite the bobbing motion of the ship and the growing pain in her bound wrists, for it was dawn when she opened her eyes again. Snarf still slept but his breathing was even, so it seemed he had taken no great harm. Hekja looked around.

Ships, lots of ships, each one far longer than even the chief's hut and as wide.[9]

The ships smelt of pine trees. Each had a giant square sail of dripping woollen cloth across the middle that flapped and billowed as the men raised them to catch the wind, and two platforms either end, with bundles stowed underneath, and a deep middle bit, which was where Hekja sat, filled with bundles too. Oars dangled from the rowlocks at either end.

Gulls screamed above them in the growing light and the clouds skidded across the sky. All around the Vikings were heading back to their ships, folding their tents on shore and splashing through the shallows, their arms full of whatever they had stolen – cooking pots and cheeses, calf skins and dried fish. Someone had even put a ramp down into the shallows from one of the ships and was leading the chief's bull through the waves.

The poor beast looked terrified and tried to bolt, till the man gave it a whack about the rear with the blunt of his sword.

Hekja knew how the bull was feeling. Where had her life gone, the only life she'd known? Where were the villagers? Were they all dead, except the girls up on the great mountain and the witch?

Hekja looked up the hill, but no smoke hovered up above the witch's fire. Either she had the sense to put it out, or else they had killed her too.

Men yelled. Two youths chattered in their strangely accented language on the next ship. A man lumbered past. Hekja shrank back.

It was the man Finnbogi, who had killed Hekja's ma. He still had Ma's blood on his shirt, but he didn't even glance at Hekja as he passed. She was just one more piece of loot among the many.

No one seemed concerned with her at all. They were busy setting sail, stacking goods and settling themselves comfortably against the bundles.

Suddenly Hekja saw the woman Freydis who had captured her the night before. She was the only woman on board, standing amidships and directing men to stow this here and stow that there. A tall, short-bearded man Hekja hadn't seen before stood by her side, bellowing orders.

Hekja looked on wide-eyed. What was happening? Where were they going now? To raid another village, or a monastery perhaps? Where did the Vikings live? But there was no one to ask.

Finally the ships began to wallow out from the calm of the bay and plunged into the wild ocean waves. Hekja had lived her life by the sea, but this was the first time she had been on it. In her village, boats were for the men. Hekja stared at the distant shore as the village grew further and further away. But nothing moved there. The shore was still, except for the eagle circling above. Even the gulls seemed to have flown. Then suddenly she saw a figure striding out onto the cliff top above the waves, her cloak wrapped tight about her.

It was the witch. As Hekja watched she lifted her arm and waved, a small woman growing smaller, and smaller still.

One of the men yelled something and pointed. But they would not turn back for an old woman. They had got all that could be stolen from one poor village and had their sport. Now they wanted to be gone.

"Arf?" said Snarf softly. Hekja bit her lip. She would not let the Vikings hear her cry.

How much had Tikka guessed when she named a fat little puppy Riki Snarfari? thought Hekja. *How far are we going to travel now?*

Chapter 12

UNDER SAIL

The sky and sea swallowed the great mountain. Now there were only grey waves and the grey sky above.

Finally Freydis strode across to Hekja. Even on the swaying ship her walk was confident, as though she had been born on one. She carried a dipper of fresh water and some dried fish dangled from her hand. She held the dipper up to Hekja's mouth and let her drink deeply, and then she let Snarf drink as well.

"Well?" she demanded, staring down at Hekja. Even the Viking women, Hekja thought, were taller than a village man. "If I untie you, will you scream and jump overboard? It's too far to swim to shore, you know, even if you can swim, which I doubt."

Hekja said nothing. Some of Freydis' words were strange, so she was not sure what they meant.

Freydis laughed. It seemed she liked laughing, though not everyone might like the things she chose to laugh at. "Hikki!" she called. "Come here!"

"Yes, mistress?"

A young man, with dark hair and eyes the same colour as the villagers', made his way uncertainly across the boat.

His face looked slightly green from the motion of the ship. He was taller than any village man, even Bran, though he was not as tall as even the shortest of the Vikings.

He glanced at Hekja curiously, then saw the dried fish in Freydis' hands. He dashed to the side and vomited into the sea.

Freydis laughed even louder. "Stop feeding the fish, Hikki!" she shouted. "I ordered you to come over here!"

The man wiped his mouth and staggered back. Freydis pointed to Hekja. "You're from her land originally, are you not?" she demanded.

"Yes, mistress, though I have lived in Norway for many years."

"And now you no longer live in Norway. You are my brother's thrall, on my ship, and you will do what I say. Untie her, explain things to her, get her to eat. Teach her our language."

Hikki stared. "She should understand you already, mistress!"

Freydis shrugged. "These tiny villages on these islands only use half a dozen words. She probably doesn't know a loom from a codfish. Tell her what she needs to know."

"That will take some time, mistress!"

"Then the sooner you begin the better," said Freydis without much interest. "Feed her too!" She thrust the dried fish into Hikki's unwilling hands then strode back to the front of the ship and sat staring at the sea, as though she could understand its waves.

Hikki put the fish down and untied the rope from Hekja's hands. The rope was wet and the knots hard to undo, but finally he managed it. Hekja gave a small groan as the blood flowed back into her hands and feet, then bit her lip. She wouldn't give the Vikings the pleasure of hearing her pain. But none of them were listening; they were chattering to themselves or pulling ropes about the sail.

"Who are you?" demanded Hekja softly, as Snarf sniffed the young man's feet, rejected them, and took a fish to chew instead.

"I am Hikki, runner for King Harald the Fair Hair,"[10] said the young man proudly. "Now a gift to Leif Eriksson, the son of the great chief Erik the Red, the founder of Greenland. Leif brought many goods to trade with Norway, and Erik the Red sent his son to the king with gifts of walrus ivory and furs. The king gave me to Leif in return. I am the fastest runner in the whole of Norway. I took messages from one end of the land to the other."

"Norway? Greenland? What are these names?" asked Hekja, bewildered.

"They are countries, far from your village. Norway is where this ship has sailed from," said Hikki patiently. "Greenland is where we are going. It's a new land, found only eighteen years ago. My master and your mistress have holdings there, near their father's farm at Brattahlid. The Lady Freydis is your mistress now. She is my master's sister."

"We are going to another land?" Hekja had to force her voice to stay steady.

Hikki nodded. "The Norsemen know how to sail far across the sea and find their way even when there is no land to guide them. From Stad in Norway it is seven days' sailing to eastern Iceland, then four days' sailing to Brattahlid in Greenland."

Hekja blinked. It was too much to understand.

"We were sailing to Brattahlid but the storm blew us off course," Hikki continued. "The Vikings had to shelter in your bay, so my master says now we will sail well to the south of Iceland and, God willing,[11] see land in eight days' time."

Hekja shook her head. "Eight? Seven?"

Hikki sighed. "They are numbers, for counting. You have a lot to learn." He held up his fingers. "You see — one, two, three, four, five. Ten are the fingers of two hands. But there are bigger numbers. Erik the Red took four hundred followers with him to Greenland. That is a larger number by far."

Hikki patted Hekja's hand, till she drew it back. "I was as ignorant as you are when I was taken as a boy," he added.

Hekja stared at him. "The Vikings captured you too?" Hikki nodded. "I am a slave, a thrall like you."

"A slave! Why didn't you run away then," Hekja demanded, "when they landed at my village? You said you are the best runner in... in wherever it is!"

Hikki looked superior. "And live among the rocks and hares? Greenland is an empty land, my master says. If I serve him well I will be freed and may claim land of my own,[12] and have a proper farm, not a hut with a scraping of barley behind it. Even... " he looked calculatingly at Hekja, "a wife."

Hekja ran her hands across Snarf's ears. They at least were familiar and comforting. "So I am a slave," she said slowly. "What does a slave do?"

"What her mistress tells her to do. What did you do back in your village?"

Hekja shrugged. "I herded the cows, paddled the butter, made the cheese, dug the turfs... what everybody does."

"Then doubtless you will make cheese in Greenland. It sounds a fine, green place," said Hikki enthusiastically. "There must be mountains of grass all year round, to have a name like that."

"And the father of your master and my mistress, you said he is a chief there?"

Hikki nodded. "His name is Erik. They call him Erik the Red. A great man, by all accounts. A hero. My master Leif Eriksson is a hero too," he added proudly. "Leif made a voyage to yet another new land, Vinland, just last year. That is where he traded for the fine furs he took to Norway this summer, to trade for other things."

"What things?" asked Hekja. She picked up one of the dried fish and began to pull it apart, nibbling some of it and feeding the rest to Snarf with her fingers.

"Flour for bread and malt for beer, iron, linen, wax and tin, weapons, cooking pots, glass beads for the women, a good horse to ride and one to pull the plough. Many things," said Hikki. He looked at Snarf, as the big dog chewed the second fish. "That is a fine hound," he added.

"He is mine," said Hekja proudly.

Hikki shook his head. "You are a thrall, a slave. He is Freydis' dog now." He gave a shrug. "A good dog like him is worth more than a thrall, though not as much as a runner like me."

"He is mine!" flared Hekja.

Hikki looked at her consideringly. "You will learn," he

said at last. "Now, you must study the Norse words, as your mistress ordered."

For a moment Hekja wanted to argue. She didn't want to learn the strange new words. She didn't want Hikki's company either.

But at least he wasn't a Viking. And perhaps he could tell her something that might be useful. Somehow... somehow, she had to get away.

Chapter 13

STORM

The day dragged on. Hikki droned more words. Some she knew, and some she didn't, but she repeated them anyway, even the ones she knew, just to pass the time. The wind lashed at the boat and the salt spray splattered them. The bottom of the boat where Snarf slept slowly became a puddle.

There was no land, though Hekja searched the skyline. The world was featureless, grey, and grey and more grey. How could the Vikings know which way to go in a world like this? Maybe, thought Hekja, they would sail like this forever, and the world would never change. She was too numb now to even care.

Someone handed Hekja a dipper and told her to bail out the water. The ship was heavily loaded, and already rode low among the waves. Hekja dipped and threw and dipped, and Snarf rested his face on her lap as though to say, "I'd help you if I could."

There was dried fish to eat that night. Hekja had eaten dried fish all her life, either smoked by the fire or just hung in the wind outdoors till it was too hard and dry to rot, but in the village dried fish was soaked in milk or water to soften it. Here on the ship the fish were so hard you had to gnaw at them. Hekja shredded some of hers and took the bones out for Snarf to eat. Some of the Vikings also ate long strips of hard dried meat. But they didn't offer it to Hekja, or Hikki either.

"I am a slave," she thought. "I am a slave." The words kept pounding through her. She knew what slaves were, but had never really thought about it before. *No matter what I do, how well I make the butter or how well I guard the cows, I will be worthless, a slave.*

She and Snarf slept among the bundles. The Vikings had sleeping bags with fur inside, but no one offered Hekja any covering at all. It was dawn when she woke, the sun a red gleam on the horizon. It rose slowly in the sky till it hung high above the ship. Even through the cloud it seemed hotter than the sun over the great mountain. And there was no shade. The sail flapped and people yelled and the sea lashed and muttered over the side.

The sun sank again. The Vikings crawled into their sleeping bags once more, two to each sack, except the men who watched the sail. Even Hikki had a cloak to wrap himself in.

Hekja held Snarf to her, for comfort as well as warmth. All around them were the noises of the ship, the snores of many people, water lapping against the hull, the creak of the sail and someone farting in their sleep.

Then a voice came from the darkness. "Here."

It was Freydis. She threw a couple of rough, cured cowskins down to Hekja, then made her way unerringly through the bundles, back to her sleeping bag and husband at the front of the boat.

The skins smelt like home. Hekja wrapped one about her shoulders, and the other about her legs and Snarf, and they curled up together in the damp of the ship.

Three more days passed, each one like the one before. Only the colours changed, a sea and sky of grey or green or blue. The swaying ship didn't seem so strange now. Hekja knew its smells and movements. She even knew how to relieve herself over the swaying rail, though unlike the Vikings she waited for darkness.

Sometimes the other ships sailed close enough for the Vikings to yell at each other across the sea, cheery insults that Hekja couldn't understand. But mostly each ship was a floating world of its own.

The sun glared on the waves. The sky was blue now, bluer than it had ever been on shore, so bright it seemed to shatter on the sea. Hekja sat with Hikki and pretended to learn more words. She knew all he had to teach her now, but at least it was something to do.

Suddenly Freydis' husband, Thorvard, gave a yell and pointed high up in the sky.

Hekja followed his gaze. It was a bird.

Someone cheered, and clapped Thorvard on the back. Freydis strode down from her spot on the prow and they began to confer, gazing at the sky and sea.

Hekja looked back at Hikki. "What is all the fuss? It's just a bird."

"It's a land bird," said Hikki, looking superior. "It means that we are close to land."

"Greenland?"

Hikki shook his head. "Iceland."

Hekja shivered. The name sounded cold and strange. "Are we going to land there? Kill the people like the Vikings did back home?"

"Of course not!" Hikki looked scornful. "The Greenlanders came from Iceland. Remember? I told you so! Why would they attack their friends? No, we won't land on Iceland. The cargo boats are full already. We shall keep sailing to Brattahlid."

Hekja nodded. What did it matter? If there were Vikings in Iceland she couldn't escape there. But Greenland... it sounded different. Hikki had said it was an empty land. There would be places for her and Snarf to hide... and then... Hekja bit her lip. What then?

Snarf smelled it first. He lifted his nose and whined.

"What is it?" Hekja bent towards him. Snarf whined again.

Now the Vikings seemed to sense it too. Thorvard yelled an order and waved his arm at the sail, sagging now the wind had dropped. Freydis strode about the ship, gesturing to the store piles. Men began to tighten ropes.

"I said pull in the sail!" bellowed Thorvard. "Are none of you fools listening to me?"

"What is it?" cried Hekja.

Hikki shook his head. He mostly sat with Hekja these days. Hekja supposed it made him feel important, having someone who knew less than him. Suddenly the sail flopped down behind them. The ship stopped its onward pace and rolled a little in the waves.

Hekja gazed around. "Why are we stopping? There is no land here!"

One of the Vikings heard her. He grinned. "Storm coming!"

Thorvard clambered to the rear of the boat and hailed the ship behind.

"Leif!" he shouted. "What do you think? A bad one?"

The ship behind came closer. "Better lighten the ship!" yelled Leif. He grinned. "You can throw my sister overboard for a start!"

"I heard that, brother mine!" Freydis shouted at him. "Lighten your own ship if you want. This ship has sailors on it, not sit-at-homes, frightened of a tiny wind!"

"This storm will have even more breath than you!" yelled Leif cheerfully. "See you at home, dear sister! I'll bet you a nice new shawl we beat you back!"

"Keep your shawls to warm your feet!" shouted Freydis.

Leif grinned in return, then turned and bellowed orders to his crew.

The first gust hit. The ship lurched wildly, one side dipping deep into the water so the waves sloshed in. Hikki yelled, then grabbed the side.

The next gust was even stronger. Then the wind bit and didn't let them go.

Hekja had thought the boat shuddered before. Now it lashed from side to side. Snarf whined and crawled into the middle of the ship. Hekja followed, till they were wedged between two bundles, but they slithered too and dragged her with them.

Finally she grabbed one of the struts and held it with one hand, her knuckles white, while the other arm was stretched around Snarf. Now the rain came like a curtain, each drop so cold and sharp it bit into her skin. It was impossible to see across the ship in all the rain and spray. Where Hikki was she neither knew nor cared. Hekja held Snarf close, his warmth the only familiar thing in the world of noise and fury.

Up, up, up… Hekja had thought the sea was flat, but the ship seemed to climb a great mountain. Then down the other side, the wave crashing white around them. The ship shuddered further down into the trough, then up again…

The world had gone insane. How could waves climb as high as that? It was like mountains had risen all across the sea.

Someone screeched in Hekja's ear. "Bail!"

Hekja nodded. She held Snarf by the scruff of the neck in one hand and used a water jar to scoop out the icy water with the other. The ship was low in the water, even when the sea was calm. Now it seemed they were only inches from the water.

The ship lurched down again. A giant wave crashed behind them. Its foam lashed across the ship, carrying Snarf with it. The big dog tried frantically to paddle. Hekja caught one glimpse of his terrified face then he was gone.

"No!" Hekja dived after him, reaching through the foam. Yes… yes… her fingers touched his fur. Suddenly she had him, but it was too late. The water closed over her, and spat her out over the rail of the ship.

Down, down, down… the world was cold and water, green and grey and white. Almost instinctively she kept hold of Snarf's fur. Was this what it was like to drown, she wondered. Had her brothers felt this cold confusion before they died? Then suddenly her mind took over. No, she wouldn't die! She wouldn't let Snarf die, either! Hekja pushed downwards with her free arm and legs, forcing her body upwards, so it dragged Snarf up too. Was he still alive, wondered Hekja desperately. He was so limp, so still…

Suddenly her face met air. She gulped it in, but only for a moment. Then she was lost again, in the wild fury of the waves.

Her breath was gone. The world had gone, the sunlight and the air, gone like her father and ma, like Bran and all her village. Even Snarf had gone now, wrenched away from her grasp. Gone, gone, gone…

Then something hauled her up. No, not up. Up had no meaning in this world of waves. Something dragged her through the water and dropped her on the heaving deck. Arms reached down again, hauled Snarf up by his legs and dropped him sprawling on top of her.

Hekja gasped, though even that hurt. She rolled out from under Snarf to see Freydis still holding the hem of her dress. She must have grabbed it, Hekja realised, and kept hold while Hekja sank in the waves. Even now, amidst the wind and waves, Freydis was laughing, as though the storm and all its fury was an enemy she had conquered.

"A mermaid!" she cried. "And a hairy fish!" Hekja reached for Snarf, just as he coughed and tried to struggle to his feet. Hekja grabbed him again but her hands felt cold and weak.

"Thorvard!" yelled Freydis. "We need rope! Bring it here!"

Thorvard clambered across the ship. Even in this weather his step was firm, as though his body moved with the ship. "Tie the girl to the mast, and the dog as well," Freydis shouted.

"The dog?"

"I didn't fish him out to lose him overboard again!" yelled Freydis.

Thorvard grinned. His beard was flecked with foam. He grabbed Snarf by the scruff of the neck and dragged him over to the mast. Snarf whined and tried to get away. But at least, thought Hekja, he was still alive.

She tried to stand, then crawled instead through the water at the bottom of the ship, till she reached the mast too. It was a relief to feel the rope about her waist, tying her securely. Snarf was already tied about his neck and chest.

"Bail!" yelled Thorvard, forcing a bucket into Hekja's limp hands.

Hekja bailed. Her throat hurt, her body ached. It even hurt to breathe. But if bailing helped them survive then she'd keep on going. Half the time it seemed the waves just lashed the water back. But at least a little reached over the rail.

Waves and more waves, and waves again, some so high it seemed the ship could never climb them, or would be crashed to pieces by their weight. In between the crash of waves Hekja could see Thorvard at the rudder, forcing the ship through the storm. Even Freydis worked with the rowers now, heaving the great oars back and forth to give the ship what little power they could to ride the waves.

No, it would never end, thought Hekja. Then suddenly she thought, *the wind was worse than this a while ago*. And slowly the wind died down, and the rain stopped. But the seas stayed as high as ever.

The waves crashed around them all that night and no one slept. Black sky, black air, black sea. Only the frothing wave tops showed any white at all. But with the first grey light of dawn the worst was over.

Hekja hung limply from the rope, asleep from sheer exhaustion. When she woke the sea was calm, and men were yelling, trying to find the ships that had accompanied them before. But there was no answer except the lap of waves, and everything was white.

Chapter 14

THE ICEBERG

She had seen fog before of course. Snarf had fought the wolf in fog. But even then the world's smells had been the same, the mountain grass, the cows. This was a world that smelt of salt and ice, and fog so dense she couldn't see the ends of the ship.

"Arf," Snarf barked beside her, as though there was a monster that only he could see.

Then someone screamed out, "Berg!"

Something loomed beside them, tall as a hill and gleaming, even though there was no sun to light it. The men scrambled to their rowlocks and heaved with their whole bodies at the oars.[13]

It was as though the iceberg breathed out cold. The air about it was thick with cold. The hair on Hekja's neck rose at its strangeness, gliding so silently through the water.

Hekja scrabbled at the rope that still held her to the mast and half slid, half staggered over to Hikki. "What's happening?" she cried.

Hikki's fingers were white where he clung onto the side of the ship. He shook his head. Terror had stopped his tongue. His face was almost as white as the fog. "It is the end of the world," he muttered, through chattering teeth.

Freydis glanced at them, then strode across the ship. She lifted Hekja's chin with her fingers. "You were brave enough last night," she commented. "I like that. Let's see how brave you are today."

"What is it?" cried Hekja, gesturing towards the monster in the sea.

"Just an iceberg," said Freydis. She gave the laugh that seemed to challenge fog and ice and sea as well. "It wants to crush us. We shall see who wins." She glanced back at the iceberg as though amused at its challenge.

Suddenly Snarf barked again. It was a sharp sound in the cold air. He pointed with his nose, as he might do at a hare or deer. "Arf! Arf!"

Freydis glanced carelessly in the direction his nose pointed. Then suddenly she caught her breath as a new iceberg drifted into view. "Thorvard!" she yelled. "To port! To port!"

Thorvard heaved against the rudder. The ship veered. The iceberg passed, so close that if anyone had reached out of the ship they might have touched it. Hekja heard a faint scraping underneath the water, where the ice grazed the ship a bit too close.

The ship lurched. But at least it held.

Even Freydis held her breath at that. She let it out again and its steam added to the fog. "Well," she said. She looked at Snarf with new interest. "Do you think he can smell an iceberg?"

Hekja shook her head. "We have never seen an iceberg before. He is a good hunter though."

"But can he hunt icebergs too?" Freydis seemed to make up her mind without waiting for an answer. "Come," she said to Hekja. "The dog talks to you, I think. There is no time to teach him to talk to me. Where there are two icebergs there are more, and any one might kill us."

She strode back to the mast and untied Snarf. Snarf tried to stand, but his legs collapsed beneath him.

Hekja bent and picked him up. He was as long as she was now, so she had to haul his front while his back legs trailed behind.

Hekja half carried, half dragged him to the prow of the ship. Snarf struggled to get down, but again his back legs collapsed beneath him so he sat on his haunches, with as much dignity as he could, and stared out at the fog.

Nothing happened. Freydis shrugged. "It was just coincidence," she said. "I've never heard of a dog who—"

"Arf!" Snarf interrupted her. He pointed again, to the left this time. "Arf arf arf!"

"Far to starboard!" yelled Freydis. Another great white shape floated through the fog, though at least this was far enough away not to disturb the ship. She grinned at Hekja. "It seems it was worth saving him from the sea! A dog who can smell icebergs!"

The others in the boat were staring at them now. Snarf yipped, as though this was a great new game, and sniffed deep into the fog.

"Arf!" Snarf barked, and, "Arf arf arf!"

Iceberg after iceberg floated by. They were more blue than white, thought Hekja wonderingly, as though each had trapped a little of the sky. Perhaps that was where the sky had gone – it had been swallowed by the icebergs, leaving only the mist to take its place. Each time he sensed a new one Snarf warned Thorvard at the helm so he was able to steer away in time.

Hour after hour they sailed through the fog. Hekja found her eyes were closing. She forced them open, and tried to stare into the white. If she slept Snarf might sleep too. "Good boy," she whispered. "Good, brave dog."

"Arf," said Snarf happily, as though this was a game, like catching cow pats.

Finally Thorvard gave up the helm and wound his way towards them. "Any sign of the other ships?" Freydis spoke quietly to her husband.

He shook his head. "Either we have drifted too far apart, or they were lost in the storm."

Freydis nodded. Even she did not laugh at that.

Suddenly Snarf stiffened. He howled, a sound of fear and wonder. Freydis glanced at the way that he'd been looking.

"Iceberg to starboard!" she yelled. "Put your backs into it! Row, you sons of cow barns! Row!"

The men leaned against the rudder, so hard it creaked in protest. The ship swerved once again and only just in time.

It *was* a mountain. It loomed up higher than Hekja could see, its edges sharp and glistening. Even the islands in the bay at home had not been as large as this, she thought.

On and on it came, till it seemed the ship would never pass it. The rowers strained till they dropped, exhausted. Others took their places, their eyes bulging with the strain. Freydis rowed among them, yelling out the beat.

And then it was gone, slipping silently into the mist.

Suddenly a crack ripped the air, so loud it seemed the sky had torn apart.

No, not the sky, thought Hekja. It was the iceberg mountain. It had broken in two! One side slipped slowly down, then slap! It banged into the water, sucking the ship closer and closer to the half that still remained.

Hikki shrieked. Freydis caught him an absent-minded blow across the face and he subsided, whimpering like a puppy.

Hekja held Snarf tight.

"Hold on!" hissed Freydis urgently to Hekja.

Suddenly a wave welled up below. It bore the ship up, higher and higher still, then down again, with a slap almost as loud as the sound of ice crashing back into the water.

The ship shuddered, till Hekja was sure it was going to break apart. Then suddenly the world was still again, except for the new small waves that slapped the ship back and forth, the flap of the sail above and the creaking of the timbers of the ship.

Hekja stared back at the giant berg as the remaining side rolled slowly over, then bobbed in the waves made by its companion. Then it vanished behind them into the mist.

Chapter 15

✦

OUT FROM THE FOG

That was the worst of it. Hour upon hour Snarf watched for more icebergs, with Hekja and Freydis by his side. Day became night. Night was worse, the black and fog combined. But darkness made no difference. Snarf could smell an iceberg, even if he couldn't see one.

Slowly though there were fewer bergs, and fewer still. And finally Hekja slept, with Snarf curled around her. When she woke she found someone had covered them both with a sealskin rug, a proper sleeping sack that kept off the salt spray, unlike the cowhide blankets Freydis had given her before.

Snarf was a hero. This was a ship of heroes, Hekja thought, who faced storms and endless oceans and beat them both. But at least now they had gained some respect.

"I will call him Ice Nose," announced Freydis, as she handed Hekja their breakfast. The fog still wisped about the ship, but there was a drift of wind in the sails now and no more smell of ice.

Hekja shook her head. "His name is Riki Snarfari," she said firmly, meeting Freydis' gaze.

"His name is Ice Nose," said Freydis. Her eyes were

as cool as an iceberg, and as blue. "He can be my dog, or he can be fish food. You choose."

Hekja gasped. Was this how she rewarded them? Then she remembered the village, how Freydis had laughed even with the smell of blood sharp in the salt air.

Hekja bowed her head. "He is your dog," she said. "His name is Ice Nose."

"Good," said Freydis. "I said you'd learn." She smiled. "I'll tell Leif you were worth saving, if the storm did not swallow him and his ship." She strode back to talk to her husband and the rowers.

Snarf sat his bottom on Hekja's feet and she shared the food with him. It was better than they'd had before – dried beef as well as fish, though the beef was as tough as a bone. Hekja's face was wet, but she refused to wipe her eyes lest others notice she was crying.

They were killers, despite their bravery in the storm. And Freydis was as bad.

But things changed after the storm. Before it had been as though Hekja and Snarf were simply cargo, like bales of cloth or barrels. Now at least the crew nodded as they passed.

And then one morning as Hekja crossed the ship to throw one of Snarf's droppings overboard (a sailor had kicked him on the first day, when he had trodden in one) Freydis beckoned her to sit up by the prow.

Hekja settled herself on the damp boards, with Snarf at her feet. At first Freydis was silent, staring out at the sea, so Hekja wondered why Freydis had bothered to call her over. Finally Freydis pointed at a bird, high overhead.

Hekja squinted upwards, into the bright light. "Does that mean we are near to land again?'

Freydis shook her head. "No. It's an albatross. That bird will fly further than any ship can sail." She smiled, "My father asked Leif once, when we were children, what bird he'd like to be. Leif said a raven, and my father clapped him on the back, and gave him a new sword the next time the traders called."

Hekja frowned. "I don't understand. Why was he pleased that Leif wanted to be a raven?"

"I forget you don't know our stories." Freydis gazed at the horizon. "Floki Vilgerdson discovered Iceland with his ravens. He carried them on his boat and when he was past the Faroe Islands, he let one go. It flew straight back to the islands and so he kept on sailing."

Freydis looked at Hekja, to see if she understood. Hekja frowned. "You mean, the nearest land was there, so that's where they flew?"

"Exactly," said Freydis, pleased. "Floki sailed on. Then he let another raven go. It flew high, up into the sky, as high as a bird could fly. But it saw no land, so it flew back down on to his boat. And Floki sailed on. Finally he let a third bird go. This one flew on and on and it was not flying in the direction of the islands. So Floki knew there must be land that way. He followed the raven, and found Iceland."

"And that is why Leif wanted to be a raven," said Hekja slowly.

Freydis nodded. "My father never asked me what bird I'd like to be. Why bother with a girl? But I told him anyway."

"An albatross?" asked Hekja.

"Good girl," said Freydis briefly.

Freydis was silent after that. Finally Hekja said, "I'd like to be an eagle."

"Would you? Why?"

"Because they see everything," said Hekja slowly. "No matter what happens below, an eagle can fly high above it all."

"But eagles hunt as well," said Freydis, amused. "Yes, an eagle would suit you. You didn't scream, back in the storm, as a woman is supposed to do at danger. You didn't even shriek when the iceberg nearly dragged us down."

The albatross was just a speck now, riding the wind far beyond them. There was a new expression on Freydis' face as she watched it go, an almost wistful look.

At last she said, "Every time I look out at the ocean, I wonder what land there is beyond it, somewhere past the line where the sky meets the sea. My father found a new land and so did my brother. But I am a woman. I had to argue even to accompany my brother and my husband back to Norway, to trade the furs that Leif found in his new land. But one day…"

Hekja said curiously, "One day you will what?"

Freydis smiled at her. It was a different smile from all that she had given before. Those were smiles as Freydis challenged the world, and laughed at it. But this was a real smile for Hekja.

"One day," she said softly, "I will follow the albatross, not the raven. I will find another land, just like my father did."

Day swallowed day. The storm had blown the ship off course, so the voyage was longer than anyone had planned. Hikki shivered in his furs, sure that the ship had lost its way, and would float forever on the sea. But Freydis laughed at him as she passed on her way to Thorvard at the rudder. "I could find my way to land in a blizzard," she declared. "I can sniff out land, like my father." She grinned at Hekja. "You're not scared, are you?"

"No," said Hekja truthfully. Surely, she thought, she still felt too much pain for terror to take hold. Nothing she could do could change things now.

Freydis patted her arm. It was the first gesture of comfort or approval Hekja had ever seen her give. "Good girl," she said.

Hekja gazed out at the clouds on the horizon. What if those clouds were land, not cloud? A new land, just like Freydis dreamt of. Or an island, like her father's song, where jewels hung on trees. Suddenly Hekja realised something else was clouding out her grief.

It was curiosity, a sharp longing to know more about the new green land she was headed for. And despite her hatred there was almost admiration for the people who guided this small boat among the waves, far from any land to guide them, following the tides and winds, the sun and stars, the chants of those who had gone before.

Something in Freydis' words had lit something in Hekja's soul that burnt, as nothing had before. Even as she grieved and angered, Hekja too was dreaming of new lands and of wonders past the wall of the horizon.

Chapter 16

A LAND OF SNOW

And then one day the clouds on the horizon glittered in the sun, and Hekja realised they weren't clouds at all. It was land. Hekja waited for the grey to turn to green. Instead the land grew whiter the closer they sailed.

Freydis was up in her usual place by the prow. Hekja plucked up her courage and made her way over to her.

"Excuse me, mistress," she said. The word felt strange on her tongue. But that was the way Hikki spoke to Freydis, so Hekja supposed it was the way she should talk too.

Freydis glanced at her. "What is it?"

Hekja pointed out at the white land on the horizon. "Where is the green?"

Freydis grinned. "That was my father's trick," she said. There was pride in her voice. "He knew settlers wouldn't come to a place called Snowland. So he called his new land 'Greenland' and four hundred followed him, in twenty-five ships. Fourteen of those ships made it to shore."

"What happened to the other ships?"

Freydis shrugged. "They were lost in a storm, or turned back."

"What happened to the people?"

Freydis still gazed out at the distant land. Hekja thought she would have been happy to see land so close, but she was frowning. "They drowned."

"Do... do you think the people on the other ships who were with us drowned too?"

Freydis gave her laugh. "Perhaps. I doubt Leif has drowned though. The fish would spit him out. Besides, they call him Leif the Lucky."

The wind freshened suddenly. It came from the shore. It was warmer than the ocean wind, but it still smelt of ice, old ice, that had sat frozen perhaps since the world was made.

"Is the land all snow then?" demanded Hekja. She felt her hopes of escape begin to wither. If Greenland was a land of snow in summer, what must it be like in winter? How could she and Snarf survive by themselves in a land like this?

"There is snow and ice all year to the north, and in the high country. But in summer there is enough grass for sheep and goats and cattle."

Hekja frowned. She had never heard the words 'sheep' and 'goats' before. She would have to ask Hikki what they meant later. Freydis had a closed look, as though she no longer wished to talk.

By mid-day the coast itself was visible, with deep bays the Vikings called fiords slashed into the high, fierce cliffs. Now Hekja could finally see some green, a thin rim around the shore, but the inland was high and white, with only the steep cliffs free of ice.

The land looked fierce, thought Hekja, a fitting place for Vikings. Snarf barked beside her, excited by the smells of land.

Hekja had assumed they'd sail into the first harbour. But somehow the Vikings knew which part of the land they had come to, though it all looked and smelt the same to her, and it seemed there were no people here. Instead they sailed down the coast, past cliffs and fiords. Icebergs drifted by, the size of huts back home, and sometimes Hekja could hear them grinding when they came to shore.

Finally the ship turned in towards one of the fiords. Hekja gazed about, trying to see some sign of life. But still all there was to see were cliffs and ice. Where were all the people? She gazed about the ship, trying to find Freydis. Yes, there she was, deep in conversation with Thorvard. It was not the time to bother her with questions.

Hikki caught Hekja's eye and patted the seat beside him, but she shook her head. Hikki knew no more than she did of this strange new land. Besides, she realised, she was too excited to talk. A moon ago she had never even thought of any land beyond their village and its mountain. But now…

Suddenly she smelled it. Smoke! So there *were* people in this frozen land! She peered up at the cliffs, trying to see what lay beyond, but whatever lay above them was hidden from view.

Closer, closer. The cliffs rose even higher now. The sea was suddenly smooth, after so many days out in the ocean.

Snarf sniffed the air and yipped again, excited by the smells. Hekja too felt excitement tremble through her stomach. Even smoke smelled different here. And stronger than everything was the bitter smell of ice.

The water looked strange too, more like milk than sea and at times it sparkled, like stars that floated in the ripples.[14]

Even here deep in the fiord there were icebergs, the same colour as the sky, like frozen whales nosing at the shore.

The wind had died down as they glided further into the fiord. The sails fell slack. The men pushed and pulled at the oars at either end of the ship. Hekja hadn't realised a fiord could be so big, or cliffs so high, great slabs of rock that looked about to slide into the milky sea.

Finally she glimpsed a break in the cliffs, a tiny beach of tumbled rocks with green hills above it. There was even a pier – a stone track out into the water, where a ship could sit and unload its goods without the people getting wet.

At the other end of the ship Thorvard gave a yell. "Home!"

"Home," repeated Freydis. But her face had lost its brightness.

Still there were no people. "What have we come to, Snarf?" whispered Hekja. "An empty land of ice? Perhaps the ice has killed them all while the ships have been away."

Snarf wagged his tail. "Arf," he said reassuringly.

"Hold her steady!" bellowed Thorvard. He threw one of the ropes, thick as a man's arm, around a big rock on the pier. The big ship drew close, as gently as a calf nudging its mother. Thorvard pulled the rope tighter then looped it round some more.

The ship was home.

Two of the men shoved a thick plank across to the

pier. Everyone was cheering or chattering, hauling belongings from the pile. Hekja and Snarf sat forgotten. Freydis stepped onto the land first, then Thorvard, and then the others, till only Hekja and Snarf were left.

"Arf?" asked Snarf enquiringly.

Hekja shrugged. She had been waiting for someone to give her orders, but it seemed no one could be bothered. A new thrall and a dog were of little importance now. She stood up and tried to ignore the pounding of her heart.

Suddenly there were voices from the hill above them, shouts and laughter. People raced down to the shore. Children first, running down the grassy hill and on to the stone pier, yelling and hugging the new arrivals and peering into the ship and asking questions.

One young boy caught sight of Snarf and nudged his friend. Snarf gave a friendly woof and looked around, as though hoping there might be bones in this new land, or at least a dried cow pat for him to play with. Hekja grabbed the scruff of his neck and held on tight, in case he ran on shore without her.

Now the adults came, giant men with flowing hair or plaits and shaggy beards, with woollen caps instead of helmets. There were women too, strong-shouldered women in long dresses like Freydis wore, though these women wore hoods or scarves. Most wore aprons too and some had bracelets of gold or bronze or silver.

Still no one paid them any attention. Then Hikki beckoned from the pier. "Come," he said impatiently.

Snarf bounded off first. Suddenly he staggered.

"Snarf!" Hekja darted onto the pier – and staggered just as he had. Her legs were waiting for the ground to go up and down after so many days at sea.

Now the crowd parted. A man strode down the hill. His hair hung like snow down to his shoulders and his beard was snowy as well. Once he must have been a giant man, big even for these Vikings. Now his skin hung about him as though he had shrunk. He walked with the aid of a great stick that was carved like a dragon at the top, embellished with eyes of green stone and all inlaid with brass.

The chief back in the village was not like this. You knew this was a chief without being told.

The others all moved aside for him, except for Freydis. And suddenly Hekja saw her eyes were like the man's, though his were faded, as though all that they had seen had worn them out; the shape of her face was his too.

"This must be Erik the Red," Hikki whispered to Hekja. "Though he is red no longer."

Hekja ignored him, staring at the man.

"Well daughter?" Hekja had expected a great roar, but the big man's voice was hoarse, like it too had worn out from yelling above the wind and sea.

"It is very well, Father," said Freydis calmly. "A good voyage, and much profit."

"I know. Your brother landed two days before you."

Freydis' eyes narrowed, but she kept her face steady. "Always Leif the Lucky," she said. "It seems I owe him a shawl. Did the other ships arrive safe as well?"

"All but one. Njal Thorbjorgsson's ship was lost and all it carried. Except for him the crew were saved."

In Hekja's village the loss of any man at sea would cause an outcry, with women weeping. But Freydis only nodded. "It was a good voyage," she said. "And a safe one."

Hekja waited for her to tell her father about the storm and Snarf barking at the icebergs. But she didn't.

The men were unloading the ship now, with Thorvard bellowing orders. Freydis began to climb the hill with her father. Had she forgotten them?

"Woof!" Snarf's bark was louder than Thorvard's yells. Freydis looked around and spied Hekja still standing on the pier.

"Follow me," she said absently. Somehow she looked smaller here on land, especially next to her father.

Erik the Red raised an eyebrow at her. "A new thrall?"

"Leif didn't tell you?" Freydis grinned suddenly. "A storm drove us to shelter, and there was a village. Leif tried to catch this girl, but she outran him."

"Outran Leif!" The old man gave a shout of laughter. "A girl like that!"

"And now she is mine. I stopped her with the flat of my sword."

"Your sword?" The old man glared at her. "By thunder, your mother never wielded a sword in her life!"

"Nor did she ever go a-Viking. Mother died bearing your sons. Her only journey was following you here."

"As it should be," grumbled the man, and for the first time he sounded truly old. "And when will you have sons?"

"When I am ready," said Freydis coolly. "And that is a matter for my husband and myself, not for my father."

"If Thorvard were half a man..." Erik broke off, as Thorvard came up behind them, his arms burdened with a bale of wool, almost as large as he was, though he carried it easily. Hekja wondered what Erik meant by "half a man". Thorvard was almost twice the size of any villager.

It was impossible to tell if he had heard what his father-in-law had said. He just nodded, and said, "Sir. I'm glad to see you well."

Erik snorted. "Only one leg that works properly and breath that gives out if I so much as climb a hill, and he calls me well. I'm well enough, I suppose."

They had reached the top of the hill above the fiord now. Hekja caught her breath, for there was Erik's farm.

Farm? Hekja had never dreamt that even a village could be so big. There was Erik's great long house, as big as all the village huts put together, made of stone with a roof of turf. Smaller buildings clustered about it, each one bigger than anything she'd known. There were fields with fences of twined wattles[15] filled with strange new animals. There were grain fields too, and gardens filled with greens, familiar plants like kale and garlic, but others she had never seen before.

And there were lines of dried fish flapping, cods' tongues and whale liver, and other meat and hides hanging up to dry as well, and still more people. And the smells, so strong after the many days at sea, the familiar smells of drying fish, dunny holes and sweat, the stranger scents of boiling whale blubber and sealskins.

And above all this were the heights of blinding snow and blue-white ice, and lower hills of green, with stunted trees with dappled leaves.[16] The sun hung on the horizon, bathing it all in a golden glow.

"Arf arf!" For a moment Hekja thought Snarf was barking at the strangeness. Then she noticed a dog, almost as large as him, bounding their way. Snarf wagged his tail.

"Bright Eyes!" cried Erik. The dog bounded up to him.

"Arf," barked Snarf again. Hekja grabbed him. She wasn't sure how Erik would feel if Snarf sniffed his dog.

The dog ignored Snarf and the other humans too, and crouched down by her master.

Erik bent and fondled her ears. "Good dog," he said absently. "Well, daughter, will you come to the big house?"

She shook her head. "We will go to our own, Father."

"But a feast tonight!" ordered Erik. "There has to be a feast."

Freydis gave a laugh like his. "A feast tonight," she agreed. "I thought you would have done your feasting when Leif arrived."

"We waited for your coming," said Erik gruffly, and Hekja saw that for all his disapproval Erik loved her.

Freydis smiled suddenly. "Come," she said to Hekja. She and Snarf followed Freydis across the fields.

Chapter 17

✦

THE NEW HOME

Freydis' farm was on the other side of the fiord, through cow pasture first, then cows munching at the wiry grass. Hekja felt a pang of homesickness at their familiar chomp, chomp, chomping, and Snarf tried to sniff at every cow pat.

The next fields had stranger animals, smaller than Snarf but hairier. "Sheep," said Thorvard briefly, smiling at Hekja's obvious amazement. "Where wool comes from."

Raina and Reena, the chief's daughters, had worn woollen dresses, made from cloth traded for a side of smoked beef. But Hekja had always worn cowhide.

The sheep made a funny bleating noise, like old women complaining around the fire. Hekja peered down into the fiord. The men were still unloading the boat. The icebergs drifted by, bobbing about the milky water like Viking ships that no one had bothered to carve into shape.

They walked over the crest of another hill, with a spring bubbling from its side, and suddenly below them there were more buildings, none as large as Erik's, nor as many, but still amazing to Hekja's eyes. Each one was made of stone, with a high turf roof, all covered in grass even greener than the fields, as there were no cows up there to eat it.

There were what looked like storerooms, so many that she wondered if even Hikki's numbers could count them. There was one that looked like a dairy, with cheeses and butter barrels along its walls, and another giant empty one. And more rooms and more rooms, so many she wondered if she would ever get used to them.

Now there was a new noise, like seagulls clucking, but not quite like any Hekja had ever heard. They had reached the courtyard now. Tame birds[17] ran around picking at the ground. They were the ones who made the new clucking sound, Hekja realised. Great long walrus-hide ropes were stretched out across the courtyard to dry, with racks of drying fish and cod tongues and meat and hides, and smoke pits draped with hard tanned skins, much like the ones Hekja had known at home. Finally they came to the biggest building of all.

It was almost as big as a hill but long instead of round. Three of its walls were made of straw, and one of carved wood. Then suddenly the wood wall opened!

Hekja gasped. It was a door! The first wooden door that she had ever seen. Freydis ducked her head under the lintel and went inside, and so did Thorvard. Snarf lifted his leg on the corner of the house and produced a proprietary dribble, then he and Hekja followed.

It took a moment for her eyes to get used to the dimness indoors, after so many days in brightness on the sea. And then the house stretched in front of her, longer than she thought any house could be, and higher too, with great white rafters[18] of whalebone supporting the roof.

The walls were lined with wood, with webs of moss poking out here and there, so hardly a breath of outside air came in the house. The floor was dirt, swept hard and clean. Three fires flickered in a long, stone fire pit, halfway down the house. They smelt of wood and fish oil. Above the fire pit a great roast dangled on a metal chain and above that was the smoke hole in the roof.

Beside the fire was a great carved chair. There were benches too, with sheepskins draped across them, and a big wooden table. More skins stitched together hung from the roof beams at one end of the house, marking off a private room.

There was a platform with a strange device[19] with a length of cloth draped over it, a ladder up to a loft – there had been a ladder on the ship but Hekja had never seen it used – and two more doors with skins draped across their openings.[20]

"Welcome home, mistress!"

"It is good to be home, Gudrun," said Thorvard, as an old woman with fat ankles waddled forward. Her face was as wrinkled as an empty sausage skin, her mouth shrunk and toothless, and her thin plaits grey. Saliva sprayed from her gums in her eagerness to talk.

There was a torrent of words after that, from Gudrun to Freydis, most of which Hekja found hard to understand. It seemed to be about the farm and people and animals, but too many words were new. Beside her Snarf sat on his haunches and stared at the roast meat, in case someone decided to take it away.

Finally Gudrun stopped talking. Freydis waved a hand at Hekja. "Gudrun, this is Hekja. She's a runner from the islands. I don't know what else she's good for. She may need training before you find her much use."

Gudrun peered short-sightedly at Hekja and ran her hand across Hekja's face as though examining her features. She looked down at Snarf dubiously.

"Arf," said Snarf. He rolled over at Gudrun's feet in his dead dog position. Hekja recognised his way of saying, "I am at your command."

Old Gudrun smiled and rubbed his tummy with her booted foot. Then she looked back at Hekja.

"Well, girl?" she demanded, a bit indistinctly, as Thorvard and Freydis lifted the skins and went into their room at the other end of the house. "What can you do, hey?"

Hekja hesitated. "At home I minded the cows on the mountain. I made butter and cheese. I dried the fish with Ma and collected shellfish and... " Her voice broke off. She wouldn't cry. She wouldn't! But the tears ran nonetheless at the thought of home and Ma.

Hekja waited for Gudrun to laugh at her weakness, as Freydis might. But Gudrun patted her arm awkwardly instead with her age-spotted hand. "And where is your ma now, hey?" she asked gently.

Hekja shook her head. She made no other reply, but Gudrun understood. "Well," she said, even more gently, "there are cows to watch and cheese to make here as well as in your homeland. Perhaps your life won't be so different after all."

Hekja's face was wet. "You are a thrall too?" she whispered.

Gudrun nodded. "All my life, and my mother's too, and my grandmother, since the beginning of time. I came with the old master's wife from Iceland. But I've known others be taken from Ireland or the islands. You'll find it hard at first, but you'll get used to it. There's food enough and shelter. What more can we ask for, hey?"

Hekja said nothing. The old woman patted her arm. "Are you hungry? There's food if you like."

"Arf!" said Snarf enthusiastically. He'd recognised the word.

Hekja shook her head.

"Arf," Snarf barked again. He sniffed towards the hanging roast, as though it was a hare he'd hunted.

Gudrun laughed and patted his head. "You're hungrier than you know, after all those days of dried fish," she said to Hekja comfortingly. "You'll feel better when you've eaten."

She made her way to a cupboard – its door carved with tinier shapes than Hekja had thought a knife could make – and pulled out some cheese and a barley loaf, just like what she used to eat at home but much more plentiful, and a large hunk of cold meat too. Snarf knelt before her and slobbered on the floor.

Gudrun pulled at the small knife on the chain on her belt, and hacked off some pieces of meat and cheese. She handed them to Hekja then threw the rest of the meat to Snarf.

Gudrun was right. The food stopped Hekja's tears. And meat! All the meat she wanted, and meat for Snarf too, given so easily by one who was a thrall as well. So far Greenland was better than she had hoped.

After Hekja had finished eating, Gudrun ordered her to the outbuildings, to help store the goods that had been unloaded from the ship. The size of everything confused

Hekja at first, so Gudrun told her to sit and wipe the new weapons and tools with fish oil. Meanwhile the men carried the ship to its cradle in the giant empty shed, where it would be stripped of barnacles and caulked with rotted birch leaves to stop the water coming through the cracks.

Snarf bounded at everyone's sides, as though he was making sure that he was everywhere at once – in case a wolf attacked or an iceberg decided to invade the land. He kept an eye out for places he'd missed lifting his leg on, and snapped at passing butterflies or the tail feathers of the hens.

It was late by the time everyone had finished, though the sun still hovered near to the horizon. Despite all that had happened it was still not far from mid-summer, when the days were longest.

By now the smell of meat roasting for the feast floated across from Erik's farm. It seemed that only Freydis and Thorvard were going to go. Freydis changed her dress and put on a necklace and more bangles and different brooches made of shining metal and encrusted with sparkling stones, then she and Thorvard walked across the fields to Erik's without a word to Hekja. Freydis had more important things to do now than talking to a thrall.

"Here, boy! Sit!" Gudrun beamed at Hekja. "What a good dog he is! He comes when he is called!"

Hekja smiled tiredly. Snarf came so eagerly because he smelt the roast hanging from its chain.

"Good dog," said Gudrun approvingly, patting his head. "He's bigger than any dog I've ever seen. Do you know how to cook meat?" she asked Hekja.

Hekja shook her head. "I can cook barley bread, and fish stew. But I've never roasted meat before."

"Just keep the meat turning, then, and turn the pot so it doesn't get too hot, or the pudding will burn. You understand?"

"Yes," said Hekja. She poked the great roast of meat carefully. It spun gently as she touched it, and juice dripped down into the pot of grains and greens below.

Then a group of men came in – two thralls, and three free men who worked on the farm. They looked curiously at Hekja but asked no questions. Hekja was grateful. Her tongue felt thick with tiredness, and she was afraid that if anyone asked about where she came from she might cry again. The men sat by the smoky fire and talked about straying sheep and a sow that almost crushed a piglet – more words that Hekja didn't know. The two thralls also spoke to each other in a language the others didn't seem to understand.

"They are from Ireland," Gudrun whispered, as she passed with a platter of barley bread. Hekja nodded, though the word Ireland made no sense.

Gudrun put the meat down on to a platter and sliced it up. Her portion was minced into tiny bits, as she had no teeth to chew with. There were slabs for everyone else and the meaty bones and scraps for Snarf. Snarf gulped the meat scraps then rolled over, panting, so Gudrun could scratch his belly with her booted foot.

Each person had a spoon to eat the pudding from the pot. Hekja had never seen spoons so small. She watched how the others used them before dipping in her own.

The pudding was the best thing she had ever eaten, rich with cream and meat juices, sweet with fruit and honey, the soft grains melting with the greens. Even toothless Gudrun was able to eat it with ease, as it needed no chewing at all.

The fire burned low, till it was only coals. The house was dark, except for the twilight through the door. The men rolled themselves in sheepskins from the benches and went to sleep beside the glowing fire. Gudrun nodded to Hekja to do the same.

She felt stranger than she ever had – stranger even than on the boat, the smells of meat mingling with the scent of a foreign land, mixed with the scent of ice and smoke. But Hekja was too tired to stay awake, and the sheepskin was the softest, warmest thing that she had ever felt. She fell asleep with Snarf by her side, and didn't even notice when he rose to investigate more smells from outside, including Erik's bitch.

Even when Freydis and Thorvard returned she didn't wake, till Thorvard stumbled against one of the sleeping men, then kicked him drunkenly.

"Wake up, you lazy louts!" cried Thorvard, as he staggered past.

Hekja started to her feet, but Thorvard and Freydis were already in their room. The great wood door had been left open. Outside the sun was rising above the storerooms, and the hens were running after insects. The sheep were bleating, and the cows calling to be milked.

Her life in Greenland had begun.

Chapter 18

GREENLAND

They ate leftovers for breakfast – cold meat and cold bread and fermented milk. Hekja milked the cows as they stood with their heads through the stalls and munched at a handful of hay, while Gudrun watched.

Finally Gudrun nodded. "You know what you are about, girl," she said, hauling herself off the milking stool and on to her swollen feet. "Finish the milking yourself, then take the cows out beyond the barley fields and stop them straying. I'll ring the bell when it's time to bring them in."

"What's a bell?" asked Hekja, stumbling over the new word.

Gudrun shook her head. "What place have you been living in, hey? A bell is… a bell is… when you hear a loud noise, girl, a ding-ding-ding, then you'll know it's time to milk again."

"Arf," said Snarf, wagging his tail in case Gudrun had another hunk of meat with her. She patted him on the way out and slipped him a bit of barley bread from her apron.

One by one the cows were milked. One of the men came to take the buckets of milk back to the dairy. Hekja was just stripping[21] the last cow – a big red beast with horns that could lift a deer – when she heard a whistle behind her.

"Where is that blasted hound!" It was Thorvard. "Here, boy! Here!" He grabbed Snarf by the scruff of the neck and pulled him to his feet. Snarf grunted in surprise, then flopped back down again on to his tummy, to show he'd do whatever was wanted.

"What are you doing!" Hekja leaped to her feet, so suddenly she knocked over the bucket of milk. The cow pulled its head out of the wooden stall to watch them curiously.

Thorvard stared at her. "Get on with your milking, girl!" He bent to haul Snarf up again.

"No! Stop it! You'll hurt him!"

Thorvard struck her across the face. Her eyes watered and she staggered, but she didn't cry out.

Snarf growled deep in his throat. He could accept orders from other humans, but no one was allowed to touch Hekja while he was near.

Hekja put her arms around Snarf's great neck. "Leave him alone!" she yelled.

For a moment she thought Thorvard would strike her again. But then he began to laugh. "The dog is as big as you!" he roared. "And you think you will protect him!"

"What's happening here!" It was Freydis.

Thorvard stopped laughing, but his grin was as wide as a cheese. "It's your new thrall here. It seems she objects to my disciplining the dog. Perhaps you would like to fight me for him, hey, thrall?"

Freydis looked at Hekja coolly. "I thought we had this out on the ship. This dog is mine now." Her words were hard, but her eyes were amused.

Hekja shook her head, confused. "I… will fight… if you want me to," she stammered. "But you are not to hurt Snarf."

Suddenly Thorvard seemed to understand. He lifted Hekja's chin with his fingers. "I was joking, girl. But the dog needs to be trained if he is to be of use."

"What will he be used for?" demanded Hekja.

Thorvard glanced at Freydis. "She doesn't give in, does she?" There was admiration in his voice now. "He is a hunting dog. He needs to learn the hunting commands. Do you really want him to sit with you all day, a fine dog like that, while you watch the cows?"

Hekja was silent for a moment. Then she said slowly, "In our village the chief's dog did what the chief commanded at the hunt. But I never knew how to teach Snarf what to do."

"I know dogs, girl," said Thorvard. "My dog, Silvertail, died on our way to Norway. I will train your dog well."

"My dog?" enquired Hekja. She wasn't sure if she had heard correctly.

"Your dog," Thorvard said seriously. "But you are my thrall, so he is mine as well. Understood?"

"I understand," said Hekja.

Thorvard shook his head. "What is the world coming to? Making bargains with a thrall." But he was grinning.

Freydis looked at Hekja. And then she nodded. "I think," she said, and there was approval in her tone, "I may have won more than I realised when I captured you from my brother."

And so Snarf went to work with Thorvard, learning to come when he whistled, to sit when he clicked his fingers, to run at his heels until he gave the signal to chase. He learned to follow the scent that Thorvard chose, and not to be distracted; to bring game back and drop it at his feet; and to point properly when he sensed an animal in the bushes.

Finally Thorvard took him hunting. That, it seemed, was what most of the free men did in this new land, while the women ran the farms.

The men hunted reindeer; and polar bear, with their thick white coats; or walrus, prized for their ivory tusks and tough skin that was made into leather ropes and belts. They tracked the auk as well, giant birds who were too docile to even run away, with their precious feathers and their meat that stank of fish, and seals and eider ducks as well. The soft duck feathers were as valuable as the waterproof sealskins, and earned much silver from Norwegian traders.

Sometimes the men rode horses[22] – shaggy beasts as tall as Snarf, but with broader backs. But mostly the horses were kept for ploughing or for stallion fights, the great horses nipping, kicking, striking and rearing to see which one was strongest.

But after every hunt, as the men and women of Brattahlid streamed out to greet the hunters and exclaim at what they had brought back, Snarf would sniff out Hekja. She would hug him and he would lick her face as though to say, "No matter how far I have hunted, I am still your dog." Even when Thorvard whistled for him the next day Snarf would wait till Hekja gave him her own signal that he should go.

Life was busy for Hekja too. While Thorvard hunted, dressed the skins for trade, and went fishing or whale hunting with the other men of Brattahlid, Freydis managed her thralls and men to make sure the cows were getting fat for winter, or as much as this icy land would allow; that they were milked twice a day, that the butter, cheese and skyr[23] was made and stored, and the sheep shorn.

The farm had been a gift to Freydis from Erik on her wedding day and it prospered under her care. It was Freydis who oversaw the ploughing of the fields, and their harvest too, and saw the grain ground into flour or parched and stored in barrels for the winter. It was Freydis who ordered the fish hung and dried or smoked, the bear and deer meat salted, the whale blubber boiled for oil, the cods' tongues pickled, the onions hung in bundles in the shed, the moss and rose root dried and stored for when the sunlight vanished for the year.

Gudrun helped with all of this, but she was getting old. Once Freydis found that Hekja knew how to handle cows and crops, and dry the fish, more and more was left to her – especially once she learned that Hekja would work with no one watching her, and pass on her orders to the men as well.

But there were quiet times too, that Hekja could spend with Snarf up on the hills beyond the fiord watching the cows, just as they had watched them back on the great mountain at home. Here the air smelt of ice, as well as cow, and even in summer the glaciers cracked and grumbled down to the sea.

Hekja often saw Hikki as he jogged across the hills with his messages to other farms, but he never stopped to talk – it was as if he thought his time was too valuable to waste talking to a cattle herder.

Sometimes she gazed at the mountains and dreamed of escape, but in her heart she knew it was impossible. This wasn't the green land she had hoped for, where she and Snarf might find a cave and live by foraging and hunting. Even in summer people needed a good shelter here. And winter was coming…

No, there was no escape. Not yet anyway.

Chapter 19

STRANGE SHIPS

The days had begun to grow shorter. It was quiet up on the hill with the cows, except for the stream bubbling down in the gully, all cold and icy, and the bleating of the sheep. Even the late summer air smeled sharp in Greenland, as though the ice was never far away.

Hekja let the peace seep through her body. At times like this she could almost imagine she was home. Soon Ma would come with a barley cake hot from the stone, or Bran might stride across the hill...

Somehow Hekja found that she was singing again. The tune was old, but the words seemed to come from some unknown part within herself.

> *The birds fly together,*
> *The deer run with friends,*
> *But here I am lonely,*
> *There my past ends.*
>
> *My words end in silence,*
> *No one understands,*

My life or my language,
The heart of my land.

I once walked with friendship,
I once sang with joy,
But here I'm a slave,
In a stranger's employ.

The words echoed across the empty hills. Suddenly Snarf lifted up his nose and sang as well.

"Howwwwl!"

Hekja stopped singing. Snarf hadn't tried to sing with her since the days in the far-off hut by the shore, with Ma and all the precious familiar things around them.

"Oh, Snarf!" she cried. And suddenly she was weeping, her arms linked around his neck, snuffling into his long fur.

Snarf twisted round and tried to lick the tears from her face, which made her laugh as well as cry. Finally she sat up, her arm about him, and looked out at the cows, the farm below, and the milky fiord with its icebergs bumbling through the waves.

"Sometimes… sometimes," she said, "I think I can't stand it any more. There isn't even anyone who knows my land, except for you and Hikki, and he is at Leif's farm. Every time I see an eagle or a wild goose I think, if only I were like you, I could fly back home."

"Arf," said Snarf comfortingly. "Arf arf."

Hekja wiped her nose on the back of her hand. "Sometimes I think I hate them all. They are the people who killed Ma, killed my village! But other times…"

"Woof!" Snarf barked. But this was his warning call.

Someone was coming. It was Gudrun, puffing her way up the hill, a basket in her hand. Hekja wiped her eyes quickly, and ran back down. "You shouldn't have come so far!" she cried.

Gudrun's face was red and white in blotches, but she smiled, even as she puffed. "It will do me good to get out," she said. "There was a time when I used to spend days up here, like you. I thought, I'll just see the world from the hills once again, and bring the girl some food."

Gudrun sat down, and opened the basket.

"Strawberries!" cried Hekja.

Gudrun grinned. "I saved some for you from the mistress' dinner." She laid out more food on the wiry grass. There was smoked whale tongue too, and eggs baked with cream and honey, as well as a large bone for Snarf, still with good meat on it.

"Woof," said Snarf, wagging his tail appreciatively. He grabbed the bone and took it aside to look after it.

Hekja ate while Gudrun talked. Gudrun liked to talk. Hekja sometimes wondered if she had saved up her talk till Hekja came, for surely Freydis wouldn't have been interested in the life of a thrall.

Once Gudrun talked of the time that Master Erik caught a live polar bear and kept it in a metal cage. He had it shipped to Norway to astonish the folks there and then sold it for a large sum of silver.

Another time she talked of the Starving Year in Iceland, that her mother had told her of. It was when the great volcano belched out clouds of ash all across the land and the ground trembled as though to shake all humans off its shores, and winter lasted for an entire year and all but the strongest died.

"Was that why Master Erik came here?" Hekja had asked. "Because of the volcano?"

Gudrun shook her head. "He killed men unlawfully, in Norway, and then in Iceland too. His lands were confiscated, and he was exiled for three years. That is when he discovered Greenland. But this is a good place, in spite of the cold, with enough land for everyone. In my grandmother's day in Iceland a man could claim all he could walk around in a day while carrying a flaming torch, and a woman could claim all she could walk in a day leading a two-year-old heifer. But now all the good land has been taken."

This time, as they sat on the green hill and ate strawberries, Gudrun told of the Greenland winter when she lost her teeth. "The snow came early and stayed late," said Gudrun, happily remembering what had once been horror, "and when the men went out in boats there were no fish for their nets. Master Erik wanted to kill the stock, before they all died too, with no meat left on them for us to eat. But my mistress said no. If we ate the stock we would have no food for the next year. One by one my teeth fell out," said Gudrun. "Every morning there was another to spit on to my furs. I even sucked the furs, I was so hungry. We ate the reindeer moss, we ground the fish bones in the quern. Then just as I thought I'd see the floor through my hands the traders came, in their great boat, with a huge store of grain and malt and all good things that Master Erik could buy with his wealth of silver. Oh, we ate and ate, and then were sick, and then we ate again. But since that time..."

Hekja gasped.

"What is it, child?" cried Gudrun.

Hekja was looking out to sea. "No," she whispered. "No!"

Gudrun peered out to sea with her faded eyes. "What can you see?"

"Ships!" cried Hekja. "Ships!"

"They'll be hunting whales then," said Gudrun, puzzled at Hekja's distress. "The master took his harpoon and the sealskin floats from the storeroom this morning."

"No! These ships are different! They've come to attack us, just like before!" cried Hekja. "I have to tell Freydis!"

Suddenly she was running, almost as fast as a bird could fly, down the hill. Snarf bounded after her.

"Hekja, come back!" called Gudrun.

But Hekja kept on running. Down the hill, over the grass, which was scattered with cow droppings and sheep dung, then past the barley field, then the sheep yard. The men stared at her as she ran past and some cried out. But Hekja didn't stop.

Into the courtyard she ran, past the flapping lines of drying fish. The hens scattered, squawking and dropping feathers.

"Freydis! Freydis!" yelled Hekja.

That was not how a thrall addressed her mistress, but Hekja didn't care.

"Freydis!"

"What in thunder is all the yelling about?" Freydis pushed open the dairy door and stood staring.

"Arf!" Snarf leapt over a startled hen. "Arf!"

"Freydis!" panted Hekja. "I'm sorry, I mean, mistress…"

"What is it?" Then Freydis added, "Shut that dog up!"

"Ships! Five of them, out on the horizon!"

"Five?" Freydis looked interested, not alarmed.

"Are they invaders?" cried Hekja.

Freydis laughed. "Oh, I see, you have sounded the alarm. Well, thank you, I suppose, but there was no need. Who would dare come a-Viking here, to Erik's den? No, they'll be traders, from Iceland perhaps, or even Norway. I must go and change. You," she added, to a staring thrall, "go and watch the cows. And you, Hekja, wash the cow dirt off your face. I think," Freydis gave a smile, "you will be needed."

Chapter 20

THE TRADERS

Freydis soon came out, wearing a clean apron and a red and green silk scarf about her head, and a gold chain hanging around her neck and her best brooches too. She hurried across the fields down to the pier. Others from Leif and Erik's were heading that way too, as well as from the smaller farms that Erik owned and others worked.

Gudrun arrived back with the basket, panting and exclaiming that Hekja was not to worry. By now Hekja was embarrassed to think she had panicked at the sight of ships on the sea.

No one had told Hekja she was allowed to go down to the pier as well. So she and Gudrun collected the eggs and changed the weights and wrappings on the cheeses. Each time she peered out to the courtyard Hekja could see the ships coming further and further up the fiord. They were like the one that Hekja and Snarf had travelled in, with store boats bobbing behind them, laden with lengths of timber and barrels.

"What are in the barrels?" asked Hekja, as she dipped the cheesecloth in salty water, a Greenlander trick that prevented mould.

Old Gudrun shrugged. "Grain, perhaps, or cooking pots."

"But we grow barley here! And oats as well." Oats made a softer porridge and bread than barley, and Hekja had grown fond of it.

"Not enough to see us through the winter, not if you want to keep your belly full! That is why the masters trade, hey? The traders bring wood too, big lengths, not like the trees out there." Gudrun gestured at the stunted trees up on the hill. "Trees don't grow big enough for roof beams or barrels in this cold land."

Hekja wrinkled her forehead. "But why do the traders bring things here? As a gift?"

"To get other goods in return, of course! Did you never have traders in your village? They get good furs and walrus ivory and walrus rope, yes, and stockfish and whale oil. Ah, but you should have seen the furs Master Leif brought back from Vinland, and the wood too. Master Leif is richer even than his father now."

Gudrun glanced out the door. "They have landed already! We will have some excitement soon, hey? There'll be feasting and who knows what else." She shot Hekja a look. "You be careful, girl."

"But they're traders, not invaders. Freydis – I mean the mistress – said not to worry," said Hekja, puzzled.

"That may be," said Gudrun, "but when men have been at sea, and the ale is flowing – you be careful, child. Stay out of the way, if you can, so no one notices you. You understand?"

Hekja bit her lip, remembering some of the things she had seen when her village had been invaded. She nodded.

The crowd was heading up the hill now, towards Erik's farm. Thorvard broke from them and strode across the fields. "You, girl!" he yelled to Hekja. His hands were red with dried whale blood – he had been cutting blubber down on the beach, and had obviously had no time to wash when the traders arrived.

"Yes, master?" said Hekja obediently.

"The mistress wants you, over at her father's. Now!" he added, as Hekja failed to move at once.

Hekja handed Gudrun the last of the cheese wrappings.

"Remember!" hissed Gudrun. "Take care."

Hekja nodded. She ran across the fields, her bare feet slapping against the ground. The Greenlanders wore leather boots, strapped around their ankles, and so did the thralls. But no one had given Hekja any to wear or even warmer clothes, except for the cowskin cloak Freydis had given her on board the ship, though the days here were colder even than up on the great mountain at home. Snarf bounded at Hekja's side, his ears pricked at the noise and excitement.

Freydis stood with Erik and Leif, examining great lengths of wood. "There you are! Father, if this girl can't outrun Leif's runner I will give him my best cow."

The old man looked Hekja up and down. "You've seen her run? She has the legs for it, at any rate. But can she last the distance and find her way?"

"She will," said Freydis confidently.

Hekja looked from one to the other but didn't speak. She already had learnt that speaking out of turn would earn her a slap across the ear.

"Hikki!" roared Erik suddenly.

The runner stepped out from one of the store sheds. "Yes, master?"

"I want you to take a message. It's two days' sail north, but you will run it. Understand?"

"Yes, master," said Hikki confidently. He shot a glance at Hekja. "I can run faster than any ship can sail."

"We'll see," said Erik.

"What is the message and where am I taking it?" asked Hikki.

"The farm is due north of here, the first one that you come to up the coast, as far up a fiord as this one. The message is for my youngest son, Thorstein Eriksson. Tell him: 'The traders have come. Bring your furs and join the feast.' Understood?"

"Yes, master." Hikki glanced at the sun. "I will need dried fish, so I may eat as I run. Then I will be gone."

"One moment," ordered Erik. He nodded at Hikki. "This girl is a runner too."

"Her?" Hikki looked at Hekja in astonishment. "Girls can't be runners!" he protested.

One of the traders had overheard. He was young, only a few years older than Hekja, with hair the same shade as the butter she had churned that morning. He stared at Hekja, which made her remember that she had forgotten to wash the cow dirt off her face, as Freydis had told her to, then bent down and rubbed Snarf's ears. "A girl runner?" he asked curiously. "Do the women in your country run too?"

Hekja shook her head. Suddenly she wished she had proper shoes and a woollen dress, and a hairbrush like Freydis' so she too could pull her hair back into plaits.

"I've never heard of a girl runner," said the young man, pulling out some dried meat from his pouch and feeding it to the delighted Snarf. "Surely they don't have the strength."

"Perhaps there are things you haven't heard of, Snorri the Skald,"[24] said Freydis calmly. "Maybe girls are more capable than you think Hekja, I want you to take the message too. And if my brother's runner gets there first, you will be beaten."

Hekja met her eyes. "I'll run as fast as I can," she said. "I don't need a beating to make me run."

Snorri gave a shout of laughter. "There is no way a girl can beat a man! Uncle Nils!" he called to one of the other traders. "This girl is a runner!"

It's like I'm a strange beetle in the grass, to be exclaimed over, thought Hekja.

"Girls cannot run," said Hikki flatly. "Their skirts get in the way."

Hekja glanced at Freydis. Freydis smiled. "Run!" she said softly.

Hekja hesitated. Surely she should take dried fish too, and maybe water. But then she caught Freydis' eye. This way she would have a head start over Hikki!

Hekja ran, sprinting across the fields, with the men's laughter echoing behind and Snarf leaping at her heels.

Chapter 21

THE RACE

Once out of sight, Hekja slowed down. She knew there was no way she could keep that pace for long.

Where was she supposed to run to? North, Erik had said, and hug the coast. *That should be easy enough,* thought Hekja. And Hikki said that he could make the run in less than two days. Surely she could run that long.

But fast enough to beat Hikki? Hikki had run messages for years. He was used to finding his way across country. Somehow Hekja knew that there was more to being a runner than just putting one foot in front of another.

She was now past the familiar hills where she had herded the cattle. She crested another hill and suddenly there was a fiord in front of her, a deep gash of rock and cliffs with the waves crashing down below. Snarf began to bound down between the rocks but Hekja called him back.

"This way! Good dog! We need to go around, not down!"

"Arf," said Snarf happily, as though this was the best game he'd played for days. He galloped along the cliff edge just as Hekja caught sight of Hikki, in the distance.

He was wearing a strange shift, just two lengths of cloth tied together at the sides and fastened between his legs, so his arms and legs were free to run, and he had a sealskin pack over one shoulder. He was running further inland, so he had missed the fiord altogether, loping along as though he had done this all his life. Which of course he had.

Hikki waved and grinned, but didn't slow down. In a few heartbeats he was gone.

Hekja bit her lip. Hikki was ahead of her now and likely to remain so. But all she could do was try her best.

Over rocks and up cliffs she ran, scrabbling at the loose gravel and sliding down the slippery rock faces. Several times she had to stop and go back and find another route, each time keeping the smell and sound of the sea to her left. And all the time the thought pounded through her brain: *Hikki knows how to judge the land.* He wouldn't have to double back like this. *We will never catch him. Never.*

Hekja had seen one of the thralls beaten, when he had left an axe out in the rain and it had rusted. There had been blood down his back and face.

"I would rather run forever than be whipped," muttered Hekja under her breath. "Run up into the ice, so the ice giants can catch me, and freeze me forever…"

The sun sank below the horizon. The summer twilight filled the sky, dark enough for a few bright stars but still bright enough for Hekja to find her way, as long as she stared at the ground and not at the bright horizon.

But even Snarf was tired now. Hekja's breath came in long, deep pants. But she refused to stop.

Then Hekja tripped. "Ow!" She examined her knee anxiously but it was only a bruise.

"Woof!" Snarf lay down beside her, as though to say, "We've played enough!" Hekja ran her fingers through his fur. "We'll have to stop till it gets light. Do you think Hikki will run all night?"

Snarf scratched a flea instead of answering.

There was a clump of rocks a little way ahead, enough to shelter them from the chill breeze that was blowing up from the sea. Hekja wrapped herself around Snarf's warmth. The ground was hard and cold, and she hadn't even brought her cloak. But she was so tired that sleep came despite it all.

The first light woke her, the sun gleaming above the icy mountains. She was almost too stiff to move and hungry too. She had run for half a day and half a night, and it had been a long time since Gudrun's strawberries on the hill. Snarf was already snuffling around the rocks, hoping to find mice or lizards. But he followed her as soon as she began to run.

The shadows shrank and the day grew warmer, and the sun dried up the dew. There were streams to drink from, chilled by the falling snow, but hunger ate at her insides. Worse, it was slowing her down. Several times she stumbled, dizzy and unsure of where to put her feet.

Then suddenly Snarf stopped and sniffed the wind.

"Snarf! What is it?" Hekja whistled. "Come!"

Snarf whined. He'd come if she wanted him to. But there was something he wanted to investigate, down on the beach.

Hekja hesitated. "Go on then," she said. "I'll rest, just for a moment."

Snarf whined again, signalling Hekja to follow.

Hekja nodded and did as he asked.

There was an animal track between the rocks which led them down to the sandy beach. And there it was – the carcass of a whale. It was as long as a farmhouse and almost as high.

Perhaps it had beached itself. Or maybe fishermen had brought it in. But certainly men had taken all the meat along the spine – the tide and ravens would never have picked it off so cleanly. The only meat left was right at the head. Hekja stuck her hand into the blowhole. The meat was still warm, still fresh. The fishermen could not have left it long ago.

She would never have considered eating raw blubber before, though the Irish thralls back at the farm had talked of whale feasts on the beach, eating the whale meat while it was warm and raw. But Hekja was too hungry to care. This was food and it would keep her going. No matter how bad it tasted she would force it down.

Snarf tore at a piece of blubber and chewed it hungrily. Hekja tried to do the same, but without a knife it was impossible. Finally Hekja shared what Snarf had managed to tear off with his teeth. It tasted better than she had expected – tough but juicy. Best of all, it filled her belly and gave her enough strength to keep going.

Once she was full she finally washed the blood from her hands and mouth in the cold sea water. Snarf wiped his mouth on the grass too.

Then Hekja began to run again.

They ran all that day, fuelled by the whale meat, with only short stops to take a drink. That night they slept again, for the few hours the sun spent below the horizon. The next morning, Hekja had to force her legs to move, they were so stiff and sore.

And then they ran some more.

Chapter 22

MIST!

The mist came slowly, drifting like fine silk at first, down from the mountains and up from the sea, till it was like barley flour around them, then thicker and thicker still, till finally it was impossible to see the ground.

Hekja slowed, till she realised that the mist made little difference to Snarf. She couldn't see but he could smell, and this was quite enough for them to find their way.

Now Snarf's nose led the way, with Hekja at his tail. The path was stony in places and the lichen-covered rocks were slippery. But Hekja's bare feet were steady.

Suddenly Snarf stopped and sniffed the air. The mist clung to his fur, tiny jewels like the stones in Freydis' brooches. "Gruff," he snorted.

Hekja bent down. "What is it, boy?"

Snarf gave a short "yip" and this time Hekja heard it too. "Help!"

Snarf barked again, more loudly this time. Whoever had cried out must have heard him, because they called out louder now. "Please! Help me! Please!"

Hekja looked around in the fog, but there was nothing to see but white. She laid her hand on Snarf's head and signalled to him to be quiet, so she could listen more closely.

Girl and dog stood motionless – all that could be heard was the sound of their breathing in the quiet air, and then the rustle of a bird. And then it came again.

"Help! Please!"

"Hikki," breathed Hekja.

"Arf," said Snarf, pleased that Hekja had finally worked out what his sense of smell had known all along. He looked at Hekja, waiting for her order. Keep running or find the man?

But Hekja didn't hesitate. "Find, boy, find," she said.

Snarf bounded into the mist and disappeared. Hekja tried to follow him, then stopped, confused. "Snarf!" she called.

"Arf!"

Hekja followed the sound through the mist. Suddenly she saw something, a different colour from the mist and grass and rock, and then she saw Hikki lying twisted at the bottom of a cliff.

Snarf barked again, as though to say, "Look, he's over there."

"My foot! It's caught!" cried Hikki.

Hekja ran towards him. It was obvious what had happened. Hikki had missed his step in the mist. As he slithered down the cliff face the rocks had crumbled under him as he fell, trapping his leg.

Hekja knelt down and examined the rock fall, then pushed at the rock above his ankle. Hikki grunted in pain and shook his head. "I've tried," he said. "It's caught fast. Maybe a lever – a bit of wood to prise it off. Otherwise you'll need to go get help."

Hekja could hear uncertainty in his voice. Would Greenlanders venture out in the mist to help a thrall? In Norway Hikki had been the king's slave, and valued, but things were different here.

She looked around. There was a stand of crooked trees growing near a crevice not far away. Hekja pushed at one of the trunks until it snapped at the base, then shoved the branch under the rock, Hikki giving orders all the time.

"No, further in, the other way, no, you've gone too far. Now shove…"

Suddenly the rock began to move, just a bit at first, so Hekja could shove another rock beneath, then shove again.

This time the rock shifted, just enough for Hikki to draw his foot away. The rock crashed down. But Hikki was already free.

He sat there for a moment, the sweat dripping down his face, even though his skin was blue with cold. Then he felt his foot carefully, and the ankle too, then held his hand up to Hekja.

"Help me up," he ordered.

"Are you sure?"

Hikki nodded. "It's bruised, that's all. I can move my toes. It will swell tonight but for now I can keep on going."

Hekja helped him up. He put his weight on his foot gingerly and then more heavily.

"It's sore, but I can run," he said. He looked at Hekja for a moment without expression, then reached down and picked up the sealskin bundle by his side and unwrapped it. There was barley bread inside, made sweet with dried berries and rich with butter, as well as some strips of dried meat.

"Here." He divided it into three portions – one for him, one for Hekja and the other for Snarf. Snarf gulped his down as the others ate theirs more slowly.

"I didn't think you would get this far," Hikki said at last. "You really are a runner, even though you're a girl."

Hekja smiled. It was obviously the highest compliment he knew. "Thank you," she said, swallowing the last of her barley bread.

"It's not easy running in a new land," added Hikki. "Especially when you don't know your way and it's dark and misty and you're all alone."

"I wasn't alone," said Hekja as she patted Snarf and rubbed his ears.

"Even so," said Hikki.

Hekja waited for him to set off again, as fast as he could limp with his bruised leg. But instead he took Hekja's hand.

"Thank you," he said. He hesitated. "I would like to say that I would have done the same for you. But I wouldn't have. I would have seized my chance to be the winner and left you here. You have taught me something." He glanced at the sky as though to work out where the sun was, but the mist was still too thick. "Go," he said. "I'll wait here for as long as it takes to roast a hare, before I run again."

Hekja frowned. "Isn't your leg too sore to run?"

He shook his head. "No. I am giving you a chance to win. It surely isn't far to go now. Call it runner's honour. Now run!"

Hekja ran.

She had lost all sense of direction now, but it didn't matter. Snarf seemed to know which way to go, and Hekja trusted him. Soon she realised what he had been following – the scent of smoke, and fainter still, the smell of roasting meat. People! They were nearly there.

Slowly the mist began to lift. They topped a hill and there was the farm below.

There was no mist here, just a few drifting clouds, already almost vanished in the sky. Instead there were fields and sheep and goats and thralls cutting the grass for hay with long sweeps of their scythes.

Snarf lifted up his nose to bark, to announce that they'd arrived. But Hekja put a hand on his head.

"Ssh," she whispered. "Not yet." She turned around and walked back down the hill the way they'd come and sat and waited. Soon she heard the thud of footsteps and there was Hikki, loping through the remnants of the fog, not even puffed.

He stopped when he saw her. "What's wrong?" he demanded. "Are you hurt?"

Hekja stood up. She had worked out exactly what she was going to say. It would have been better as a song, but there wasn't time to make one. "Call it runner's honour, even if our masters never understand," she said formally. "We may be slaves, but we have both run well. Let us end the race together, so no one wins, or else we both do."

Hikki looked at her for a moment, then he nodded.

And so the race ended with the two runners striding down the hill, hand in hand, to deliver the message to Thorstein Eriksson, with Snarf running at their side.

Chapter 23

A FEAST AND A CHALLENGE

They returned to Brattahlid in Thorstein's boat, along with his bales of hides to sell to the traders, a keg of mead[25] for the feast and Thorstein's neighbours, who wished to join the celebrations.

Someone must have seen the ship as it travelled down the coast, as there was a crowd waiting for them at the pier – Freydis and Thorvard, Leif and Erik and their men, Snorri the Skald and the other traders, and Bright Eyes too, gazing down disdainfully at Snarf as he yapped in the prow of the boat. The news of Freydis' and Leif's bet had spread.

"Well, younger brother?" demanded Freydis, looking from Thorstein to Hikki and to Hekja as Snarf bounded up to greet Snorri the Skald, to see if he had any dried meat in his pouch again. "Who won?"

Thorstein shook his head. "Both of them!" he exclaimed. "I have never seen the like! They came running down the hill together, hand in hand."

"Hand in hand!" cried Freydis. "Is this true?"

Hekja lifted her chin. "Yes," she said.

Freydis' eyes narrowed. "I ordered you to win," she said. "Not play handies with my brother's thrall."

"You told me I would be beaten if I lost," said Hekja. "I didn't lose. I promised I would run my best, and so I did."

Beside her Snorri gave a shout of laughter. "She's got you there!" he cried.

Freydis looked from him to Hikki, to Hekja then to Leif. And then she grinned. "So! I get to keep my cow!"

"And I keep mine," agreed Leif. He too was grinning.

Erik clapped Snorri on the back. "Have they given you an idea for a song, skalder boy?"

Snorri smiled, as though the idea was ridiculous. He didn't even look at Hekja and Hikki as he shook his head. "I make songs about heroes, not thralls."

"And your heroes are all men," said Freydis.

Snorri nodded, his hand still on Snarf's head, fondling the big dog's ears. "Of course. Heroes like your father, finding a new land, and your brother, sailing to unknown Vinland and returning."

Freydis looked out at the ocean for a moment and was silent.

"Woof," said Snarf, sniffing at Snorri's pouch again.

Erik looked pleased at being called a hero. He slapped Snorri on the back again, so hard he nearly jolted him into the fiord. "By thunder, that was well said, boy," he cried. "Come and see how heroes feast this afternoon and you can give us your song. And you thralls too." Erik turned to Hikki and Hekja, and tapped them with his stick. "You can come and listen to his chant, in honour of your run."

"Woof," said Snarf, as though he could smell the meat already.

But first there was the milk to churn. Feast or no feast, there were jobs that must be done. Gudrun's hands were twisted with arthritis nowadays, so she was grateful for the help with the butter and she needed a hand lifting the cheese stones[26] too.

But now across the fields came the smell of smoke, and laughter. The feast was ready. Gudrun sat back on the butter stool and looked at Hekja, weilding the butter paddle fiercely like she was trying to paddle life itself into shape. "You want to go to the feast?" she asked.

Hekja nodded.

Gudrun sighed. "Be careful, child. The men will have drunk a lot – and they are men."

Hekja lifted her chin. "There is no way I will forget that," she said softly. "I wouldn't let any Norseman touch me."

"You may not get a choice," said Gudrun dryly.

"I can outrun them," declared Hekja. "Like I did before."

Gudrun looked shocked for a moment. Then she shook her head. "A thrall takes what is handed out to her."

She shook her head as Hekja shrugged. "No, child, I am quite serious. If a master wants you, you can't stop him. If you try – if you run – it will be the worse for you. A master can chop your hand off, or kill you if that is his pleasure. The only way for a thrall to be safe is to make sure she stays out of the way, especially when the drink flows freely. Why do you think the mistress hasn't given you a good dress for the feast?"

Hekja stared at her. Gudrun nodded. "The mistress is wise. In that dress you look like a child, not a woman. The men will go for better game than a barbarian who's dressed in tatters. But you take care. I knew a girl once…" Gudrun bit her lip.

"What girl?" demanded Hekja.

"Dear girl, I tell you these things only so you will be careful. She was a thrall, from Ireland, when the old mistress was alive. She had a baby, and who the father was no one knew or cared, except its mother. But winter was coming and food was short. So one night the mistress ordered the baby taken out and left on the rocks."

Hekja stared. "What happened to it?"

"It died," said Gudrun simply. "And its mother cast herself off the cliff, down by Erik's farm. See, you can see the spot over there, by that twisted tree. And no one cared, for she was just a thrall."

Hekja lifted her chin. She whistled softly. Snarf came up to her and she hugged him close. "I am only a thrall in their eyes, not in mine," she declared defiantly.

Gudrun looked worried. But she only said, "Try not to get noticed."

Hekja crossed the fields. She wasn't sure why she was going – Gudrun's words had frightened her, even though she had refused to show it, and the noise and strangers laughing held no attraction.

"I will only stay a little time," she promised herself. "Then I will sneak back."

The feast was held outdoors. Big as Erik's house was, so many people had come from farms up and down the coast for this feast that no house could have held them all.

So the sheep had been moved from a field near the farmhouse and great fires of driftwood lit there, with whale oil to keep them burning well. Two giant bears were roasting and walrus and reindeer, with great stone platters of wheat bread to soak up their juices. The traders had brought the wheat, for none grew in Greenland. It was their gift for the feast.

There were trestles of other food too – big stone pots of pickled cod tongues and oat cream puddings with onions and sorrel, which were plants the settlers had brought from Iceland, and dishes of buttered angelica and rose root, that grew naturally in Greenland. There were fat ducks stuffed with berries and fish stewed with cream; fermented whale liver, and fresh whale steaks; barrels of barley beer and mead and big stone jugs of buttermilk that had been cooling in the ice-flecked stream, and skyr too.

All the benches had been brought out as well as Erik's great carved chair, and rocks had been brought up and covered with sheepskins for people to sit on.

No one noticed as Hekja crept up to pick some scraps from a reindeer carcass, stripped of its best meat now and pushed away from the fires so it didn't scorch. The visitors all carried their own knives to cut the meat but Hekja didn't have one. But there were spare knives on the tables, as well as long spoons for scooping out the marrow from the bones.

Hekja sliced off some scraps and laid them on a slab of bread, then handed a chunk of meat to Snarf. Snorri the Skald glanced at her. He frowned, as though wondering what thrall had the impudence to help herself to food at the feast. Then he must have recognised her as the runner, for he said nothing but kept chatting to the girl at his side. It was one of Leif's daughters, with gold and brass at her wrists and throat. She had her grandfather's bright hair and a look of softness in her eyes, from her mother perhaps, thought Hekja, as there was no softness in Erik, Leif or Freydis, or Thorstein either. She overheard two women talking and nodding at the couple as they ate their meat.

"It would be a grand match for her. His family has great lands in Norway, so they say."

The other nodded. "Maybe the lad would like to mix his blood with that of heroes!" They laughed together, but Hekja could see that they were half serious.

Hikki was sitting at the back of the crowd with a big hunk of meat on a slab of bread. He raised a hand to Hekja and she slipped across and sat next to him, grateful for a friendly smile.

Hekja sat beside him, on the ground, not on a bench. The noise and crowds and laughter frightened her a little, as did the men who had drunk too much beer or mead or skyr. The women kept the men's drinking horns full and, as no horn could be put down or it would fall over, it was easier to drain it in one gulp and then call for more. The field was full of shouting and yelling, and already there was a fight, with onlookers cheering the men on.

Suddenly she heard a voice that she remembered. She peered through the wool-clad legs. There was the man Finnbogi, watching the fight, tearing at a hunk of meat with one hand, his ale horn in the other.

"Into him!" he laughed, as one man threw another

over his shoulder then pounded his face till he cried for it to stop.

Hekja tensed and hid the trembling of her hand in Snarf's fur. She forced herself to look at other things – the fire sparks streaming to the sky, the girls and women splendid in their brightest scarves, wearing their best necklaces, bangles and brooches. Even Erik's serving thralls had clean aprons on and coloured scarves, although theirs were wool, not silk.

All at once Hekja was conscious of her tattered dress, so short you could see her knees now, and her bare feet hard and callused instead of in soft boots.

Suddenly Erik yelled, "Quiet!" He banged his great stick three times on the ground.

The noise hushed. Bright Eyes, his dog, sat up straight as though to say, "Pay attention to my master!" People moved closer to Erik's chair, forming a circle around it. All that could be heard were hens muttering indignantly and a calf lowing in the distance for its mother, as the people sat in silence.

"We have been honoured," cried Erik, "by a visit from our good friends." He gestured to the traders. "May they return to us often, by thunder, with good profit to us all!"

The crowd roared their approval. Erik banged his stick again. "But we have another honour here tonight! Silence for the skald!"

The young man walked into the circle. His sea-stained clothes were gone. In their place were a silken tunic trimmed with fur that looked as soft as snow, and a blue cloak embellished with gems all down the edges. His cloak pin and rings shone in the sunlight and the handle of his dagger was carved and bejewelled, and his yellow hair was tied back with a bronze clip. He held himself proudly. *They all do,* thought Hekja, half admiring, half resentful, *every person in this land, except the thralls.* But this youth looked as though from birth he had known that he was heir to great estates.

Even the men who had been fighting were silent now.

The skald lifted his head to the sky for a moment, then began to sing:

> *A song in praise,*
> *Of heroes I raise,*
> *Of danger and death,*
> *And the ocean's great depth.*

> *But one man defied them,*
> *Though they would destroy him,*
> *For courage fills sails,*
> *With more force than the wind.*

The great crowd was silent. Hekja stared at the singer. She had heard her father sing, his voice also so true that people sat quiet even after he had finished. She had heard the men sing on the ship to Greenland. But she had never dreamed a voice could carry as much power as this.

Finally the song's echoes died away and the audience roared again, the men lifting their drinking horns to toast the singer. Erik tore off one of his great brooches and thrust it in Snorri's hand, then clapped him on the back. The young man accepted the brooch as his due and fastened it on to his furs.

Leif's daughter sang next, accompanying herself on a small harp held in her hands. Everyone listened politely, but they weren't standing motionless like they had for Snorri.

People helped themselves to food after that and drank deep draughts of skyr and mead and beer. Snarf snuffled round for crumbs. Snorri saw him and clicked his fingers at him. "Here, boy!" he called.

Snarf bounded up. The young man tossed him a hunk of walrus from his plate and laughed as Snarf gobbled it.

People called for him to sing again. This time it was a song about a prince, enchanted into ice, and the princess who learned to sing to the winds so she could rescue him. The crowd cheered again. There was a pause after that, as people waited to see if anybody else would sing.

Suddenly Hekja wondered what would happen if she began to sing. Her voice was better than Leif's daughter. But probably, she thought, singing was something for free men and women, not for thralls. And then Hekja thought: *even if I could, I wouldn't sing for them. If I sang it would be a gift to them. I will give them nothing.*

For a moment the words almost shaped themselves into a song. Hekja smiled to herself. *If I ever do sing where they can hear me*, she thought, *that will be my song.*

It was growing dark now. Someone poured more oil on the fires. Fish-oil lamps flickered on the tables to drive away the night.

A group of men were singing to one side, but their voices were too slurred for Hekja to make out their words. Finnbogi was one of them, waving his horn mug in time with the song. Hekja thrust the memories away.

Suddenly Erik's stick beat on the ground again. "Silence! Let the skald sing us another song!" His voice was more quavery than it had been earlier. Erik might have been a hero, but he was getting old.

The people nearby quietened, but the men kept on singing – their noise was so loud they hadn't heard his voice.

In a sudden fit of rage Erik picked up his carved stick and struck one of the thralls, who was bringing more food out to the tables, on the shoulder. "You! Tell them to be quiet!"

The man nodded. "Yes, master." He made his way over to the men. Hekja saw him pull the sleeve of one, to get his attention and then begin his words.

Hekja was never sure what happened then. But suddenly there was a drunken roar across the crowd.

"No one tells Olaf Njalsson to be silent!"

Metal flashed in the firelight. Hekja bit back a scream and stared across the crowd.

Erik's thrall lay on the ground. His neck was severed. The man he'd asked to be quiet stood over his body, a bloodied axe in his hands. It was one of the traders.

Hekja tried to struggle to her feet. Hikki grabbed her hand and forced her back. No one spoke. A band of silence had tightened around the crowd.

"That could have been you or me," whispered Hikki. "Sit still. This is not a time to be noticed!"

Hekja shook her head numbly. She waited for a howl of rage from Erik. She had heard him howl before, across the fields when his best axe was missing or when a thrall was slow to bring him his spear. But now he said nothing, he simply stared across the crowd at the still bleeding body and then at the man with the axe.

Snorri moved swiftly over to the trader. He whispered something urgently. The man shrugged. He bent and wiped the blood off the axe head on the trodden grass. His axe was a grand one, with carving on the handle, and there were carved bracelets about the man's wrists as well.

Snorri put his hand on the man's arm then, but the trader shook him off. "No one tells Olaf Njalsson to be silent!" he muttered again drunkenly.

Snorri gazed at him, then looked at Erik. Then he made his way through the crowd towards Erik.

"I beg your pardon," he said formally to Erik. "My companion misunderstood. I will pay compensation, on his behalf." His hand went to the purse at his waist. "Shall we say thirty ounces of silver?"

Erik stared at the young man. *Surely*, thought Hekja, *he will be angry*. The dead thrall had lived in his house, had worked for him. But Erik didn't even glance at the body again.

"The compensation for a slave is only twelve ounces," said Erik.

Snorri laughed. Despite his youth he seemed quite confident beside the older man. "Forty ounces then! Shall we call it extra compensation for a guest's rudeness to a hero!"

Erik clapped him on the back. "Well said, by thunder! Now let a hero make a gift to you as well! What will you have? Name it!" he yelled, lifting his horn in salute to Snorri, then swallowing its contents in one gulp.

Snorri raised his drinking horn in return, and drained it down. He looked around the crowd, considering his prize, then laughed. He pointed to Snarf, who was still snuffling for scraps by the fire. "Give me a hero's dog! And every puppy from his get will remind me of my hosts in Greenland!"

"No!" Hekja spoke before she thought. But what did it matter what they did to her? Nothing mattered if they took Snarf. "No!" she yelled. "No!" She leapt to her feet, but Hikki again forced her down. He thrust his hand over her mouth, muffling her words.

"Hush," he hissed, "or it will be your body on the ground next."

But it was as though no one had heard Hekja's outburst. *I am invisible*, thought Hekja. *Who hears a thrall?* She struggled against Hikki's grip, but he held her hard.

Across the crowd, Snorri didn't even glance her way. He just continued as though he hadn't heard her cry. "On second thoughts, what use is a dog to a singer? Will he make my songs for me?"

Snorri smiled and pointed to the harp that Leif's daughter held. "No, lend me that instrument, so I can play it while I am here, and when I'm gone, you can play it to remember a singer who once had the privilege to play in a hero's hall."

Hikki's hand still covered Hekja's mouth. She stared through the sea of skirts and trousers. Had she heard correctly? Was Snarf still hers?

Leif's daughter laughed and blushed as she handed the singer her harp. A mist of tears and anger clouded Hekja's eyes. Why had Snorri changed his mind? Had he heard her cry? Or had he simply thought of another way to compliment Erik's family? Dimly, she heard Hikki say,

"If I let you go will you be silent?"

Hekja nodded and he took his hand away from her mouth.

"I'm sorry," he whispered. "But I had to do it. If you had tried to argue they'd have killed you." His voice dropped even further. "Or worse."

Across the fire, Erik was delighted. "Well said, skalder boy! Sing us another song of heroes then! Daughter! My mug is dry!"

"He doesn't care," whispered Hekja. "He doesn't care about the poor dead man, or me, or Snarf. We don't exist. We're nothing." Suddenly she wanted to run, as fast as she could, and never stop. But if she ran now the men would notice her and take it as a challenge. And this time one might catch her.

"Why should he care?" said Hikki, and for the first time Hekja heard bitterness instead of pride in his voice. Grand runner he might be, but he was still a thrall.

Hekja got to her feet. For the third time Hikki pulled her down. "Stop," he hissed. "If you go now you'll attract attention. Wait till the skald is singing."

"He should sing of the dead thrall," whispered Hekja. "He should make a lament for his death."

"Forty ounces of silver is all the lament he'll get," said Hikki grimly. "Skalds don't sing of thralls."

Freydis went to fetch her father more mead. Across the crowd another thrall, a woman, bent down towards the dead thrall's body. She was crying. But Hikki was right – the skald didn't even glance her way. He smiled at Leif's daughter, and stroked the harp strings with his fingertips, as he began to sing:

Stand upon the mountain,
Gaze beyond the sea,
There is a new land calling,
Singing "come to me".

Raise the sails, my shipmates,
Fill the barrels well,
I'll sing of the far horizon,
And what to us befell...

The song went on and on. Hekja sat silent in the shadows. Now that the crowd was watching the singer Hikki got up to leave, and held his hand out to help Hekja to her feet. Hekja shook her head at him. *Just one last song,* she thought. *After this I'll go.*

Hikki sat down next to her again. Snarf wandered over, unaware of his part in anything that had happened, and curled up beside them, his ears pricked.

Another thrall arrived and helped drag out the body. The singer finished and the last echoes of the harp died away.

"Well sung, by thunder!" roared Erik. His face was flushed but there were shadows under his eyes. He looked around the crowd. "A song of heroes! Are there any here who will do what I did, and my son? Sail the unknown waves to find new lands beyond the clouds? Found a colony where none have ever been before?"

It was not said as though he expected an answer, except maybe a few 'here here's' as people remembered how brave he'd been, before he'd shrunk with age. But suddenly Freydis spoke up.

"I will!" she cried.

People muttered. Someone laughed at the edge of the crowd. Freydis ignored them.

"I challenge every man here!" she cried. "Who will join me? We will sail south, to the lands my brother found. Lands with trees as tall as mountains and salmon that leap like birds. We will explore the land and make our fortunes! And once we have settled there our ships will explore even further!"

Suddenly everyone was still. Then someone cried, "Will you take your husband too?"

Laughter rippled through the crowd.

Freydis turned on them, her eyes flashing. And then she turned to Thorvard. "Well, husband?" she challenged.

Thorvard stared at her, as though considering. And then he grinned. "Well said, wife. I will come. Who will join us?" His voice rose to a bellow.

No one spoke. And then the singer, Snorri the Skald, pushed forward and joined his hand to Thorvard's. "I'll come," he shouted. "What is the use of singing of heroes, if you refuse to be one!"

"My ship will follow them!" someone else cried.

"And mine!"

"And mine!" It was the man called Finnbogi.

"Four ships then!" roared Erik. "Or five? Leif, will you lead a colony to the land you found?"

"I will," said Leif. "And I will take my household with me."

Chapter 24

A GREENLAND WINTER

Hekja could feel Hikki stunned and silent beside her. Was this the end of Hikki's hopes of a farm and freedom in Greenland? All about people chattered, and cheered those who'd said that they would join the expedition. She whispered, "Will we have to go as well?"

Hikki nodded. "Yes. We are runners. They will need runners to explore this new land."

Hekja bit her lip. "Vinland is even further away, isn't it?" she whispered.

"From what?" asked Hikki.

"From home," said Hekja quietly.

Hikki's eyes were sympathetic in the firelight. "A thrall's home is with his or her owner. It just makes unhappiness to think otherwise."

Hekja was silent for a moment. Then she said, "What is this Vinland place like?"

"I have spoken to Leif's men who were there," said Hikki. He sounded happier now he could instruct her again. "It is a wonderful place, they say. Rivers thick with salmon, weather so warm the cattle can eat grass right through the winter, and all the grapes that you can eat."

"What are grapes?"

Hikki shrugged. "Berries I think, that they make a drink called wine from. But it is a good place. No ice, no snow." It was as though he was trying to convince himself. "There will be free land there too. Better land than here." Hekja could see he was remembering Leif's promise to free him, and give him land if he worked well.

Hekja gazed up at the mountains. The ice gleamed, even in the starlight. "Why don't they all go to this Vinland then, instead of staying here?"

"Because it is so far away," said Hikki. "And Leif only discovered it three years ago. Maybe they will all follow us in time." He was looking brighter now. "But by then maybe I will have a farm of my own. I will be free. Maybe," he added, "maybe we will both be free."

Hekja had assumed they would set out at once, but it seemed that it took a long time to plan an expedition like this. Besides, it would be winter soon and the seas would be too full of ice to sail. Summer was the time to go a-Viking, when the days were long.

The traders sailed away two days after the feast, with their walrus ivory and walrus-skin ropes, their sealskins and eiderdown, but Snorri the Skald stayed with Erik and Leif.

Now autumn was half over it was harvest time. The days of hunting parties were gone. Thorvard had the household up each day as soon as the world brightened, but there was no need to urge the men to work. Thrall, free man and husbondi[27] all would starve together if summer's harvest wasn't stored in time for the bitter Greenland winter.

The cows were left unmilked so that they might put on fat to help keep them alive in the hard times ahead. Hekja too was set to gathering the grass that men cut for hay, to feed the animals when the snow lay on the ground. The cut grass was left to dry in the sun, then raked into heaps, then stacked by Erik's man Arnkel the Strong Hand, who could make a haystack so tight that water flowed off it and the hay inside stayed dry and sweet.

Whale blubber was boiled down for oil, the beaches were scoured for driftwood. Even twigs were bound together and dried for faggots. More fish was smoked or dried, and whale tongues too, as well as strips of blubber to chew in the cold weather.

Then there was the grain to thresh and more grass to cut, and more grass again, till it seemed to Hekja that all of Greenland was either ice or rock or drying haystacks.

Sometimes she heard Snorri sing as he swung his scythe, for in this season even honoured visitors had to work in the fields. At times Hekja found she was humming the tunes too. It made her long for music even more. But there was no chance to sing her own songs with everyone else around.

Snarf enjoyed the grass cutting. The mice had bred up as the grain ripened and the scythes sent them scurrying. He could catch a bellyful on a good day, then bounce around the cows that grazed the stubble from the crops, and the hens pecking the grain that had fallen on the ground.

But the best was still to come, from a dog's point of view, for it was time to slaughter the bull calves and lambs and the oldest of the cows and sheep, and most of the hens and pigs as well. There was no way to store enough grain and hay to feed them all.

So their necks were slit and the hot blood collected, mixed with oats and herbs to make blood puddings and stuffed into lengths of intestines that had been washed clean in the streams. They were then hung to dry up in the rafters, while Snarf watched and drooled and begged for leftovers.

Calves' stomach was kept for rennet, to turn milk into curds then cheese, the legs and back strips smoked and salted and hung to dry above the fire, the head boiled down for brawn, the fat boiled to a hard white lard and the lean meat cut into thin strips and hung to dry, along with fish, either gutted or with their roes, so you could hardly see the houses for the lines of drying food.

All through summer the crocks of butter had been buried in the cool soil by the stream, and every second day a new cheese hung up in the dairy. Now the eggs were buttered too and stored in straw, the onions dug, their stems plaited and hung up in the storerooms above the casks of sorrel dried into whispery flakes, and watercress, angelica stems and rose root leaves.

Then one morning Hekja woke and found the world outside was silent.

The household was still sleeping. Hekja tiptoed over to the big wood doors and peered outside. Everything was white. Even the air was white, the snow still falling, muffling every sound.

Someone stepped up behind her. It was Thorvard. He took one look outside, then yelled, "Blizzard! Hurry! We have to get the animals inside!"

He began to pull his cloak and over boots on, while inside the men groaned then scrabbled for their cloaks as well. But Freydis called Hekja back.

"Here." She thrust some sealskin boots at her, that were lined with fur, and a long calfskin cloak too. It was not much of a cloak – the hide was barely trimmed – but it was warmer than the one she had. "Thank you, mistress," said Hekja.

Freydis shrugged. "If you lose your toes to frostbite you cannot work," she said. She nodded at the boots. "Mind you dry those out before you put them on, or your toes will freeze. We keep no crippled slaves in this household."

Hekja didn't ask what happened to a crippled slave. She slipped the boots over her feet, fastened the cords of the cloak and ran outside after the others, awkwardly at first, till her toes got used to the clumsiness of boots.

It was so bright in the daylight that her eyes hurt. Hekja helped the men drive the cattle in to their byres – the poor things were shivering and glad to escape the snow. The pigs had already found their way into the pig shed. The sheep were driven into the house – they would live at one end and the humans at the other, to help keep each other warm.

That first snow melted by the afternoon and there was no more for days after that, so the last of the hay dried out and was brought in. But the next snow lay upon the ground and the one after too, and then it was just constant days of more snow and ice. The snow piled up so high about the house that the men spent most days just digging out the door and tramping the snow flat to make a walkway to the byres and sheds, so that Hekja and Gudrun could feed the animals their winter rations of hay and grain.

The household woke in darkness now, till Freydis lit the fish-oil lamp, but only one, as the oil had to last till summer came. By early afternoon it was dark again. They lived in shadows, for even when it was light outside there was little light indoors. It was a darkness that dragged at you and made you long for summer.

The men sat by the fire and played chess or told stories of storms at sea or plundering villages. Even as they played or talked their hands were busy, carving wood or walrus ivory into spoons, or runners for the sleighs, needles or jewellery.

The women worked too. Hekja mostly spent her days combing wool for Gudrun to spin into thread on her spindle, while Freydis sat up on the weaving platform with the loom, weaving the cloth for the household or for sails. Sometimes Gudrun sewed trousers or made dresses and aprons. She tried to teach Hekja how to use a sewing needle too. Hekja wasn't very good, but she kept working at it, as one of the woollen dresses was for her, with a proper headdress too. She had almost outgrown the dress she had worn since her capture.

Sometimes Hekja combed Snarf with the wool comb, which made Gudrun laugh, and threaten to spin his long hair into thread. But Snarf was not always there.

In the first break from wind and storm Leif sent a thrall to see if Thorvard would join him and others on a hunt. Thorvard put on his furs and snow shoes, gathered his sleeping bag and leather tent, and a store of marrow fat and berries mixed with oats.

And then he whistled and called out to Snarf, "Here, boy."

Snarf looked up at Hekja, as he always did, for her permission. She could see that already he was excited at the thought of bounding through the snow, hunting scents again in the cold air.

"Go," she whispered.

The men were gone for days each time they hunted. By now the days were so short it was impossible to travel far in one and most of the game about the farms was gone. The seas were now frozen so they could hunt seals across the ice, for the meat and their fur, winter soft and waterproof. Sometimes there was other game too, though as winter drew on most animals lost their fat. But the fresh meat was welcome after so much salted and smoky meat that had to be soaked for hours or days to make it soft enough to eat.

Freydis never hunted with the men. But sometimes, when the hunters' cries echoed as they strode out of the courtyard, Hekja saw her face go blank, as though she was dreaming of a time when she would not be bound in a small house with mundane sewing to keep her busy and the sheep and thralls for company, when she too could stride out across the world.

Mid-winter brought the Yule feast. "And it's a grand one, hey?" said Gudrun happily. "A whole week long, our household and Master Leif's and Master Erik's!"

"And barley beer enough for everyone and a bull calf kept to roast," said Conlan the Irish thrall longingly, from his place by the fire. "If I eat another fish I will turn into one and go swimming down the fiord with the mermaids."

Hekja looked up from the spindle she was twirling. "Do thralls go to the feast as well?"

Conlan nodded. "We do indeed. And we can eat and drink as much as we want to, with singing and games too."

The wind died down Yule morning. The snow had formed a crust and Hekja's feet left deep holes as she padded out to see to the animals. Even though the sun had risen low on the horizon the day was dim, as though the darkness had crushed all brightness from the air.

But today there was the scent of roasting meat from Erik's farm across the fields. Hekja felt like dancing through the snow! It had been so long since she had left the house, apart from brief visits across the yard, so long since she had seen a person who was not from her household. And there would be fresh meat and feasting food, instead of hard dried fish. And music too…

Freydis stepped out from her and Thorvard's curtained room as Hekja took off her wet boots. Freydis had on her best cloak and all her jewellery, and Thorvard his best furs. Freydis picked up her cloak then glanced at Hekja, who was putting on some dry boots – she had worn Gudrun's spare pair to keep her new ones dry.

"Not you," said Freydis shortly.

Hekja looked up. "Mistress?" she enquired.

"Someone must stay and keep the fire alight and tend to the animals."

Hekja took the boots off again and came back to the fire pit. She felt the disappointment like a blow.

Gudrun patted her hand. "It will be your turn to go to the feast next year, perhaps," she said.

"Next year," said Freydis, "we will be in the new land." And suddenly her face glowed, as Hekja hadn't seen it shine since the days on the ship.

Chapter 25

YULE FEAST

They left her then.

"Eat what you want from the storeroom," were Freydis' parting words. "It is yuletide, after all. You may keep a lamp alight, and the fire, but use no more wood or oil than you must. Feed the beasts and give them fresh hay but don't bother to muck them out – the men can do that when we return. A week of dung will do no harm."

The door closed behind them. Hekja could hear them chattering as they slid on the fresh snow, and Thorvard's laughter as he picked his wife up in his arms to keep her feet dry.

At least they had left Snarf, Hekja thought. She felt guilty at that, for she knew Snarf would have enjoyed the excitement of the feast. But without Snarf she would be quite alone, except for the sheep. And sheep, thought Hekja, were even stupider companions than cows.

It was quiet after they had left. *No, not really quiet,* she thought. The sheep bleated. The wind came up again and howled, though the sod roof kept it out. The fire flickered and a mouse rustled in the moss, chinking between the stones. Snarf snuffled after it, then put his nose on his paws and dozed by the fire, with one ear pricked to make sure the sheep didn't push past the hurdle that kept them in their part of the house.

Hekja sat by the fire and twirled her spindle. There was nothing else to do now the animals had been fed, except go to the storeroom of the main hall to fetch fish for supper. There were dried berries in a basket and she took a handful of those too. After all, Freydis had told her to eat what she liked. It was little enough for a Yule feast, thought Hekja, as she chewed the hard, tough berries.

The day passed slowly. Hekja felt its gloom sweep through her. Winters were so long and dark in Greenland, far longer than at home. At least she'd had the feast to look forward to. Now there were just more dark dull days – the tomorrows seemed endless.

Finally she went to sleep with Snarf and the sheep for company. It seemed so much darker and colder, Hekja thought, without other people near.

There was no snowfall during the night, so the doorways were still clear in the dimness next morning. Hekja fed the cattle crammed up in their stalls, and the hens too, and carried in fresh hay for the sheep, while Snarf lifted his leg on the doorposts. But today, despite the cold, Hekja hesitated before going back indoors. The hill looked so inviting, white and pure despite the darkness of the day. She could run up there, just for a while, into the peace and freshness, just her and Snarf like they used to do…

"Arf," said Snarf encouragingly. He leapt up and licked her face. "Arf arf!"

Hekja shook her head. It wasn't worth the risk. She had seen how worthless thralls were. She had been told to guard the house and keep the fire alight. If she left without permission Thorvard or Freydis could kill her and no one would even question what they'd done.

It would be easy to escape, now everyone was gone. But where to? Only into the snow and ice and dark where they would surely die.

Hekja went indoors again and sat down by the fire. But this time she didn't pick up her spindle. Why bother with the boring work when there was no one to order her around? At least she could spend this time as she liked.

She would sing. But not an old song, not one of Pa's. They belonged to the past. No, she'd sing a new song, for herself and Snarf. She reached out for the words and then the tune came too.

> *Snow on the hillside,*
> *Mountain and sky,*
> *The whole world shivers,*
> *As winter flows by.*
>
> *Empty and longing,*
> *Lonely as I,*
> *The wind howls as it searches,*
> *For…*

"Hooooooowwwwwwl!"

It was impossible to tell if Snarf was joining in or complaining about the noise. Hekja broke off singing. She laughed and hugged him. The mouse rustled again and Snarf darted after it. Hekja began to sing again.

The door opened.

"Who is that?" demanded Snorri the Skald. "Who is singing?" He was dressed in furs, a fur hood and fur-trimmed boots and mittens, and there were flakes of snow on his face.

Hekja stood up respectfully. "No one, Master Skald," she said. "My dog was howling, that was all."

"Arf," welcomed Snarf, his mouth full of mouse. He swallowed it. "Arf arf."

"It didn't sound like a dog," said Snorri. He stepped inside. The sheep moved restlessly as they watched the newcomer. The snow was melting on Snorri's face and he wiped it off.

"Maybe it was the wind," offered Hekja. She picked up the spindle and began to twirl it.

Snorri looked at her curiously. "Perhaps. Or maybe the ice giants were calling, up in the mountains."

"Are there really ice giants?" asked Hekja cautiously. Gudrun had told her there were, but she had never quite believed it.

Snorri smiled. "Not that anyone has ever met. Not anyone sober at any rate. Or maybe they have, and haven't lived to tell the tale."

He walked down the hall, then sat down in Thorvard's chair, and looked around the house. "There is a legend that poetry was stolen from the dwarfs," he added. "Maybe the dwarfs sing in this land, in winter when the people are indoors."

"I wouldn't know," said Hekja. She looked down at her spindle as though it was the most fascinating thing in the world. "I have only been here since past mid-summer."

"Where are you from?"

Hekja shrugged. "I don't know the name your people give to my island. No one bothered to tell me," she added bitterly. "They simply came and killed and left." She lifted her chin. "Perhaps you would like to make a chant of that? A tale of heroes, fighting girls and women and men who have no swords."

For a moment Snorri looked shocked. Then he looked angry. Suddenly Hekja realised what she had done. *It was the song*, she thought. *I forgot I was a thrall when I was singing.* Now she was here alone with a Norseman, one that she had angered and insulted.

Could she reach the door before he grabbed her? Then the anger left his face.

"You don't understand," he said gruffly.

Hekja nodded. "No. That is true." She spoke respectfully, and hoped he didn't sense what lay underneath.

"All men fight," said Snorri, "it is what men do. And the best men win. How can a man test his courage except in battle? And the brave deserve their reward."

And what of those who lose, thought Hekja, *or who never wanted to fight at all?* But she kept twirling her spindle. Snarf sniffed Snorri's feet, then lay down again at Hekja's side.

"Tell me truthfully," said Snorri, now in a gentler voice. "Was it you singing?"

"Yes," said Hekja. There was no point denying it now.

Snorri shook his head. "What is your mistress thinking of?" he cried. "She should have brought you to the feast! A voice like yours would drive the dark away!" He stood up, and made his way back to the door. "And I'll tell her so at once," he added. "Yule isn't a time to spend alone."

"Please…" Hekja ran to the door and called after him.

He turned. "What is it?"

"Please… please don't tell them I can sing."

Snorri stared. "Why ever not?"

Would he understand? Or would she anger him again?

"Because… because a slave has nothing. No belongings, no past that anybody cares to know, no future unless her mistress gives her one. My songs are all I have. If you tell them, they will own those too."

Snorri stared at her as though he had never seen a thrall before. Then he turned and stamped through the watching sheep and out the door. Hejka watched him trudge across the snow through the endless twilight towards the feast.

Would he tell Freydis to punish her? She couldn't tell.

Hekja went back to the fire and stirred it up so the sparks rose in the smoky air. The wind was rising; it muttered down the smoke hole, sending a gust of snowflakes through the house. Hekja threw on more wood – the updraught of a good fire kept even a blizzard out.

Suddenly the door opened again. It was one of Erik's thralls, an old woman, with almost as good a beard as Erik, though his was soft and hers spiky like a seal's whiskers. "Your mistress says you are to go to the feast," she said. "I will stay here in your stead."

Hekja stared. "When did she say this?"

"Just now." The old woman smiled. "Off you go, girl. It will do me good to have a rest, away from all the noise. I will mind the house and animals."

"Did the mistress say anything else?" asked Hekja. "About singing, maybe?"

The woman shook her head. "Nothing else."

Hekja pulled on her boots and fastened her cloak. Snarf bounded out after her and they set off across the snow.

Light gleamed through the doors of Erik's farmhouse. *There must be dozens of lamps burning,* thought Hekja, *driving away the winter dark.* She could hear men's voices singing; and the scent of bread and roasting meat filled the air that the heavy snow had left odourless.

Freydis was sitting just inside the door, a mug of mead in her hand. She nodded to Hekja. "The young poet there suggested someone else take your place." Freydis sounded amused. "I should have thought of it myself," she added. "Old Sigrun is more than happy to snooze Yule away by a fire."

Gudrun smiled at Hekja from the seats by the fire pit and Hikki moved over to give her space on his bench. Hekja glanced at Snorri, but he didn't even glance her way – he was too enthralled by Leif's tale of the farmhouse further up the fiord that had been crushed by a glacier which had grown unexpectedly, killing all inside. He even ignored Snarf when he sniffed hopefully at the pouch where he had once kept dried meat.

So Snarf went to sniff Bright Eyes instead, and for once she didn't growl at him to go away.

It was a grand Yule feast. There were games with the other thralls, and music from the skald and Leif's daughter, and stories from Erik in his great chair. Once Leif spoke of Vinland, its giant trees and lush grass, and Freydis' gaze burned as bright as the fire. And then the week was over, and no one had mentioned Hekja's singing at all.

Chapter 26

A HERO'S FAREWELL

Erik the Red died towards the end of winter. Many people died at winter's end, from poor food or not enough, and from the bitter cold. But Erik died from none of those. He was in his chair, playing chess, pondering his next move, just as he had pondered settling a new land twenty years before. And then he gave a cry, toppled from his chair and died.

Freydis was weaving and Hekja and Gudrun were spinning when the thrall came running with the news. "Mistress," he panted, as Freydis looked up from her loom. "His Lordship... his Lordship's dead!"

There was no doubt which Lordship he meant – The Lordship always referred to Erik. Freydis stood up, her face expressionless. Thorvard had been carving a new runner for the sleigh. He stood too and looked as though he might make a move to comfort her. But she shook her head at him.

"Come," she said shortly. "We will help with the funeral." She reached for her cloak and gestured to the men to come as well.

It took both households three days' work to prepare Erik's grave. He was a Christian – his wife had built the first church in Greenland – but it was fitting that he be buried as a Viking hero too.

Hekja and Hikki were sent to run to every household within a day's journey, to let them know of Erik's death. The seas were too frozen to send out ships.

This time both ran together – running in winter was dangerous, and both carried ropes in case the other fell into a fissure in the snow. If it had been summer the whole colony might have been invited to the funeral, but this was not possible in blizzard season.

It was strange running in the winter silence. Even the trees and rocks were white, and the ice mountains gleamed in the sunlight, and always behind the silence the rumble and grind of the glaciers as they carved their way out to the sea.

The husbondi of the last farmhouse they reached offered them a place in his sleigh, so Hekja was back at Brattahlid for the funeral.

The thralls had dug a pit, a giant one, and Erik's ship was lowered into it. His grave goods were piled around, his sword and shield, the carved chair he had sat in since his house was built, his sleigh and snow shoes, even his sleeping furs.

Snorri carved a funeral poem in runes in the shape of a snake on to a stone. No one told Hekja what they said, but she imagined that they spoke of heroes.

There was some talk of killing a female thrall as well, to keep him company in the afterworld. Hekja's face whitened when she overheard this, but nothing came of it – not because a thrall was valued, but because it was a pagan custom and too many disapproved.

Finally, as women wailed, Erik's final ship was covered by a mound of dirt, outlined with big stones and a cross put at the head.

Freydis stood silent as the frozen dirt was shovelled back into the pit. Even when Thorvard tried to comfort her as they watched the grave being covered on the hill, she shook him off and went to stand alone on the hillside, staring down at her father's grave.

What was she thinking, wondered Hekja. Of songs and games when she was young? Of how her father hadn't lived long enough to see his daughter claim a country too, as he and her brother had done?

It was impossible to tell.

Finally the echoes of the last song had died away and the mourners left the graveside.

Erik the hero, discoverer of Greenland, founder of the colony, fighter and chief, was gone.

It was fully dark when Hekja heard the noise outside. The lamp had flickered down and the hall was quiet. At first she thought the men were singing another lament for Erik. But this sound was different.

Hekja made her way across the hall and passed the restless sheep as quietly as she could, then looked outside. The night was lighter than indoors, for the full moon cast shadows on the snow.

The noise came again. "Hoooooowwwwwwwwwwl!"

Hekja peered across the fields to Erik's grave. Bright Eyes and Snarf sat on the great mound. As Hekja watched they lifted up their heads again and howled for the dead master.

The sound floated past the farms, over the fiords, up to the mountains of ice and snow, across the glaciers, above this cold and foreign land that Erik had made his own. The dogs sang their own song, one that had no need for human words. A song to honour a hero, in the best way they knew how.

The rest of the household was still asleep when Snarf slipped indoors. When Hekja cuddled him his fur felt like ice, and so did his nose. She hoped that Bright Eyes had found someone to give her comfort too.

Chapter 27

❦

AFTER THE FUNERAL

Freydis was rich now. Erik's big house and the main fields would go to Leif. Freydis inherited two smaller farms, with the allegiance of the men who worked them, as well as the farm Erik had given her on her marriage. Erik's wealth of silver was divided between Leif, Thorvard and Freydis.

Hekja watched Freydis at her weaving the day after the funeral. Freydis had never shed a tear since the news had come of Erik's death, not that Hekja had seen.

Freydis' face was still expressionless. She said nothing all morning until it was time to order Gudrun to serve the meal – fish stewed in water and thickened with reindeer moss, for now at winter's end all of the meat was gone. The household was spooning up the tasteless stew from the big pot when Leif bent his head under the door lintel. No Norse door was ever tall enough to walk through with one's head held high – it was easier to slice off an enemy's head if he had to duck to come in the door.

But today Leif was no enemy. He took off his cloak, shook off the snowflakes and came in to stand by the fire.

Freydis didn't offer him fish – Erik's, or rather Leif's, household had many times as many thralls and beasts as hers, and was better supplied. While her household ate dried fish, Leif's still dined on meat.

"What is it?" Freydis asked her brother shortly.

Leif took a breath. "The Vinland expedition – it is impossible now. We must send runners to the other households to let them know."

Freydis didn't even look up from her fish. "Why?"

Leif stared. "Surely you must see that! I must take Father's responsibilities here. I can't go wandering off beyond the horizon."

"Why not?" said Freydis coolly. "That is what Father did."

"Father was outlawed for three years and had his lands forfeited for unlawful killing. He had no choice but to leave Iceland. But I have my duty here."

Freydis put her bowl aside. "Then we will go without you."

Leif stared at her. "A woman, lead an expedition?"

"Why not?"

"You know why not! How will you get men to follow a woman? You have never been to Vinland! How will you even find it?"

Freydis laughed. "You forget, brother. You've been boasting of your voyage for two years! You gave the poet every detail, so many days to the south, so many to the west. In fact I am sure we can do better than you, and sail straight to Vinland, without your troublesome adventures on the way."

"Freydis…" Leif looked at Thorvard. "You are her husband! Say something! Tell her it's impossible."

Freydis didn't give her husband time to reply. "The ship is mine," she said shortly. "And the farm men are mine as well. Whether my husband chooses to come or not, I am going."

"I am coming," said Thorvard, just a bit too softly. He held Leif's eyes as though in challenge.

Freydis' gaze was triumphant. "We shall see how many choose to follow Erik's daughter, instead of staying mouldering at home with his son."

"But…" began Leif. He stopped and shook his head. "There is no arguing with you. A proper wife would…" He stopped at the expression on Thorvard's face.

Thorvard's fingers inched towards his axe. "You may be her brother, Leif Eriksson, but I will have no man insult my wife and live."

Leif turned on his heel, grabbed his cloak and left.

Chapter 28

FREYDIS' FOLLOWERS

It seemed to Hekja that one day they lived in twilight, then all of a sudden the days were so bright they hardly needed the lamps at all. Gudrun laughed at her surprise. "It's the ice giants," she explained, "they sit up in the ice mountains and watch the winter sun. They are so big they hide it from everybody else. But as soon as the sun begins to rise higher in the sky for spring they sit down again. And bump! The days are longer, hey?"

Hekja longed for spring to come properly. By now the salt fish was so hard it needed soaking for three days. Most of the household had coughs from months of breathing smoke and fish-oil fumes, and her voice was hoarse as well. The house and every person in it stank of sweat, sheep and fish.

The snow melted in the warmer days, dripping down the smoke hole then freezing again into icicles overnight. More snow fell; this time it looked like silvery puffs that the fresh sunlight turned to magic, then that snow melted too.

Finally the patches of mud amongst the drifts of snow turned green, then the green all turned to flowers. Butterflies hovered just out of reach when Snarf tried to snap them. His fur was falling out in big thick handfuls, and finally Gudrun made good her threat to spin some into thread. It looked quite fine, but smelt so much like wet dog that Freydis refused to weave it.

Thorvard and the thralls carried the cattle out on to the green grass – the cows were too weak to stand by now, much less walk, for there had been little hay and no grain at all for the last month of winter. The pigs staggered out as well and began turning the fields to mud. Only the sheep were still steady on their feet. They too had gone short of food, but at least they had been warm inside the hall.

Spring was busy and hungry too, despite the first leaves of sorrel and rose root shoots and onion tops. But after the first reindeer hunt there was fresh meat, even though it was winter tough and stringy with not a speck of fat. There was fresh fish to eat as well. The hens were well fed on fish guts and reindeer heart and soon began to lay as the days grew longer. A whale was sighted out past the fiord, too, so even if there was no grain or milk or cheese there was more whale meat than anybody wanted. Hekja could no longer feel Snarf's ribs through his fur, or her own underneath her dress.

She was glad of the good food, for now that the snows had partly cleared Freydis sent Hekja running, and she needed all the energy she could get. She ran to the farms of the men who had promised to join Freydis' expedition, to tell them of her plans and bring back details of what men and ships they each would bring.

But each time, Hekja came back with a refusal. Freydis took each message calmly, but with each setback her face grew stonier than before. Without Leif's leadership the men had changed their minds.

Hekja was sent to Finnbogi's farm last, as it was further away than the others, up north where the snows kept their grip for longer. He and his brother relied more on hunting seals than on farming, and it had been to sell their sealskins that Finnbogi had accompanied Leif on the voyage when Hekja had been taken.

It took Hekja four days to run to Finnbogi's. Each night when she stopped to rest she saw him in her dreams, his face above her mother, his laughter and the blood. Finnbogi had made no sign he ever remembered chasing Hekja or killing her mother. Hekja was just another thrall now, among so many. At least she hoped so.

Finally Hekja came to the fiord with the black rock slope and the glacier above it, white and cold, just as Thorvard had described. There was the farm too, a big main house with a few thin cows and long lines where sealskins flapped in the wind. Down below Finnbogi's ship rode the milky fiord water. Even this early in the season it was evident they had been fishing or sailing north to seal. Whatever else Finnbogi was, it was evident he was an excellent seaman.

A young thrall opened the door, no older than Hekja, but thinner faced. It seemed Finnbogi's household didn't eat as well in the winter months as Freydis'. She stared at Hekja in astonishment.

"Who are you?" she cried.

"I am Freydis' runner," said Hekja, as calmly as she could. She kept wondering every moment if Finnbogi would appear, "With a message for your master."

Another thrall came to the door. She was a few years older than the first, but still young. Hekja swallowed her contempt. She had learned enough from Freydis to know that older, experienced thralls were more valuable in a good household. It seemed that Finnbogi's thralls weren't chosen for their skill at making cheese. The young thrall also stared at Hekja, as though she had never seen a female runner.

Now another woman pushed the thrall away. She was middle-aged, with thin grey hair plastered to her scalp, a sharp face and narrow lips. This must be Finnbogi's wife, Hekja realised, the mistress of the house, though she wore none of the fine brooches or bracelets like those of the other mistresses she'd met.

Hekja gave her message again. Finnbogi's wife shrugged her bony shoulders. "He is in the fletching shed.[28] Gunnhild! Go fetch the master!"

Hekja waited for the woman to ask her in, and offer food and drink. But she just stood there staring, till Hekja heard Finnbogi's footsteps from the shed.

Finnbogi's hands were bloody. *It is just seal blood from the fletching shed,* Hekja told herself. But she still shivered.

"Well?" demanded Finnbogi abruptly.

"My mistress Freydis has sent a message," recited Hekja, as she had so many other times. "She intends to sail when the first crops are sown, after the next new moon. She wants to know if you will still join her."

"Why not?" asked Finnbogi coolly. "I have sailed with Leif before."

Hekja flushed. "Master Leif will not be going. Master Erik died this winter and Master Leif must look after the farms. But he has said his sister can use the long houses he built in Vinland, and he gives all his claim to the land to her."

Finnbogi gave a bark of laughter. "I see! And I bet none of the others will follow a woman. Neither will I!"

Hekja felt relief course through her. She hated to bring more bad news to Freydis, but at least she need never see this man again. She bent her head politely. "I will tell my mistress..." she began.

"Not so fast! Tell her I will come as her partner. We each bring thirty men, no more. All profit will be split equally, half for her, half for me. Go tell your mistress that and come back if she agrees."

He turned his back on her and walked back to the fletching shed. Hekja waited a moment in case his wife invited her in to rest and have a meal, as every other household had done.

But his wife just stared at Finnbogi's departing back. "There had better be a good profit," she muttered to herself. "Better than a life of seal porridge and whale blubber." She turned her back and slammed the door.

Hekja jogged out of the courtyard, trying to ignore her hunger. She had eaten all the food Gudrun had packed her as all the other households had given her food for her return. But at least she hadn't had to linger at Finnbogi's.

The scream of a bird made her look up. Hekja grinned to herself as she clambered carefully down the fiord cliffs. It was spring! She knew where there'd be food to find now.

Sure enough, there were gulls' eggs on the first ledge she found. Hekja gathered them in her skirt and climbed away from the furious parent birds before she sucked one from the shell. Had it only been a year ago she had eaten eggs at home? Homesickness bit deeper suddenly. Freydis could wait just a little longer for her answer, she decided.

She made a driftwood fire, lighting it with the iron and flint she carried with her these days, far enough from Finnbogi's so no one would see the smoke, and baked the rest of the eggs in the coals. She wished Snarf was with her, to eat them too, just as he had before. But Snarf was hunting with Thorvard.

Hekja peeled the eggs one by one and nibbled them as she gazed out to sea. Home was there, across the water. Or was it? What was left of everything she knew? Perhaps even the girls were gone, to husbands further up the coast, the cows serving as their dowries, or even to other islands. Maybe even Tikka's hut was empty.

Hekja shut her eyes and let Ma's face float before her. But when she tried to think of Bran, Snorri's face was there instead.

Hekja opened her eyes, annoyed. Snorri had a golden voice and his songs were… good, Hekja admitted. But that was no reason for him to slide into her dreams. Besides, it was time for her to get going.

As Hekja ran down the hill, Freydis was sorting out the best cattle to take to Vinland. They had been put to the bull late this year so they would not calve till the expedition landed. Freydis had found tenants for her other farms, and they would care for the cattle that were left.

Freydis stood silently as Hekja repeated Finnbogi's message. Then she said abruptly, "Go and eat, and sleep. Hikki can take my message back."

"Please, mistress," said Hekja. "What will the message be?"

For a moment Hekja thought Freydis might rebuke her. But then she said, "Hikki can tell him yes. Tell Finnbogi I agree."

And so the preparations for the voyage went ahead. There would only be two ships now, but at least Freydis had her expedition.

There were the fields to plough, the crops to sow, though the best seed was kept for Vinland. Finally the seas were clear enough of ice to sail. It was time to go.

Chapter 29

LEAVING GREENLAND

It had been arranged that Finnbogi and his brother would set sail from their farm the day after the full moon. They would meet Freydis at Brattahlid and both ships would sail on from there.

Full moon came and went and the moon grew thin again. But there was no sign of Finnbogi. Finally, Freydis ordered that the ship be loaded. They would wait till old Thrand Egilsson, who was the most experienced sailor in the Brattahlid district, declared the weather would hold for the next few days. Then they would sail, whether Finnbogi came or not.

There was nothing for Hekja to pack. She had the dress she wore, her rags from home, her boots, her cloak and that was all. But the morning they were to leave, Freydis beckoned from her curtained room at the end of the long house. She handed Hekja a pile of clothing. "Here," she said.

"Should I put them in your packs?" asked Hekja, thinking that Freydis wanted her to store them in the waterproof sealskins for her.

"No, they're for you. Two dresses," said Freydis. "New

ones. There's no point giving you old dresses of mine – I'm twice your size. There are aprons too, and boots, and another cloak." She handed Hekja another bundle, smaller than the first. "This is for you too. It's a tunic like the one Hikki wears, when he runs. People would have been shocked if you wore it here. But in Vinland it will be useful when you are scouting out the land."

"Thank you," said Hekja.

Freydis hesitated. "The other women coming with us are not thralls," she added. "But you'll be passing on my orders to them. It will be easier for you to have authority if you're dressed well. I'd also like you to have these."

Freydis handed Hekja a hairbrush. It was backed with walrus ivory and carefully carved. Hekja's eyes widened at its beauty. Then Freydis undid one of the brooches on her apron. Hekja stared. The brooch was gold.

"For me?"

Freydis nodded. "Partly because a brooch like this indicates your status. But also…" Again Freydis hesitated. "Because I trust you," she said at last. "And I think in this new land I will need someone I can trust. Someone who'll do what I say unconditionally, even though I'm a woman." Freydis paused again, as though trying to find the words.

"We are founding a new land in Vinland. Always with new lands there are more men than women, at least at first. There'll come a time when a man asks to buy you from me, so you can be freed to marry. But a runner can't run when she's pregnant. I ask that you do not commit to any man for three years. After that, you will be free."

Hekja looked at the ground, and then at Freydis. "What if I don't want a husband?"

Freydis blinked at that. "Why ever not?" She smiled one of her rare true smiles. "It's what free women do."

"Some might say that women don't lead expeditions," said Hekja. "I… I saw what Norsemen do to women in my village. I want none of that."

"Ah," said Freydis quietly. And then she said, "It is not always like that with men and women. Do you think I would put up with a man who treated me like that?"

Hekja shook her head. "No."

"You'll have many offers down in Vinland. Do well by me and I'll make sure you have silver or cows or land enough to take to your marriage to ensure respect."

"But if I don't want a husband?" persisted Hekja. "Can I still be free?"

"Free to do what?" Freydis was genuinely perplexed.

Hekja was silent – thinking of her home. Then she said, "Just be free."

Freydis thought a while. It was clear she had never thought what a freed woman thrall might do, except to marry. "Very well," Freydis said at last. "If you marry I'll give you land and cows or silver. If you do not, you can have them anyway. But I expect good service and total loyalty." She walked swiftly from the room and out of the long house without waiting for a reply.

So on her last day in Greenland, Hekja was finally dressed like a true Greenland woman as she left the house, in her new wool dress and boots, her apron and her scarf, and the gold brooch. But she would never truly look like she belonged, she thought, not with her dark hair and eyes. She had grown in the past year, but still only came to Freydis' shoulder.

It was hard for Hekja to say goodbye to Gudrun. Gudrun was too old and crippled to be of use in Vinland, but she had given Hekja more kindness than anyone had shown since she had left her own village.

"Take care, dear girl," whispered Gudrun as Hekja hugged her in the doorway. "Watch out for those fierce unipeds."[29]

Hekja left Gudrun gazing from the doorway as she followed the men down the hill to the waiting ship by the pier. It was a large ship, but it looked so small to be venturing out on to the wide sea.

The towboats were already loaded with sacks of seed and tools. Now the cows and bull were led on to the ship too, and the hens in their boxes. The animals had to come in the big ship, as they would need water during the voyage and quieting when things got rough.

Most of the folk of Brattahlid had come to see them off. Leif's daughter was there, talking earnestly with Snorri the Skald. Hekja wondered if she was coming too, but Snorri boarded the ship alone. He hardly glanced at Hekja, even in her new dress, and when he did it was as though he deliberately forced his glance away.

Hekja and Snarf were among the last to board, still standing with Freydis and Thorvard on the hill above the pier when Leif arrived. He was alone, except for Hikki and Erik's dog, Bright Eyes, who kept close to Leif's side now.

The dogs sniffed each other, almost as though they exchanged news, thought Hekja, amused. Bright Eyes had had a litter of pups in early spring, and Hekja wondered if they were Snarf's. Suddenly she saw Hikki coming down the hill, his rolled sleeping bag and cloak in his arms. She hadn't been able to speak to him since

Yule, but no one had told her that any of Leif's household were coming to Vinland too.

It seemed that even if Leif were not coming, his runner was, a gift from Leif the Lucky.

"Thank you," Freydis was saying to her brother.

Leif nodded. "I will keep an eye on your farms of course," he said.

"So you have promised," said Freydis coolly. Brother and sister looked at each other for a moment. Then Freydis said, "Try to understand. You spent your youth a-Viking. Am I to be suffocated in the house and cheese room, with nothing but my loom to occupy me?"

"It is what women do," said Leif uncomfortably.

Freydis smiled. "Our father was outcast from Norway and from Iceland for doing what he wanted, not what people thought he should. We are both his children."

Leif said nothing. He just hugged her roughly and slapped Thorvard on the back. Then he marched back up the hill, without staying to watch them leave.

Freydis boarded the ship now, with Thorvard after her. Suddenly Snarf stared at the boat, as though he had just realised Hekja expected him to get on board too, and live on fish again instead of meat.

"Arf," he said unwillingly. But he followed her as she walked across the plank, and felt the rocking of the ship again under her feet.

There were three other dogs on board. Snarf ignored them. This was his second summer and he had reached his full great height, taller than any other dog around.

Hekja had thought the ship she had arrived in was crowded, but every inch here was crammed, so the ship rode low in the water. She wedged herself on to a sack of oats next to Hikki, then shifted again so there was room for Snarf too. "I didn't know you were coming!" she said. "Did you ask to come?"

Hikki shook his head. "I didn't know myself till this morning. I think Leif had only just decided."

"Do you mind?" Hikki shook his head again. He seemed preoccupied. "There are more than thirty men on board," he said.

Hekja looked around. She could count now, but had to concentrate to get to thirty.

"The agreement was thirty men each," said Hikki quietly. "Freydis has broken it."

Freydis' men were all young and strong, and carried weapons. About half had brought their women. Hekja realised she and Hikki were the only thralls. This was a company of warriors, as well as farmers and hunters. "Perhaps Freydis doesn't trust Finnbogi," she whispered. "Besides, if he doesn't come we will need more than thirty men."

Hikki shrugged. "Maybe she wants to make sure that she is Mistress of Vinland and has the men to back it up. I'm glad," he added. "It is good to be on the winning side."

The oarsmen pushed at their oars. The sail flapped and filled, the cargo boats with their high-piled load of crates and barrels bobbed behind the ship, and suddenly they were away. Snarf rested his paws on Hekja's shoulders as they watched the land vanish behind them. The others were chattering, but Hikki and Hekja were silent.

Then Hekja said, "I hated this land. But I am almost sorry to leave it. It's beautiful in its way."

Hikki shrugged. He was not impressed by beauty. "Land is just something a runner passes through to get to his destination. Leif has promised me land and my freedom, after a year's work with his sister," he added. "Perhaps Freydis will grant you freedom as well."

"Perhaps," said Hekja noncommittally.

"It would be worth working hard to please your mistress," Hikki added meaningfully. "I can take a wife when I am freed."

Hekja said nothing. She looked around the ship. Her glance settled on Freydis, sitting by the prow, her face glowing as it hadn't done since their last time at sea, then on Snorri with his butter hair, sitting at Freydis' side, as though he was storing every second as inspiration to make up a song.

Hekja turned back to Hikki. "But first," she said, "we have to survive."

Chapter 30

THE JOURNEY

For Hekja, ships meant storms and icebergs and fog. But this journey was different. The ship sailed to the Western Settlement first, to take on more fresh water, and so people could stretch their legs and have a night on shore. Then they sailed south.

Icebergs were plentiful, so Freydis called Snarf and Hekja to the prow again so Snarf could sniff them out during the night. But the ship met no fog, or storms – the old man had been right when he told Freydis when to sail.

They sailed straight southwest after that. Leif had sailed further west and come to other lands before he came to Vinland. But now Freydis knew there was land to the south, she had courage enough to shun the coast and cross the open sea. This meant a shorter voyage, even though they had to navigate without a coastline to guide them.

The ship sailed for eight days without a sight of land. Leif had calculated it would take them six, with good winds.

Each day Freydis threw the ship's log into the water and counted slowly as the ship sailed past it.[30] The ship was sailing as fast as Leif had expected. But there was still no land.

Nor had there been any rain, and fresh water was running out. Freydis had taken as many barrels as the ship would hold but the cows, hens and sheep had needed water too.

People began to mutter. Not loudly, not so Freydis or Thorvard might hear. Norsemen were used to sailing out of sight of land. But they were not used to trusting a woman leader. Thorvard might accompany his wife, but everyone knew whose expedition this really was.

Dusk began to settle on the ninth evening. Freydis handed out the rations: a dried fish each, and a dipper full of water.

"If there had been only thirty men we would have more than a dipper full to drink," muttered one of the men.

"What did you say?" demanded Freydis sharply.

The man's face was blank. "I said nothing," he said.

"Good," said Freydis. She pulled up another dipperful and handed it to Hekja for Snarf.

Thorvard bent low. "Do you think that is wise?" he whispered, though Hekja could still hear his words. "The other dogs get a quarter ration. The men are talking."

Freydis met his eyes. "If any of the men learn how to sniff an iceberg they can come and tell me. Till then this dog gets what we do." It was the first time, Hekja thought, that Freydis had openly overruled her husband's advice.

Snarf drank his water, then ate the fish from Hekja's fingers after she'd taken out the bones. Then he dozed, till someone trod on the deck behind them.

Snarf yipped a welcome. It was Snorri the Skald. He shoved a rolled sleeping bag out of the way, and sat on the deck next to Hekja. It was the first time he had sought her out since mid-winter, though she had sensed him watching her during the voyage.

Was he waiting for her to misbehave, she wondered, so he could tell Freydis of her rudeness to him at Yule? He puzzled her. Most times he acted like any Norseman would. But at others...

Snorri looked at Snarf instead of Hekja, and rubbed his ears, so it almost seemed he had come to talk to the dog rather than to her. "Well, noble hound," he said half jokingly, "can your nose smell out land for us?"

"Arf," said Snarf willingly.

Snorri laughed. "So, you understood that, did you? But was that a yes or a no? What do you say?" he asked Hekja. "Can your dog smell land as well as ice?"

"I don't know," said Hekja honestly. "I think he might be able to."

"It will be useful if he can," said Snorri lightly, but Hekja could hear the urgency behind his words. "Some of the men are saying we've reached the endless ocean, with all hope of land behind us."

"Then you should have stayed safe at home," suggested Hekja, then bit her lip. They were harsh words for a thrall to use to a free man, almost like calling him a coward. Somehow she spoke without thinking when Snorri was around.

But Snorri just raised an eyebrow. *Perhaps,* thought Hekja suddenly, *he doesn't think I matter enough to be angry at.* Then he said, "One day I'll go home again. In a year, perhaps. I'll sing of this voyage and the settling of the land and the adventures. That is what songs do, tell others of what lies beyond their narrow lives."

Hekja said, as though it was no concern of hers, "You don't intend to stay in Vinland then?"

Snorri looked surprised. "No. I never did. I am my father's heir. One day I must run the estates."

Hekja said nothing. Despite what she had said to Freydis, sometimes, in the dreaming moments before sleep, she had wondered if in this new land a free man might ask her to be his wife. But if that happened it would not be Snorri the Skald, heir to Norwegian riches.

The darkness grew deeper about them. People were unrolling their sleeping bags, and settling for the night. It was time to go up to the prow with Snarf, for their evening watch. There had been no icebergs for days now, but Freydis was still uneasy about what might happen in the dark. "What will happen," Hekja said at last, "if we don't find land? Do any of your chants tell of sailors who never found a shore?"

Snorri shook his head. "How could they? My songs have to be about the ones who came safely home, to tell their stories."

"And dead men don't sing songs," said Hekja quietly. "Maybe those alive should sing them for them. Men with dry mouths, aching for rain, their eyes longing for a glimpse of land. Bleached bones floating on old ships, with only the sun and waves to see them."

Snorri was silent for a moment. Then he said, "You almost make it sound like a song."

"No," said Hekja. "These are your heroes, not mine. Nor my songs neither."

"You don't think what we are doing is worth a song?"

Hekja shrugged. "I didn't say that. But your heroes are not my heroes."

"And who would your heroes be?" asked Snorri softly.

Hekja smiled. She laid her hand on Snarf's back and scratched him just above the tail. Snarf stretched in ecstasy and laid his head on her lap.

"Snarf is a hero," said Hekja. "He saved me and my friends from a wolf when he wasn't even full grown. He must have been scared, but he still went for that wolf's throat. Our chief was a hero. He took his boat out in the high seas to save three fishermen. My mother was a hero. Even as they were killing her she used her last breath to tell me to run. But what do I know of heroes?" added Hekja, "I am just a thrall."

Hekja stood without waiting for Snorri to reply, and made her way up to the prow with Snarf following her. Freydis and Thorvard were there already in their sleeping bag. Freydis nodded to her, and closed her eyes. The only sounds now were creaks and snores and the slapping of the sail and waves. Hekja rolled herself in her cloak and sat with Snarf as he stretched out and smelt the darkness.

One bark would wake Freydis and warn the man on the tiller there was ice ahead. But for now Snarf seemed to smell nothing, except the sea.

Or did he smell fear as well, wondered Hekja, as the ship quietened about her. These men were brave. Fighting was their joy and even death at sea was an adventure. But even they were frightened of a slow death, their sides shrinking from lack of water, their bellies screaming for some food. Soon they would demand that the ship turn back, rather than keep sailing into the unknown.

185

The waves washed at the ship. The mast creaked, the sails flapped. A hen squawked, awake for a second, and then was quiet. Snarf seemed to sleep, but his ears were pricked, and his nostrils twitched as well, and Hekja knew he would fully wake at any hint of danger. And so she dozed.

Suddenly Snarf leapt to his feet and pointed, as he might at an iceberg or a deer.

"Arf!" he barked. "Arf!"

Hekja rubbed sleep from her eyes. Freydis threw off her sleeping bag, then stood and peered out into the darkness. In a heartbeat Thorvard was at her side.

"He is pointing west," he muttered. "The iceberg must be far on our right side. There is no need to worry about it." Thorvard slipped into his sleeping bag again.

"Arf!" Snarf barked louder than ever.

"Good dog," said Freydis, absently rubbing his ears. "We've heard you, now go to sleep."

Snarf sat and growled, deep in his throat, then stood and barked again.

Freydis sighed. "Some of us need to sleep. Can't you get him to be quiet, Hekja?"

"No!" urged Hekja. "Please. It's something different. It's not his iceberg bark."

"Arf!" Snarf strained his body towards the west, then looked back as though willing them to understand.

"Please!" Hekja pleaded. "Listen to him!"

Freydis laid her hand on Snarf's head and gazed into the darkness. Suddenly she seemed to understand. "Land?" asked Freydis softly. "Do you smell land?"

"Woof! Woof! Woof!" Now the other dogs were barking too.

"Hard aport!" yelled Freydis suddenly. "You at the tiller! Move!"

The ship slowly swerved till it faced the wind. Snarf's nostrils flared, as though whatever he smelled became stronger now. As the ship moved he moved with it, and he kept pointing in the same direction – west.

All over the ship men woke up and rubbed their eyes. And still he pointed into the darkness. It was only when he was sure that they were headed in the right direction that Snarf sat and rested his nose on Hekja's lap, while all about him the people waited for the day.

Dawn came behind them, the sun rising out of the sea. But even in the faint light before sunrise they had all seen it, like a line of clouds on the horizon.

But these clouds were land.

Years later Hekja would make a song of how her dog discovered Vinland. Their ship had been headed too far east. If it hadn't been for Snarf's nose they would never have come to land at all.

Of course others had discovered Vinland before Snarf. Hekja would make songs about them too, the Skraelings and Bjarnin Herolfsson then Leif.

But for Hekja, Snarf would always be the true discoverer of Vinland. What did it matter that he was not the first?

Chapter 31

LAND!

The land came closer and closer still. The sea changed colour, brighter, greener, till Hekja could see waves, all white-tipped about this shore. The wind smelled of soil and trees. The land was bright with them, more trees than Hekja had thought possible for a land to grow. It was a strangely flat land too, with green hills instead of proper mountains, like the other lands she'd seen.

By the time the sun was high they had come in close enough to see the beach. Here was another strangeness – sand that glowed the same colour as the sun, not stones or rock, great beaches that stretched to the horizon, instead of coves and fiords where a ship could rest. The ship sailed for a whole day and all they saw were trees and sand.

But this, it seemed, was what Leif had described. No one minded the lack of water now.

There was no safe harbour where the ship could rest that night – the waves rolled into the shore and the wind was strong and besides, there seemed to be no streams or rivers where there would be fresh water anyway.

Freydis ordered the sails lowered though, so the ship didn't drift far in the night. There might be rocks or sandbars, where the ship might run aground, and in any case she was looking for the island that Leif described, that led to Vinland's harbour. It would be easy to miss it sailing on at night.

Dawn saw the ship not much further than they'd been the night before, but the wind was still strong. By mid-morning they discovered Leif's island, sitting like a fat blue whale on the outer edge of a great harbour.

Everyone cheered and clapped each other on the back, as though no one had ever doubted they'd land safely.

Freydis ordered Thorvard to steer to the landward side of the island, and told the lookout to watch for sandbanks and rocks. Now they could see a headland, with twisted trees blown out of shape by the wind, and below the headland a great beach of rippling sand and a river, wider than Hekja had dreamt that any stream could be. Far up the river something gleamed among the trees – the lake that Leif had also described.

Vinland!

The wind was behind them now, fresh and gusty so everyone had to yell above its howling and the flapping of the ship's sail. Thorvard shouted, "Look at the colour of the water! Best wait till high tide before we travel up the river, or we might run aground as Leif did!"

Freydis grinned. "Leif the Lucky, stuck in the mud." But she gave the order to pull around and Thorvard steered the ship back to the island till the tide rose higher.

Finally it was safe to cross the sandbanks into the mouth of the river.

Hekja peered down into the water. It was so shallow still she could see the sand, all rippled like the waves had carved it, and a few fish too, with silver scales that glistened in the shallows. Hekja leaned down and lowered a dipper into the river water and tasted it. "It's salty!" she spluttered, spitting it out.

Freydis grinned. "It's too near the sea. Don't worry, there'll be fresh water further up."

People were shouting now. You could smell the excitement, so strong it could carry the ship to shore without the wind.

"The trees!" cried someone. "Look at the size of the trees!"

"And the ducks! Enough feathers to bed an army!"

"A land of plenty," breathed someone else. It was Hikki. Hekja could almost hear his dreams: land here, and far richer than any he had known.

"It's beautiful," said a voice behind her. It was Snorri.

Hekja nodded. "The colours – it is all gold and green and blue. Like every colour has been dyed twice to make it glow."

Suddenly the men gave a cheer. There on the river banks, in a clearing among the tall, tall trees, were the two big long houses that Leif had built and promised to his sister, and smaller huts for smelting iron and carpentry and storerooms. Smoke sifted into the sky above the green sod roofs and there was another boat pulled up in the shallows.

We're here, thought Hekja. *And Finnbogi has arrived before us.*

Chapter 32

THE FIRST NIGHT IN VINLAND

Finnbogi's men came running out of the long houses and in from the forest, where they had been cutting timber, and stared at the ship as it came up the river. Thorvard pulled it close enough to the bank to cast a rope ashore, and one of Finnbogi's men tied it around a tree, while another shoved out a plank so the passengers could come ashore.

Freydis' men and women clambered on to the dry land. There was more back-slapping; men gulped river water and splashed their faces to wash off the salt, and paced around the trees, exclaiming at their size. The women marvelled at the lush grass and what milk and cheese the cows would give on such a pasture.

But Freydis stood back as the others rushed to shore. Even now she stared down the coast, past the great river, as though wondering what new lands might be there. She caught Hekja watching her and smiled slightly.

Hekja stood back to let her pass, holding Snarf by the scruff of the neck to stop him bounding out, and let the others climb out first. She watched as Freydis stepped across the gangplank and narrowed her eyes at the smoke coming from the long house's smoke hole.

"Men," she muttered. "That's all that Finnbogi has brought, it seems. Where are the women, hey? Thorvard!"

Thorvard had been staring around the clearing. "What is it?"

"Tell the men to fetch their weapons," said Freydis in a low voice. "One by one, so no one notices."

Thorvard stared. "What's wrong?"

"Where are Finnbogi's cattle? His sheep?"

"Perhaps he thought he would share ours," said Thorvard.

"Exactly," said Freydis quietly. "Whether we agreed or not."

Thorvard's eyes widened. "I will tell the men," he said softly.

Hekja shivered. Was their new life to begin with killing?

Freydis beckoned to her. "Come with me," she ordered. She started for the long house, Hekja hurrying after her, with Snarf sniffing at the new scents along the way.

They reached the long house just as Finnbogi stepped out.

"Welcome," he said, grinning. "We made it here before you!" He waved a hand at the giant trees, the grass that looked like it had never known the snow of winter. "It is just as Leif described! Even the grapes, great bunches of them on thick vines, hanging from the trees."

Freydis ignored the talk of grapes. "Why didn't you call at Brattahlid, as we agreed?"

Finnbogi's grin grew wider. "Is that what we agreed? I must have forgotten."

"It was," said Freydis coldly. She looked around. "I see your men, Finnbogi, but no women. No cattle either. How can you settle a new land with neither cows nor women?"

Finnbogi looked down on her from his great height. He looked like he was enjoying himself. "A man can make riches with neither cows nor women. Besides, my wife is here, and her thralls. That is enough for me."

"And for your men?"

Finnbogi shrugged, and glanced at Hekja. "If you have brought women then perhaps we'll have to share."

Hekja felt her skin prickle. But she gave no sign that she had understood.

"We will share profits," said Freydis crisply, "and that is all. Why have you put your belongings here?"

"Where else?" Finnbogi looked her up and down lazily.

"These houses are my brother's," said Freydis. "He said that I could use them – me and my people."

Finnbogi shrugged, his grin even wider. "Then you should have set out earlier. You can build your own houses. I am here now, me and my men."

"I have men of my own," said Freydis evenly.

"Men who follow a woman," snorted Finnbogi.

"My men followed me to Vinland. They will follow me now," said Freydis quietly.

"Then perhaps you should have brought them with you," said Finnbogi.

"We are partners, Finnbogi," said Freydis, still in that too quiet voice. "Do I need men with me for you to honour your word?"

The two stood there. If they had been dogs they would have growled, thought Hekja, their hackles raised. But these two only stared.

"Do not cross me, Finnbogi," said Freydis finally. "My men have their swords and axes and are waiting for my word. Where are your men's weapons? Hanging up inside the houses? You have a choice. We can start this colony with your men's blood upon the ground. Or you can leave my long houses, according to the law."

Finnbogi stared at her for a moment without speaking. Then he pushed past her, out on to the path down to the river. Hekja heard him shouting at his men to leave the unloading and come and take their things from the long house.

Freydis smiled, but her eyes were worried.

Finnbogi and his brother and their men, and the five women who were with them, loaded their belongings back on to their ship.

"Watch them," Freydis told Hekja. "I want to know exactly where they go."

Hekja ran out to the bend of the river and watched Finnbogi sail further down the shore then into the lake. The trees were too tall to see where they headed after that, but soon smoke rose up into the air. It seemed Finnbogi had set up camp on the lake shore. Hekja ran back to tell Freydis.

The cattle had been unloaded now, their legs unsteady after the voyage. Freydis ordered the bull tethered to a tree, while young branches were stripped from the trees

Finnbogi's men had cut to make a rough fence to keep the cattle and sheep in. The hen boxes were placed on a platform of big rocks, and the hens let loose to scratch around. They would roost in the trees at night and come back to their boxes to lay.

"Come," said Freydis to Hekja again. They left the others to their unloading and entered the biggest of the long houses.

It was far larger than the farmhouse in Greenland, and twice as high, with a framework of great tree trunks and wooden walls as well. There was a big attic room where the men could sleep, as well as the storerooms and the hall below, and bed closets each closed off by wooden walls for the couples, the first that Hekja had ever seen, and a big room at the end of the great hall for Freydis and Thorvard. All along the hall there were benches of rough wood to sit on and big tables, just half-round slabs of wood resting on tree trunks.

The fire pit was massive too – there was certainly no shortage of wood to burn in this rich land. Finnbogi's fire was still burning in the fire pit.

"Tell the women to build the fire up high," ordered Freydis. "Then they can choose their bed closet."

Hekja nodded. She supposed that if the couples slept in the closets she would sleep alone in the great hall with Snarf.

Hekja went out to give the orders. They were the first she had ever given, but no one seemed to notice. Some of the men had already caught salmon in their nets in the river – giant fish that glistened in the sun. You only had to throw in a net, they said, for it to fill up with fish.

Soon the salmon were hanging on the roasting chains above the fire, tended by the women. Freydis ordered a barrel of barley beer be broached, to celebrate their arrival, then went out to check the animals were safely fenced. One by one the men came in and sat before the fire, with horns of ale and platters of cooked fish. And then Thorvard carried in the great carved chair that had sat by the fire pit in the farmhouse in Greenland. He placed it in the spot of honour, facing south. The men waited for him to sit in it. But instead he sat on one of the benches, like the other men.

Then Freydis entered. She walked steadily up the hall, to the fire pit, then sat in the great chair, just as though she were a man, while the women turned the fish on their great chains and filled the horns with beer.

No one spoke. The silence grew, then Snorri's voice rose clearly through the dimness of the long house. He had left the harp in Greenland, as he had promised. But Snorri had no need of a harp, thought Hekja.

> *Over the trackless ocean,*
> *Over the endless sea,*
> *Food for ravens we travelled,*
> *But none flew as far as we.*
>
> *Warriors boast of beating,*
> *Weaker foes than ours.*
> *A man's strength is fleeting,*
> *Against an ocean's powers.*
>
> *Now we have a new land,*
> *Ours to change and watch and grow.*

Let only they who dare to follow,
Question how we go.

No one cheered. The words meant too much for them to toast the singer, so they gave him the even greater compliment of silence. And Hekja stared across the fire at Snorri, heir to great estates, further from her than Bran had ever been.

And so she spent her first night in Vinland, in a house much like the one that she had left, the men snoring in their sleeping bags above, the couples whispering in the bed closets, wrapped in seal furs by the coals of the fire, the smoke drifting lazily until it found the smoke hole, the sounds of cows outside and the crowing of the rooster, who thought the moonlight was the sun.

But there were new sounds too – new frog calls that she had never heard before and insects that chittered through the night. When she opened her eyes again the big wood doors were open. It was dawn and different birds were yelling. And there in the early light stood Freydis, Erik's daughter, gazing around as though to say, "This land is mine."

Chapter 33

EXPLORING VINLAND

Breakfast was leftover fish. By the time Hekja rose Snarf had breakfasted already. Like Freydis, he had been out in the dawn already, and Hekja noticed feathers on his fur.

Then Freydis gave her orders: some men were to put up more fencing, for the cows would calve soon and the ewes have their lambs, and the animals would need more grass. Others to hunt, for the party needed fresh meat as well as fish; and the last of the men to build byres for the animals, to shelter them when winter came. The women were to feed and tend the animals, set up the looms, and choose where the summer crops could be sown, so the grain had time to ripen before winter.

Leif had said that animals could be left out all winter in this mild land, as there would be grass for them to eat all winter long. But Freydis wanted to take no chances. It was a long way to Greenland to get more cows or sheep.

The animals were eating as though they had never seen grass like this before. Hekja grinned. She supposed they hadn't. Even the bull didn't lift his head when she walked past to fill a bucket from the river. She was carrying it back when Hikki came jogging over to find her. He looked happier than she had ever seen him.

"Come on!" he yelled. "It is time for us to run the land!"

Hekja went back inside and changed into the running dress that Freydis had given her. It had two loops and buttons to fasten the material between her legs and at the sides, but her arms were bare, and so were her legs when she moved. The women shaking out the sleeping bags stared at her and giggled, but Hekja paid no attention. She was stronger and faster than those house women would ever be.

Freydis looked her up and down, then nodded.

"Tell Hikki to come in," she ordered.

Hikki too had changed into his running shift. He looked even more different from the big, fair Norsemen now, with his dark hair and small features and his strong runner's legs, so unlike the muscles of the men who exercised with sword and axe. He nodded respectfully to Freydis. "Which way should we run, mistress?"

"Run south along the coast for two days," ordered Freydis. "Then inland for two days, then run four days north, and make your way back along the coast. But if there is anything worth investigating you may take longer."

"What sort of thing, mistress?" asked Hikki.

"Birds' nests, lakes of fish. My brother said that there were fields of wild grain and berries. There's a whole land out there waiting to be discovered," Freydis said softly. "And you will see it first and tell me all about it."

"We are to run both together?" asked Hikki.

Freydis nodded. "If one has an accident, the other can

help." She smiled at Hekja. "And yes, you can take the dog too. But be warned," she said quietly to Hikki, so none of the house women could hear her words, "if you so much as look at her I will pull your guts out through your mouth and feed them to the fishes."

Hikki glanced at Hekja, then back at Freydis. "I would never do anything without your permission, mistress."

"See you don't," said Freydis, amused.

Hikki set off at a jog as soon as they were outside. Hekja followed him, with Snarf bounding happily at her side. The whole camp stopped work, it seemed, to watch them go. Hekja could feel their eyes on her bare legs.

Snorri was stripping bark from a fallen tree for the new fencing, just beyond the clearing. He must have just chopped it down, for his axe lay next to his shirt. Hekja nodded at him politely as she passed, and Snarf gave him a happy "arf". Snorri only nodded in reply. It wasn't till she passed that she heard him call, "Take care!"

She stopped and turned. He was still staring at her. "Would you tell a warrior going to battle to take care?" she asked.

Snorri frowned. "No." And then he grinned. "Though maybe I should. Come back safe," he added, and now he didn't grin.

Hekja felt herself blushing. "I will." She turned back and followed Hikki through the trees.

It was easy running on that first morning. This time Hekja carried a pack like Hikki's, with a cloak, knife, a water bladder[31] and another bladder filled with oatmeal mixed with salt butter. Hikki also carried flint and ironstone.

The sun was barely high when they reached the beach. They ran along the sand where it was firmest, just above the waves. For a while there was little to see, for the sand dunes rose between them and the land. All that was visible were the scattered islands, most no larger than a whale, and the piles of rotting seaweed for Snarf to nose at. The sand was almost the colour of the sun and the waves rolled smooth and even and splashed their ankles.

When the sun was high Hikki announced a rest stop. They crossed the sand dunes, up into the edges of the forest, where the sand met the first black soil, and flopped down into the shade. Snarf shook himself, and wet sand flew from his fur and into their faces, then he flopped too. He had found a dead seagull and had carried it proudly in his mouth for the last part of their run.

Hekja kicked it further away. "If you're going to eat that," she said firmly, "you can sit over there."

"Arf," said Snarf reproachfully. He trotted over to his seagull and sat down to chew it.

Hekja opened her pack and pulled out her water bladder. She untied the top and drank a few gulps, then tied it up again and rested against a tree and shut her eyes. She opened them to find Hikki staring at her.

"You don't use your arms," he said abruptly.

"My what?"

"Your arms. When you run. That is why you are so tired now. You need to let your body balance, so it pulls you along."

"I don't understand," said Hekja.

Hikki shrugged. Then he said, "The singer... what do you think of him?"

Hekja hesitated. "I think he has the most wonderful voice I have ever heard," she said honestly, and watched Hikki's face darken. "I also think he is a Norseman, and my enemy."

"Perhaps. But you still have to live with these people," said Hikki. He studied her face closely.

"I know," said Hekja softly. "For a while I hoped I could go back home. But my home no longer exists. If I ever have a home again it will be here. But not with a Norseman."

Hikki said nothing. He took a single gulp of his water, then put it away. Then he smiled at her. "Come on," he said. "Now I will show you how to be the finest runner in the world."

Before she'd met Hikki, Hekja had thought that all you needed to run well was strong legs, and some practice running after cows. Now she learnt differently.

This time, as they ran along the beach, Hikki showed her how to push with her bare toes, to propel her body forward; how to swing her arms so they pushed her body too; how to angle her body against the wind so it almost seemed that she might fall, but somehow ran faster, and easier too.

Most of all he showed her how to pace herself, so that she ran at an easy speed without having to stop and rest. Suddenly it seemed as though their feet ate up the beach, as headland after headland disappeared behind them.

But it seemed that there was even more to learn.

Mid-afternoon they splashed across a creek, its leaf-brown water trickling across the sand. It was the first fresh water they had found since they left the river. Hikki glanced up at the sky. "Time to stop," he said.

"But it will be light for ages yet," protested Hekja.

"And we have days of running ahead of us. Best stay here, with fresh water, and collect driftwood for a fire and start at first light tomorrow." Hikki nodded at Snarf. "And perhaps your friend here might find dinner for us too."

"Arf." Snarf wagged his tail, as if to say, "I'm sick of running on sand. Let's go hunting instead."

Hekja followed Snarf into the trees, while Hikki gathered driftwood. Suddenly the world was dappled shadows, and cool after the glare on the beach. In places the undergrowth would have almost been too thick to push through, if it hadn't been for trails that the animals had made.

Finally Snarf bounded ahead. He was back a few minutes later, carrying something in his mouth. He dropped the dead animal at Hekja's feet.

It was big and furry, like a hare but with a bushy tail. Hekja skinned it with her knife, but left the guts in so Snarf could eat them later with the head and the feet. She hesitated with the skin, for it looked soft and valuable. But finally she left it there, rather than carry it as she ran.

The smell of smoke and roasting led them back to the sand dunes and the fire. Hekja stared at the creatures Hikki had placed over the coals.

"What are they?"

"Crabs. One of Leif's men told me about them. They have their bones outside, not inside. They're supposed to taste like fish."

They did. Hekja poked the last of the flesh from the claws while the furry creature cooked, and Snarf gulped the guts then settled down to doze, with one ear up so he didn't miss anything and his nose pointing away from the fire so he could smell the new scents.

"It's beautiful," said Hekja at last. "The golden sand and the waves. I never thought anywhere could be so beautiful. Do you think we are the first people ever to see this?"

Hikki shrugged. "Maybe. Leif's party explored too. But it is a rich land, true enough. There is wealth enough for everybody here." Then he added, "My muscles are sore – they grew too soft aboard the ship." He stood and began to undo his tunic.

Hekja stared. "What are you doing?"

Hikki grinned at her. "I'm going to bathe. Have you ever tried it?"

Hekja shook her head.

"It stops your muscles from aching," said Hikki. He shrugged and added carefully, "But the waves are probably too rough for a girl."

Hekja glared at him. "If you can bathe, I can too."

She undid a button on her tunic, and then looked up. Hikki was still staring at her. "Look away!" she ordered.

Hikki grinned. "Why?"

"Because Freydis ordered it," said Hekja. Then she added, "And because I ask you to."

"Then I will obey you, not Freydis, this time," said Hikki seriously.

Hikki pretended to look at the sky while Hekja undressed, then raced down the sand without looking behind. Hekja followed him. They waded out till the waves crashed against their waists. Hikki ducked down till only his head was showing and Hekja copied him, while Snarf splashed at the shallows and looked worried in case they planned to run right out to sea.

"It's cold! But good!" yelled Hekja.

"I told you it was," said Hikki smugly.

Hekja wondered if he could see her shape under the water. But she could only dimly make out the white of his body, so she supposed the water hid her too. The last naked man Hekja had seen had been her older brother, years before, but that was different.

They ran back after that, Hekja first, then Hikki when she called that she was dressed, and sat by the fire while Snarf gnawed at the bones. The shadows grew deeper as they talked of the villages where they had been taken from, and of the families that now were dead. It was the first time that Hekja had talked so freely since her capture, and somehow it seemed to take away most of the pain.

Hikki talked too about the farm he'd have soon, when Freydis gave him land and freedom. But Hekja never mentioned that Freydis had said she would free her too.

The moon hovered above them, so bright it made shadows, just like the sun. Hikki leaned over, and threw more wood on the fire. An owl hooted. It sounded strangely like an owl from home.

Down on the beach the waves pounded out their own music. And suddenly Hekja felt a new song sweep through her. The words had come to her as she had run that afternoon, but now the tune carried them along.

> *My heart was crying,*
> *As they took me from my home,*
> *But my mouth made no sound.*

I would not sing for Norsemen,
Not of sorrow or of joy.

Today our heels have flown,
Across white sand and gold,
Today my soul is free,
And I can sing again.

The music died away. Hikki gazed at her, his mouth open as though it was the first song he had ever heard. Finally he said softly, "The Norsemen prize good singing. You would not have had to mind the cows if they knew that you could sing like that."

"My singing is mine, not theirs," said Hekja, just as she had said to Snorri with his butter hair.

"But still…" began Hikki.

"No," said Hekja. The song had left her empty. "No discussion." And she lay down to go to sleep.

Hikki slept too, with Snarf dozing but alert beside them.

When morning came they set out again. By mid-morning they came to a great river, cutting deeply through the sand, so wide it would need a boat to cross it. They turned inland then and ran along the river bank.

At first the river flats were mostly sand and grass, where floods had swept them clean. Then the big river broke off into small ones, with trees along their banks. Finally they came to marshlands full of reeds and waving heads of grain.[32] Hekja picked a bunch and placed it in her pack to show Freydis.

They headed northwards now as Freydis had instructed, over low hills, along animal trails again that were hidden among the trees. Suddenly Snarf stopped and barked. "Arf!" It was his danger call.

Hekja looked back. "What is it, boy?" she demanded.

"Arf!" Snarf barked again, then growled warningly.

Hekja looked around. But there was nothing to see.

Snarf growled again.

"What's wrong with him?" called Hikki.

Hekja shook her head. "I don't know," she admitted. "I can't see anything. It must be something he can smell." She bent and patted Snarf's head.

"Maybe he's hungry," suggested Hikki.

"Maybe," said Hekja doubtfully. She gazed around again, but there seemed to be nothing wrong so they began to run again.

Snarf bounded after her. But he seemed wary now, no longer leaping carelessly through the trees or bringing back branches for Hekja to toss.

That night they slept on a hill above a marshy lake, but Snarf only dozed. And when Hekja woke at dawn he was awake, his hackles raised, and growling.

Chapter 34

THE SKRAELINGS

"What is it, boy?" whispered Hekja, sitting up in her sleeping bag. Hikki was still asleep.

Snarf whined and pointed into the forest with his nose.

"Hikki, I think you should…" began Hekja, in her normal voice.

Snarf whined again more urgently, to tell her to be quiet. This time she understood.

"What's wrong?" she whispered. And then she smelled it too.

Smoke.

She and Hikki hadn't bothered with a fire the night before, so the smoke could not be theirs. She pushed her way out of her sleeping bag in alarm and looked around.

Snarf pointed again, the way Thorvard had shown him. Hekja nodded and crawled over to Hikki. "Wake up!" she whispered. "Shh! Wake up!"

Hikki knows how to be silent, thought Hekja – years as a thrall will teach you that. He woke up blinking, but didn't speak, till Hekja whispered, "Smoke!"

"Where?" hissed Hikki.

Snarf growled, deep and low, and walked forward a few steps and looked around, as though to say, "Follow me."

Hikki beckoned to Hekja. "Place your feet down on their outsides like this," he whispered, as he demonstrated what he meant. "It's quieter that way. Move your body as little as you can, especially your head – it's movement that attracts attention."

Hekja nodded. They grabbed their packs and followed Snarf through the trees and then around a hill.

And then they saw them. It was a hunting party of seven men, and dogs too. Now Hekja knew why Snarf had led them upwind – so the dogs wouldn't smell them as he had smelled the fire and cooking meat.

The men's fire was nearly out, but they had been feasting well. A deer's carcass, mostly charred bones, lay next to its pelt, rolled up to carry away, and there was another carcass hanging from a tree.

The hunters looked different from any men that Hekja had ever seen. Their hair was long and black instead of red or blond like the Greenlanders, or brown like Hekja's and Hikki's. They were shorter than Norsemen too, and had darker skin, and their eyes were brown, not blue or green. They were dressed in softly fringed skins, tied above their chests or around their waists, and their hair was shaved to make a long crest on top, with feathers poked behind their ears and they wore strange markings on their wrists, legs and chests.

Hekja froze, hardly breathing. She knew how Snarf felt now, for the hair on the back of her neck rose at the scent of danger just like his.

The men called lazily to each other as they picked up their bows and stone-tipped arrows, birch-bark containers, the deer carcass and the rolled-up skins. They moved off down the hill. Hekja stayed perfectly still until she heard their calls slowly die away.

"Who were they?" she breathed.

"Skraelings," muttered Hikki. The word just meant 'natives' or ones who lived in this place. "Leif's men didn't mention Skraelings."

"We have to follow them," whispered Hekja. "We need to know more."

Hikki hesitated. "If we get too close they'll hear us, or the dogs will smell us if the wind changes suddenly. These men are hunters." He looked at Snarf, staring through the trees, and came to a decision. "We'd best wait, till they get a distance away, and trust Snarf to track them. Can he do that?"

Hekja nodded.

The sun rose, the mist dissolved into the hot clear air. "Follow, boy!" whispered Hekja. Snarf put his nose to the ground on command.

It was easier than Hekja had thought it would be. Snarf moved quietly and confidently through the forest, as though the hunter's trail was as clear to him as a path through the trees. Finally they reached a track, leading past a marsh. Hekja bit her lip. Perhaps the trails she'd seen a few days earlier hadn't all been made by animals after all.

The sun rose high as they crept along the trail, twisting through the trees and over grasslands, taller than Hekja's head, then through the trees again. Now the track led up a hill. Snarf stopped suddenly and whined, just as Hekja pointed.

The Skraeling village was below them.

"It's enormous!" whispered Hikki.

Hekja nodded. This village was even bigger than Brattahlid. The houses were quite different from any she had seen – long huts, not made of stone or logs, but of tree branches with rounded roofs made of branches as well.

All around the houses there were fields, with tall yellow flowers[33], and grain[34] higher than a Norseman's head, and green-leaved plants[35]. Smoke from cooking fires rose into the air.

And people. More people than she had ever seen!

The men were dressed like the hunters, but there were women too, with bare feet and breasts, leather skirts and strings of beads, their heads shaved across the top and with markings on their skin just like the men's. The children were mostly naked, running around the village, yelling and playing games.

Hikki and Hekja looked at each other then edged back into the trees. Then they ran as swiftly as they could, back the way they came.

The sun was low on the horizon before they stopped. "Freydis has to know of this at once," said Hekja.

Hikki nodded. This land had a people – and they looked like warriors too.

They ran more slowly now, as night fell. Finally it grew too dark to run safely. They stopped on a small rise, and slid into their sleeping bags. It was impossible to risk a fire now. They ate and drank quickly from their packs, then Hikki pointed at the stars. "Look, see that star there..." he began.

"Can't it wait?" snapped Hekja. She could hardly stay awake.

Hikki shook his head. "If we are separated you need to know this," he said. "The stars can tell you how far you have run, and which way you have to go. Now, find the north star and…"

Neither slept well that night, despite their tiredness. They knew that there might be danger in the forest now – and more than Snarf could protect them from. As soon as daylight came they ate the last of their travelling food, and ran as swiftly as they could.

By mid-morning they came to the swamps again. These gave way to a small lake, edged again with reeds and grain. They trotted around the water's edge till the first lake opened into an even bigger one.

"This looks like the one near camp," said Hekja hopefully.

Hikki glanced up towards the sun then nodded. "I think so too," he said. "Come on. We need a break."

"I can keep going longer," said Hekja.

"Perhaps," said Hikki. "But we need reserves of speed too, in case we have to run for our lives. Come on, let's sit up there." He pointed to the hill above the lake.

"Did you ever have to run for your life?" asked Hekja, as they jogged up the rise.

"Once," said Hikki shortly. "I had to take a message from the king to a man he hoped wasn't his enemy."

"Yes?" encouraged Hekja.

"By the time I reached him, he and his men were already marching towards the king. So I had to run again, even faster this time because they'd seen me, to tell the king. But I outran them all, even with their horses. A man can cross cliffs and take shorter ways where a big horse cannot go."

"Why didn't you just keep running?" asked Hekja curiously. "Run away so you could be free?"

"I told you before. A thrall can't outrun his master. I don't look like a Norseman. Anywhere I went I would be hunted down, unless I had a master's protection."

It was good to sit and drink, even if there was nothing to eat. Hekja hardly felt hungry now – it was as though the running had driven it away, though she felt faintly light-headed from lack of food. Snarf drank from the lake and then sniffed about the trees before spreading himself out in the shade next to Hekja to doze.

Suddenly something dropped on his nose. Snarf snapped at it, half asleep, thinking it was a beetle, then sat up and spat it out on to Hekja's lap.

"Errk," she said. She peered up where it had come from.

"Hikki! Look!" she cried.

Hikki stood and reached up. He brought down a bunch of purple berries. "Do you think we can eat them?" he asked.

"Snarf spat his out," said Hekja dubiously.

"Snarf is a dog," said Hikki dryly.

"He's smarter than most humans," flared Hekja at once.

Hikki laughed. "But still a dog!" He put one of the berries in his mouth, then wrinkled his nose.

"What are they like?" asked Hekja curiously. He handed her a bunch and she picked one off. "Errk."

Hikki grinned. "I think the green ones aren't ripe yet. Try a purple one instead."[36]

Hekja tasted another, and considered it. "It's alright," she said at last. "Not wonderful. Do you think these are Leif's grapes? The vines of Vinland?"

Hikki nodded.

"Why did Leif make such a fuss about them? I'd rather have strawberries," said Hekja frankly. "These are too tough skinned."

"Yes," said Hikki slowly. "But I think they would make fine wine. I tasted wine once, back in the court of the king. It's made of grape juice."

"What did it taste like?"

"Rich," said Hikki. "Rich as you would expect a king's drink to taste."

Hekja laughed. "My father sang about an island of clouds, where jewels hung from trees. I didn't know what jewels were then – I thought they were a sort of cheese! I think... I think Pa would have liked this land."

Hikki nodded. "It's a good land, Hekja. Worth fighting for."

Hekja looked up at that. "Fighting!" she whispered.

Hikki looked surprised. "Of course. That is what the Norsemen do. They fought for land in Ireland and England and the islands. They drove off the first Icelanders to take the land instead. So they will fight the Skraelings for this land too." He shrugged. "Did you notice? The Skraelings had no iron weapons. The Norsemen do."

"But there is plenty of land here! Enough for everyone!"

"Norsemen fight," said Hikki, as though this explained it all.

"But Freydis is in charge now," said Hekja slowly. "Maybe... maybe things will be different."

Hikki shrugged.

Hekja looked out, through the trees to the hills beyond, with the glint of water and the glades of grass. "It is so beautiful," she said softly. "It seems impossible there should be hatred and violence here. Does every land have its own beauty? The crags of the mountain at home, the islands of rain and sun in the grey sea, the white of the ice against the sky in Greenland, the green and richness here. All different, all beautiful."

Hikki said nothing. He pulled her down more grapes, purple ones this time, and handed them to Hekja. She sat sucking out their juice and spitting out the skins, while Hikki pulled off more grapes from the vines that clambered into the other trees as well.

Hikki tied the bunches together, and put some in his empty pack to take back to Freydis, then shared the rest with Hekja.

Finally Hekja stood up. "Come on. We've rested enough." She grinned at him wickedly. "Or are you too tired to keep running?"

Hikki glared at her for a moment, his pride stung, then realised she was joking. "I'll race you to the next hill," he offered.

Hekja grinned and shook her head. "No competition. You run faster than I do Hikki, I admit it."

"I'll give you a head start. Come on, go!"

Hekja ran. Snarf bounded with her. She could hear

Hikki running too, but could tell that he wasn't running his fastest.

Hekja made the hill first. She turned to wait for Hikki, laughing. "You are getting old, Hikki!" she taunted.

Hikki smiled. "No," he said simply, "my life is just beginning."

They ran again properly after that, refreshed by the rest and the grapes, an easy lope that covered a lot of ground. Soon Hekja could smell more smoke and see it across the lake. It was the smoke of Finnbogi's camp. She glanced at Hikki and he nodded. They were nearly home.

They stayed up on the hills, for it was easier going there than in the thicker brush down by the lake shore or along the river banks. By mid-afternoon Freydis' camp was below them. Hekja began to trot down the hill, but Hikki put his hand on her arm. It was the first time he had touched her since they had left the camp. "Stay a moment," he said.

Hekja turned. "Why?"

For the first time Hikki looked embarrassed. "Would you sing again?" he whispered. "A song from our land, a song like my mother might have sung."

Hekja smiled. She sat on a log, fallen in some past storm and covered with moss, and looked out over the camp and the river to the sea, just as she might have looked out at the harbour from her ma's doorway. This time she sang a song that her ma had taught her, about a fisherman who caught a seal with a gold ring in its mouth.

The fisherman knew this was no ordinary seal. He kept the ring and let the seal go, and as it swam through the water it turned into a beautiful woman. The woman swam back to his boat and held up her arms to him. The fisherman married her and from that day no fisherman of their family was ever drowned.

Hikki watched, as Hekja sang, then Snarf joined in.

"Arooooh!"

Hekja began to giggle, and even Hikki laughed. Suddenly Snarf leapt to his feet. "Arf Arf!"

For a moment Hekja thought it might be Skraelings again. Then she realised this was a bark of welcome.

It was Snorri. He had been cutting timber, for he carried his axe and he smelled of wood sap as well as sweat. He had been standing behind them as she sang.

"Arf, arf, arf," barked Snarf loudly, embarrassed that Snorri had snuck up without him noticing.

But Snorri stared at Hekja. "I thought you wouldn't sing for anyone?"

"Not for a Norseman," said Hekja softly. Then without asking Snorri's leave – for he was a free man and, even though she was obeying Freydis' orders, she was a thrall – she began to run down the hill.

"Master," began Hikki, unsure of what to say.

"Go," said Snorri shortly.

Hekja could feel his eyes on them as they ran down the hill to Freydis.

Freydis was checking the new sheep fields. The sheep had been shorn recently, and were due to lamb, and the new fences had to be closely woven to stop the lambs from wriggling through them.

She leaned against the fence and stared at them. "Well?" she demanded. "What's wrong?" She smiled slightly as Hikki gaped. "You are back before I told you to return. It's not much of a guess that you found out something I need to know at once."

Hekja let Hikki talk – he had more experience than she did in fitting all that had happened into a short account. Freydis looked thoughtful when he had finished.

"Fetch Thorvard," she said at last to Hikki.

"Should I go?" offered Hekja.

"No," said Freydis. "Stay." She questioned Hekja again about every detail of the Skraeling camp till Thorvard arrived, and then they had to tell their story again.

Thorvard listened in silence too. And then he grinned. "So," he said, "we fight."

"No," said Freydis flatly.

Thorvard stared at her. "If we want this land we have to take it!"

Freydis shook her head. "This isn't like Ireland, or England or the islands, with the best land taken. There is rich land enough here for us and the Skraelings too. Besides, we have no reinforcements here. We have only forty men…"

"And Finnbogi's," put in Thorvard softly.

"And Finnbogi's. But from what the runners say the Skraelings have more men than in the whole of Brattahlid ten times over. There is no way we can take this land by force."

"We are not cowards…" Thorvard began.

"It has nothing to do with cowardice!" interrupted Freydis. "If I thought we could defeat them I'd say let's attack their village now, take them by surprise, and burn it to the ground. But where there is one village there will be more."

"Then what do we do?" asked Thorvard unwillingly.

"We wait here until they find us," said Freydis flatly. "And we try to look like friends, not enemies."

Chapter 35

THE SKRAELINGS ARRIVE

It took the Skraelings half a moon to find the Norse camp.

It was early morning when they paddled their skin-covered canoes up the estuary, then along the river. They came slowly, as though they were in no hurry, so Hekja had plenty of time to find Freydis after the lookout called.

Some of the Skraelings put their oars down as the canoes drew closer to the big Viking ship, and waved sticks that made a noise like the sound of barley flails that blew the chaff off the grain.

Freydis shaded her eyes against the glare and stared at them, then turned to Thorvard.

"What do you think?" she whispered.

Thorvard stared out at the massed canoes. "I think each man needs to fetch his weapons," he muttered. "There are more than twice our number there."

Beside him Snorri gazed, fascinated by the newcomers. "Maybe the noise is a sign of peace," he hazarded. "If they were going to attack surely they'd try to be quiet."

Freydis flashed him a smile. "My thinking too, skalder boy. Go fetch the white shield hanging by the fire," she ordered Snorri. "Maybe they will recognise it as a sign of peace. And yes," she added to Thorvard, "tell the men to fetch their weapons too, but two at a time only, so the Skraelings don't think we are preparing for a battle. The women are to stay in the long house."

Hekja wondered whether that meant she was to go to the long house too. But Freydis made no sign that she was to leave, so she stayed where she was. Snorri came running with the shield. Freydis held it high, while all the camp gathered behind her. Each man had his shield and sword or battle-axe ready to hand, but on Freydis' orders held them low, so as to not look too ready for war.

Hikki edged up to Hekja. "If they attack, run towards the hills," he whispered. "We can hide among the trees."

Hekja stared at him. He shrugged. "The free men have their swords and axes. We have nothing but our legs."

Hekja bit her lip and said nothing, but stared out with the others.

The canoes were almost on them now. The Skraelings leaped out and pulled their canoes up on to the bank, while their leader strode towards Freydis. He was taller than the other Skraelings, almost Viking size, with many strings of big white beads[37] about his neck. He stared at the cows as though he had never seen cattle before, then he stepped up to Thorvard and said something.

The words made no sense to Hekja. Thorvard shook his head too. The Skraeling leader nodded, as though he had expected this. He signalled to his men.

The Skraelings pulled out piles of pelts from the boats and carried them over to their chief, then put them down at Thorvard's feet.

Thorvard glanced at Freydis. She handed the white shield back to Snorri and picked up one of the pelts and stroked it. She nodded at Thorvard. "These are good furs. It seems he wants to trade."

The chief pointed to Thorvard's sword and said something sharply.

Freydis stepped forward. "No," she said, and though the chief must have found the word strange her meaning was obvious. "We will not trade fur for weapons."

The chief spoke again, more angrily. He pointed again at Thorvard's sword, as Skraelings yelled behind him, stamping their feet on the ground. Hikki began to edge away. "Time to run," he hissed to Hekja.

"Not yet," said Hekja urgently. "Stop! If we run now the Skraelings will think that we are scared."

Hikki hesitated as Freydis beckoned Hekja.

"Fetch some cheeses," she ordered. "Quickly! And fresh milk as well."

Hekja ran. She yelled to one of the women staring from the long-house doorway to bring out a bucket of milk, while she grabbed a cheese, a big one nearly ripe, and carried it to Freydis, Thorvard and the chief. Behind her two of the women struggled with great buckets of fresh milk.

Slowly, very slowly, so there should be no misunderstanding, Freydis pulled out the small knife from the chain that dangled from her brooch. She cut a wedge of cheese, sliced off a tiny piece and put it in her mouth, then handed the rest of the wedge to the chief.

The chief sniffed it suspiciously, then bit it.

Then he smiled.

Freydis smiled too. She took a bucket of milk from the women behind her and handed that to the big man too, with a gesture for him to drink.

The chief lifted the bucket. Hekja heard him gulping. When he finally put it down his smile was even wider.

It was easy after that. The Skraelings brought out more bales of pelts from their canoes and Freydis emptied the dairy of milk, cheese and butter to trade for them.

"There will be no cheese for us," whispered Hikki, staring as fascinated as the rest.

"No matter," said Hekja. "Vinland has more than enough food." She gazed at Freydis. "She was wonderful. The Skraeling didn't even look at her. But she made him see that she was in command. They could have killed us all. But instead they are leaving us with furs – and all for cheese."

"Indeed," said a voice. It was Snorri the Skald. Somehow he always seemed to be near Hekja now, though whenever she glanced at him he was looking somewhere else.

Hekja turned, as though she hadn't known that he was there. "Worthy of a song?" she asked softly.

Snorri stared at her for a moment without speaking. Then he said, "Perhaps. Or perhaps a woman should sing about another woman's deeds."

Hekja said nothing. Then Freydis beckoned her again, to get more cheese.

Chapter 36

VINLAND DAYS

The Skraelings came often after that. They brought more furs and, as the summer melted into autumn, some of their strange grains as well, one that grew on long stalks and could be cooked when young and tender, or ground to flour when it was older[38] and another kind that came from flowers[39] that were eaten raw, or made into an oily paste like butter.

They brought gourds too – dried ones carved with strange designs to store grain in, or milk or water, and others that were soft and yellow inside when they were cooked, and tasted sweet, and still others that had white flesh too.[40]

If there wasn't enough milk or cheese they traded for strips of bright red cloth, which they tied around their heads. But milk and cheese were prized more than anything else the Norse folk had.

Mostly Snorri the Skald conducted the trading. Unlike the other Norsemen he was learning Skraeling words. The Skraelings even took him hunting. They showed him how to shoot at giant salmon with their stone-tipped arrows, while in return Snorri showed them how the Greenlanders dug fish traps in the sand, that filled with fish at each low tide as the waves retreated down the beach.

"Do the Skraelings have music too?" Hekja asked Snorri one day. She had seen him climbing across the sandhills, trying to balance two big baskets of the clams the Skraelings had shown the newcomers how to dig. It was only polite, she told herself, to run and help him carry them.

Snorri grinned as he passed over the smaller basket. "Not like ours. The first time I heard one of their songs I thought the man had stuck an arrow in his foot! But they thought the same of my songs."

"They didn't like them!"

Snorri's grin grew even wider at her surprise. "No! Too different. But when I heard their music again, I don't know, I still can't say I enjoy it. But I can see it has a beauty, a complexity, of its own. It is like the Skraelings themselves, Hekja!"

"How?" asked Hekja.

Snorri turned to her eagerly. "They are different too. As different from us as this land is from Norway, or Iceland, or Greenland. The more I see of them the more fascinating I find them!" He laughed, and threw his hair back over his shoulders. "To think I came here thinking I could make songs about a new land! Now I can sing about a new people too when I go home to Norway."

So, thought Hekja, he was still planning to leave. They were nearly at the long houses now. Snarf bounded out to meet them. He had been supervising the young lambs, and making sure they knew that dogs were boss.

"Hekja," began Snorri. "If you would like… I mean, I could tell you more about the Skraelings, perhaps…"

"I'm sorry," said Hekja hurriedly. "I must see if Freydis has any orders for me. I'll put these by the fire pit tonight." She forced a smile. "I think there is roast deer tonight, as well as a salmon and these too, and Helga has made a bread with the first of the new wheat, and a flummery.[41] There is so much to eat in Vinland it's hard to know what to taste first!" She walked off too fast for him to reply.

This was indeed a land of plenty. Hekja heard the women commenting that the new fields had given more barley and wheat than any in Greenland or Iceland either, or even Norway. The cows and calves were so fat they almost rolled around on the grass and there was plenty of hay, and chickens running everywhere you looked.

The crops of oats and wheat had been brought in, more than twice as much as similar fields would have given back in Greenland. As the weather cooled great flocks of swans, geese, ducks and cranes flew to the estuary, so many that the men boasted they could throw a spear with their eyes shut and still hit two or more. The long houses smelled richly of roasting meats and bread.

The storerooms were full of skins to trade back in Greenland when the ice about its shores cleared enough next summer. There were great lengths of timber too, felled and dressed and left to cure on rocky platforms.

The people in the long houses slept on bearskins now, or even softer furs, and ate from platters of carved gourd. Even Snarf had a carved gourd to lap his water from. Hekja had seen Snorri carve it. But he had never given it to her, just filled it with water and left it where Snarf would find it.

Hekja made sure she avoided him now. Even if friendship between a thrall and a skald was possible, it would only lead to loss next spring.

But life was still good – better, in many ways, than it had ever been. She had responsibility now, and friends, and Snarf. Snarf had filled out even more in the Vinland summer. His chest was broader than a wolf's now and his legs much longer. None of the Greenland dogs was anywhere near his size.

Several of the women were pregnant, too. *Soon we will be a proper village,* thought Hekja longingly, *with children running between the houses.* There were plans for more buildings. This colony would grow, just as Greenland had, but faster and more prosperously, for Greenland was a poor land compared to this.

It was almost, thought Hekja in surprise, coming to seem like home.

Chapter 37

✦

WINTER FEASTING

The first leaves were changing colour when Freydis ordered a feast.

"The best of everything," she said to Hekja. "Three days from now. Tell the men we need meat to roast, deer and bear and swans. We will have wheat bread and barley beer, and the first of the young wine. Vinland wine from Vinland grapes!"

Hekja nodded. Then she said, "Why?"

Freydis frowned. "Why what?"

"Why have a feast now?"

Freydis smiled at her. "Always questions. Anyone could guess you were never born to be a thrall! Because I say so." Her smiled deepened. "There is another reason too. But I will announce that at the feast."

"I will give the orders," promised Hekja. She hesitated, then asked, "Should we ask Finnbogi's people too?"

Freydis frowned. "I have given a lot of thought to that. No, I don't think so. It would be different if the Skraelings were unfriendly, if we needed to join with Finnbogi to fight them off. But Finnbogi will never accept my authority. It's best to keep our groups apart."

It will be a fine feast, thought Hekja, the first feast since the one on the great mountain where she had felt truly part of it.

The fires were lit at first light, and by the time the sun had risen high the coals were ready for the meat. All through the morning the women loaded the big tables with wheat and oat breads, the roasted Skraeling corn and pumpkins, the shellfish, with wheat puddings sweetened with grape juice and rich with eggs. The grease from the roast meat caused the flames to flicker higher and lick against the meat, and the smell of cooking filled the camp.

By afternoon the meat was ready. Hekja helped the other women serve, and kept the drinking horns filled too. The dogs lay underneath the tables and as the men got drunker, fed on the spilled puddings and bread soaked in meat juice, and the bones. This time Freydis didn't serve with the other women, but sat in the great carved chair and was waited on like a chief.

When the best of the meat had been eaten Snorri the Skald stood up. Hekja had noticed he had drunk less than the other men, and eaten less too. The men quietened, even those arguing at the tops of their voices. The sun began to sink in a haze of golden. Snorri began to sing.

He sang to Freydis, at the head of the tables. He didn't even look at Hekja, but somehow she knew that the song was meant for her.

It was a song about a prince who had to defeat the enemies who had stolen his kingdom and his family and the princess he was to marry. He met a white swan, who showed him where the forest kept its treasure, so he could have enough silver to pay an army. The swan flew above the enemy camp, so the prince knew where his army should wait in ambush. When the prince finally won the battle the swan taught him a song to sing to his princess, to tell her he loved her.

Then the swan flew away and the hero realised it was the swan that he had loved all the time.

And so Snorri sang, his butter-coloured hair gleaming in the moonlight:

> *Across the sea I came wandering,*
> *For glory and heroes and fame,*
> *But I knew not for what I was searching,*
> *For love was only a name.*

Finally the swan heard the prince calling her from across the mountains, and flew back. The lovers were reunited. They were swans in summer, flying across the world. In winter they turned into a prince and princess and lived in the prince's kingdom.

Hekja's eyes were bright when the song had finished. She stared at Snorri across the fire, hoping no one could see her in the dark.

Freydis stood and waved her horn mug in the air to silence the cheering. "Thank you, Snorri the Skald," she cried, "for brightening our feast. Maybe one day you will judge our deeds to be worthy of a song too!"

The men cheered again. Someone called for another song, but Freydis waved him silent.

"There will be time enough for singing," she called. "But now I have an announcement."

The whole crowd was quiet now. *Does Freydis plan*

another expedition, to explore further still? thought Hekja. She remembered Freydis staring at the sea to the south, on their first day in Vinland.

But Freydis smiled and said, "This land has given us riches beyond our dreams. Soon it will give me something more. For in five months, Thorvard and I will have a child."

The cheering nearly lifted the roofs off the long houses. The men would have cheered the wind by then, for they had drunk so much and were in a mood for cheering. Thorvard alone didn't cheer. He stood and grabbed his wife from her high chief's chair, and swung her round, his face so full of joy it almost seemed to glow. Then he held her high in his arms and the crowd cheered again.

The men sang a drinking song after that, loud as a battle almost, thought Hekja. She and the women slipped indoors as the men grew drunker and the fights began.

"And let's hope no one has his legs chopped off this time," said Helga matter of factly to Hekja. But as she said the words Hekja heard Freydis raise her voice outside, calling a halt to the fights and drinking.

"For we depend on each other here," she cried, "our duty is to live, not die, like heroes."

Freydis ordered the fire banked down for the night after that. She and Thorvard went to bed in their curtained room, and the couples went to their bed closets, and the men climbed to the attic. Hekja could hear them laughing upstairs, and more fighting, but nothing much, in case Freydis should hear.

Snarf was lying by the fire, chewing a deer bone, and Hekja was combing her hair with the brush Freydis had given her, before she plaited it for the night, when the ladder creaked. Snarf looked up. Someone was coming down from the attic.

"Arf," he barked, but softly. He wagged his tail too. It was Snorri.

"I wanted a mug of water," he said. "I'm thirsty after all that ale."

Hekja nodded. She put the brush down, and began to divide her hair into braids. Snorri dipped a mug into the water barrel, then sat on a bench and watched her in the faint glow of the coals.

"Did you like the song?" he asked at last.

"Yes," said Hekja, paying attention to her plaiting, and not to him. "But I think it was a pity you didn't let the swan sing, as well as the hero."

Snorri smiled at that. "True," he said. "Swans are supposed to be wonderful singers. Is it my fault they rarely let humans hear them?" He took another sip of water, and then said softly, "If you had been the swan, what would you have sung?"

Hekja did look at him then. "I think her song would have said 'You are a prince, and I am a swan, and two people so different can never be happy together'."

Snorri looked at her seriously. "Maybe they would discover that they were not so different after all."

Hekja shrugged, trying to seem as if she didn't care. "Perhaps they'd be happy for a while. But then the prince would go back to his kingdom. And the swan would be alone."

"You didn't listen close enough," said Snorri gently. "In my song the swan and the prince go home together."

Hekja froze. He couldn't mean that she might go back to Norway with him? "Imagine his parents when their son brought them home a swan," she said tightly. "They'd be horrified."

"Until they heard her sing," said Snorri. "I think they would love her then, as he did. But yes, a swan would need courage to marry a prince."

"I think," said Hekja softly, "that they would be happier with their own kind, swan with swan, prince with princess. And when he got back to his castle the prince would know it too."

"Is that how you would sing the song?" demanded Snorri.

Hekja nodded. "A lonely prince, far from his own kind, who falls in love with a swan because there's no one else to fall in love with. But when the prince saw the princesses of home again," she shrugged, "he'd soon lose all interest in beaks and feathers."

"No!" cried Snorri. "That's cowardice! You're scared to risk…"

A voice from behind the curtain interrupted him then. "Will you be quiet out there!"

It was Thorvard. Snorri flushed and put down his mug of water. Hekja concentrated on her plaits as the ladder creaked as he went back upstairs.

Snorri spent more time with the Skraelings after that, so that sometimes he was gone for days. When he was back he spoke to Hekja politely, as he did to all the women. He neither avoided her nor sought her out. Nor did he sing again.

The days flowed into each other. Freydis' belly began to swell, so she had to tie her apron looser, till finally one of the women made her a bigger one.

Pregnant or not, she was still in command. She had promised to bring her men to Vinland, sailing far from land, and she had. She had promised riches, and they were there. She had dismissed Finnbogi, had traded so well with the Skraelings that there were furs beyond imagining waiting to be taken back to Greenland.

Now the trees turned gold and red, brighter than any autumn colours anyone had seen.

"Even the trees are richer in this land," said Hekja, as she stirred the rennet water into the fresh milk to start its journey into cheese.

One of the women smiled at her. "Gold leaves don't buy iron pots," she said, but she meant it kindly. The women were all older than she was, and they were free born, but the women liked Hekja. Today they were making soft cheeses that would be ready in a few days, instead of taking months like the hard cheeses. The Skraelings loved the soft cheeses as much as the hard ones.

Women were kept busy in this new land, for making the cheese and the red-dyed cloth were all women's jobs, not men's.

Snarf lay on the cool stone floor of the dairy, and panted and watched it all. He had rolled in bear droppings the night before and was enjoying his rich new smell.

Suddenly someone stood in the dairy's doorway, blocking out the light. Hekja looked up, and there was Hikki. She had seen little of him lately. Freydis had him running south and north, spying out the land, but she had kept Hekja with her.

"Can you come?" Hikki asked Hekja abruptly.

Hekja put down the cheese wrappings. "Come where?" she asked.

"Somewhere," said Hikki mysteriously.

Hekja looked curious. "If Freydis looks for me," she said to the women, "tell her I have gone with Hikki, and will be back soon." Snarf hauled himself to his feet as the women looked knowingly at each other.

"Where are we going?" asked Hekja again, as soon as they were beyond the fenced fields of the camp. Hikki shook his head. "You'll see," was all he said.

Hekja sighed, and looked at the glowing forest instead. "It's hard to believe autumn could be so bright," she said. "Do you think the birds will stay on the estuary all winter?"

"Maybe," said Hikki. "If they don't fly further south. But they have been here for weeks already. I think this is where they will stay till spring time."

They were climbing a hill now, down towards the lake. The wild vines hung thickly here, though their fruit had long been eaten by the birds. Down in the gully a stream ran through the bracken, smelling of autumn leaves. Small furry beasts chattered from the branches. Snarf woofed at them, and they chattered again, too high for him to reach.

"Here we are," said Hikki finally.

Hekja laughed and looked around. "Where is that? There's nothing here!"

"There will be. This will be my land," said Hikki solemnly. "I will build my house here, on this hill by this stream. My thralls will clear the timber, and plant my wheat and oats."

"Your thralls?"

Hikki nodded. "We will all have a share of the silver after next summer, when the furs and timber are taken back to Greenland and Iceland. Enough to buy thralls and tools and everything we need. All of us who came here first will be rich, Hekja. All of us."

"I see," said Hekja slowly. She sat on the leafy ground, her back to one of the great trees, and looked around.

"Do you think you would be happy here?" said Hikki quietly. "I am a thrall now, but I won't be one next summer. In time I will be as rich as any man in Vinland. We belong together, Hekja. We understand each other."

"Do we?" asked Hekja softly. "I suppose we must. We come from the same land. We are both runners, both have known what it is to be a slave. It's just…"

"What?" asked Hikki quietly.

"I want to see my home," whispered Hekja. "My real home. I want to go back to my village."

"Why?" asked Hikki, more gently than she had ever heard him speak. "What is left of your village now?"

"I need to know!" cried Hekja fiercely. "The girls up on the great mountain survived. Maybe others did as well."

"Are the girls so dear to you that you will leave all this, to go back to them? To live in a stone hut, and eat barley cake and fish and kale? Think what a life we could have here! Furs for your bed and wheat bread on the table. All the meat that you can eat. Thralls to serve you…"

"I could never have a thrall!" cried Hekja.

Hikki shrugged. "Some people would rather be a slave than free," he said. "They like to have someone tell them what to do."

Hekja was silent, thinking of Gudrun. Then Hikki said, "Would you really prefer your village to this?"

Hekja looked around, at the tall trees in their brilliant autumn cloaks, the sea beyond, the golden beach, the waves that stretched from sand to sky. Was her village just an excuse, so she didn't have to give Hikki an answer?

"No," she admitted finally. "You're right – I wouldn't want to live there now. I don't know! Hikki, I promised Freydis I would stay with her for two more years. After that – if you still wish it – ask me then."

Hikki grinned. "I will still wish it! By then I'll have your house built, the fields cleared. Two years – yes, I can wait that long."

"I must go," said Hekja abruptly. "Freydis will wonder where I am."

They started down the hill, Hikki laughing and talking of the house that he would build, the storeroom here, the dairy there. It was as though he assumed that Hekja had said yes.

Hekja was silent. But she let Hikki hold her hand as they walked down the hill. And even when she saw Snorri watching, she didn't pull her hand away.

The trees lost their leaves. Now there were finally cheeses in the storerooms, for the Skraelings had stopped coming to trade.

"Perhaps they move away in autumn," said Freydis.

Hekja shook her head. "Their village looked too substantial to leave every year. Snorri might know," she added, trying to say his name carelessly.

"Snorri has never been to their village," said Freydis comfortably. "Only on hunting parties. He hasn't seen any sign of them either." She shrugged. She had become more relaxed since her pregnancy. "They'll come back in their own time, I'm sure. Not that it matters. We have more than enough trade goods to fill our ships next spring. And then…" Freydis looked out, past the harbour, at the sparkling sea.

"Then what?" asked Hekja. But she guessed.

Freydis laughed. "And then our ships will bring back more silver than we have ever seen – and more ships, and more men too. This is just a start, Hekja. My father founded one colony. By the time my child is grown I will have villages all down this land. And maybe there are still more lands to be found."

To Hekja's surprise Freydis put an arm about her shoulders, and gave her a brief hug. "You will tell your grandchildren you sailed with me, Hekja," she promised. "And by then you will be one of the first families of Vinland."

Each morning now Hekja's breath turned white as she went to milk the cows, and each night a giant log was dragged into the fire pit, to smoulder all night and warm the house. But Leif had been right. Even through winter here the grass stayed green, and the cattle and sheep stayed fat in their fields. There would be milk all through winter, it seemed, in this rich land.

Then one morning the Skraelings attacked.

Chapter 38

THE ATTACK!

Snarf heard them first. Hekja rolled over on her furs when she heard him bark, then shut her eyes again. It was a, "Hey, look who's here!" bark, not a, "Watch out! Danger! Enemies!" bark. Perhaps, she thought, some of the men in the other long house were setting out on an early hunt.

Suddenly Snarf barked again, more urgently now. He ran up to the big wooden doors as though telling her to open them.

"Do you want to go out? Wait a moment then." Hekja shrugged off her sleeping furs. She yawned as she crossed the silent hall, and pulled at the wooden doors.

Suddenly she froze. The grey river was black with Skraeling canoes, silent and purposeful, their men with arrows ready at their bows. "Skraelings!" she screamed.

"What is it, girl?" One of the men ambled past her out into the dawn. "Another trading party? A bit early, isn't it?" He blinked into the dim light, then realised what she had seen. "Thor's boots!" he yelled, scrambling back into the long house. "Attack! Attack! Everyone to arms! Attack!"

Freydis stumbled from her bedchamber. Already men

were scrambling for their swords and shields and axes. "What is it?" she shouted.

"Skraeling raid!" someone yelled to her.

Hekja grabbed Snarf by the scruff of the neck, and shrank back against the wall, to keep out of the way. Thorvard was yelling orders now. Freydis was the colony's commander, but she had never fought a battle or led a raid or even seen one, apart from the accidental landing at Hekja's village.

Thorvard had. Hekja bit her lip. Thorvard was a good man, but not a man that others followed. Could he lead them now?

Freydis gazed around, then picked up her skirts and ran out the door – ungainly as her belly was now so large. She was going to the other long house, Hekja realised, to warn them too. An arrow landed on the door behind her. Hekja darted after her, but was caught in the rush of people pushing through the doors. She struggled through them, into the courtyard, and looked around for Freydis. Men were pouring from the other long house now.

Suddenly Hikki grabbed Hekja's arm.

"Come on! Run!" he yelled. "None of them can catch us!" Hekja shook her head.

"There are too many of them!" Hikki shouted. "Don't be a fool! Run!"

"Freydis…" began Hekja.

"You owe her nothing!"

"No!" cried Hekja.

Hikki hesitated, then sprinted across the fields without her towards the trees.

An arrow fell at Hekja's feet. Someone screamed – one of the women, with an arrow in her stomach. She doubled over then fell to the ground. An arrow whizzed past Hekja's face, close enough to feel its wind. She heard the wet smack as it buried itself in a man's shoulder.

Another woman made to go back into the long house. One of the men grabbed her. "No!" he yelled. "You'll be trapped in there! Into the trees! You can hide up there!"

The woman began to run after Hikki. The other women followed her, lifting their skirts high so they could scramble through the bracken. Suddenly Hikki screamed. It was a long scream and it went on and on. Hekja turned and saw him just as he staggered forward a few steps, trying to get to the safety of the trees. Then he collapsed, the feathered arrow in his back.

Hekja hesitated, then pushed forward to try to get to Freydis, just as another rain of arrows showered all around. The Skraelings were out of their canoes now, but for the moment they came no closer. Why run towards the Viking swords when their arrows could kill them at a distance?

A Norseman crumpled to the ground, and then another.

"Hekja!" It was Snorri. He grabbed her, putting his body between her and the Skraeling bowmen, just as an arrow thudded into him, below his heart.

Hekja screamed as he slumped next to her. She bent to try to help him, but one of the men pulled her away. "Run," he yelled. "There are too many for us! We all have to run to the trees!"

"No!" Freydis stumbled from the other long house, her pregnant belly big before her. "Why do you flee, brave men like you?" she yelled. "You should be able to slaughter them like cattle!"

No one seemed to hear her. Hekja crouched on the ground, as though to shield the dying Snorri from more arrows. His eyes were open and he saw her, though there was blood trickling from his mouth.

"Run," he whispered. "Run."

"Harrrrrrrrrrr!" It was a wilder shriek than Hekja had ever heard. She looked up. The fleeing Norsemen stopped and stared.

Freydis shrieked again. She ripped her dress open, so the bodice hung down and showed her pregnant belly. She bent down and picked up a sword from a man crumpled at her feet, then stood and slapped it three times against her naked breast.

"If men will not fight then women must!" she called. "Hekja!"

Hekja blinked. Part of her lay there with Snorri. Snorri, who had sung of heroes… Suddenly she seemed to find herself. She grabbed Snorri's sword from his limp hand.

It was a big sword, too heavy for a woman. But Hekja held it above her head and could not feel its weight, and shrieked as Freydis did.

And then they charged.

A pregnant woman and a girl charged a horde of Skraelings, Freydis shrieking like a storm up on the mountain, and Hekja too.

Snarf ran as well. Where Hekja went, he went, even to the jaws of death.

The Skraelings stopped. Perhaps, thought Hekja, they think we are enchanted and arrows can't pierce us. They are thinking there's no other way a pregnant woman and a girl could run at a band of warriors and show no fear. Surely it must be magic!

But mostly she just ran. Was this what Snorri meant, she thought exultantly. *Is this what heroes feel, the final exhilaration of battle before we die?*

Suddenly there was a noise behind her. The Norsemen were running too. But now they ran towards the enemy, not away. The Skraelings picked up new arrows and began to fire. But now the arrows fell on shields, not flesh.

The men were overtaking Freydis and Hekja now. Thorvard flung himself in front of them, so his shield protected Freydis too. His was the first sword that crashed into the enemy, but there were others with him. Axes chopped through flesh. The flow of arrows stopped. Arrows don't work when the enemy is on you. Wooden clubs are no match for swords and axes.

Hekja faltered, lost in the tumult of men and blood and weapons, too short to see what was happening. She was only conscious of Freydis panting at her side, still sheltered by Thorvard's shield, of blood and noise and pain.

Suddenly the Skraelings were running, back to the canoes, dragging their dead and wounded with them. There were just enough alive to speed the canoes back up the river, as silently as they had come.

Chapter 39

AFTER THE RAID

Freydis let the sword fall from her hand as though she had forgotten it, as Thorvard ran with the other men after the fleeing Skraelings. Hekja stared at them, unable to believe that she was still alive. Then she ran back to where Snorri lay upon the ground.

He was still breathing. He must have pulled the arrow out himself when Hekja ran on with Freydis. Now he lay unconscious, his blood in a dark pool on the soil. Hekja pulled her apron off then knelt by his side and began to press the apron against him to try to staunch the flow.

Freydis had lost the fire that drove her towards the Skraelings. She almost staggered now, back towards the houses. Suddenly she leaned against the long-house wall. Her face was white, and even in those minutes dark shadows had grown beneath her eyes. One of the women ran to her, as though to help her walk, but Freydis shook her head and forced herself back up, fastening her dress again with hands that shook.

"Bring the wounded inside," she ordered, resting her hands for a moment on her belly. Her voice was hoarse but steady.

"What if they return?" called someone.

"They won't for now. I want the rest of you to bring the logs we cut for timber. I want a fence around the houses by nightfall, as high as three men and pointed at the top, so no Skraeling can climb over it. Drive each log deep into the ground and leave a gate that can be barred." She caught her breath, as though in pain, then added, "A lookout. Build a lookout too. We will not be taken by surprise again." She walked awkwardly over to Hekja and peered down. "What are you doing, girl? Smelling him?"

Hekja looked up and nodded. "A wise woman told me that is how you can tell how deep a wound is. If it smells bad the gut is pierced. If not," she bit her lip, "then he may live."

"Well?" asked Freydis more gently.

"Maybe he will live," whispered Hekja. "Perhaps the arrow was almost spent and didn't go too deep."

"I hope so," said Freydis coolly. "His family is important in Norway. They will be useful when we need to trade." She beckoned to two of the men to help Hekja carry Snorri indoors and did not object when Hekja commandeered almost every sheepskin in the house to make him comfortable by the fire.

People looked at Hekja differently now. Before they had listened when she passed on Freydis' commands. But now they obeyed Hekja's wishes too. Hekja was still a thrall, but none of the people there that day would ever think of her as such again. Hekja had run side by side with Freydis as they led the fight against the Skraelings. Now they did her bidding and, almost without realising it, Hekja expected them to do so.

Hekja cut Snorri's shirt away as gently as she could. She bound the wound again properly with clean linen, as Tikka had once shown her how to do, so long ago. The best that she could do was stop the bleeding, Hekja thought. There were no healing herbs here, like the ones the witch used back on her mountain. Perhaps the Skraelings knew of some, but she did not.

Hekja still sat with Snorri while outside men yelled and carried poles for the new stockade, and Freydis walked white-faced from group to group, checking that all was done according to her orders. Snarf followed Freydis for a while, but as the day grew hotter he trotted back inside again, and lay by Hekja. Her eyes were on Snorri, his face almost as white as the sheepskins.

At midday one of the women, Helga, knelt beside her, and handed her a horn of buttermilk. Hekja shook her head. "He can't drink it," she whispered.

"For you, not him," said the woman gently. "It has an egg in it. You need to keep your strength."

Hekja sipped without tasting, then realised the woman still sat beside her. "Hikki?" she asked.

The woman shook her head. "I'm sorry, Hekja. He is dead."

"I see." Hekja thought she should feel something, some kind of sadness. But it was as though every emotion had been used up.

"How many more are dead?"

"Two. Thorhild Gunnarsdaughter and Njal Valgardsson. Three wounded – Ketil, son of Thorgeir and Thorkel Gilsson. And Snorri Skald."

Hekja thought of Hikki, his face glowing as he talked about his farm. "Bury Hikki up on the hill above the gully," she whispered. "It will be his land. Let no man take it for their farm."

The woman stood up. "Yes, Hekja. I will tell them."

Hekja finished the milk, then with some soft leather sponged away the blood that seeped from under Snorri's bandage and stared at him, as though storing up the sight to last her all her life. Then Snorri opened his eyes. For a moment he did not seem to see her. And then his gaze steadied and he gave an almost smile.

"Valkyrie," he whispered.

Hekja frowned and bent closer to hear what he had said. "What is that?"

"The maidens who take dead warriors to paradise," whispered Snorri.

"I would rather live with a warrior here than carry off a dead one," said Hekja firmly, but her eyes were gentler than her words.

Snorri tried to smile then grimaced instead. "Maybe you are a berserker then," he whispered. "How is it that you sit with me now, when you scorned me before?"

"Because I saw you dead," said Hekja softly, "and knew my life was empty. Wherever home is, it is with you."

Snorri nodded drowsily. Hekja wondered how much he had understood. But there was happiness in his smile now as well as pain. And when he slept this time somehow his hand was holding Hekja's.

Hekja beckoned Helga with her other hand. She came at once, even though she was free born.

"What's a berserker?" asked Hekja softly.

Helga smiled. She guessed what Snorri had whispered. "They are the greatest warriors of all. They dress in animal skins and fight with such ferocity that no one can touch them, for they are protected by Odin."[42]

Hekja shook her head. "Freydis and I were not dressed in animal skins," she said quietly.

Then Freydis screamed.

Chapter 40

A CHILD IS BORN

It was not a scream like the one that she had given before. This was a cry of pain.

Helga left Hekja and ran outside. The other women followed her. Hekja glanced at Snorri, to check he was still sleeping, then ran as well, with Snarf at her heels.

Freydis stood by the first tall posts of the new stockade, clutching her belly. At her feet was a pool of water and blood.

Snarf whined, frightened by the new smell. But to Hekja's relief the older women didn't seem worried. Two of the women and Hekja helped Freydis indoors and up on to her bed platform, while another fetched fresh cloths and yet another warned the men to stay outside.

For all that day Freydis strained and gasped. But apart from that first scream, she made no other noise at all. Hekja divided her time between checking on Snorri and patrolling the stockade, to make sure Freydis' orders were carried out, then reporting back to Freydis.

Even as the sweat ran down her face Freydis gasped out instructions: "The... gate... must... be... as... high... as the... fence. A shield about the... lookout." Freydis strained again and clenched her hands. "To keep him safe from arrows. I want a… lookout… Now!"

Each time Hekja checked on Snorri she found Snarf with him, his head on Snorri's furs. Snarf looked up as though to say, "Don't worry. I'm guarding him for you. Nothing – not even death – will get past a dog like me."

The shadows were thickening as Freydis' child was born. Freydis did scream then, but as much in triumph as in pain. Hekja fetched Thorvard – he had been trying to work on the stockade and listen for the sounds indoors too. He knelt beside Freydis and looked at the red face of his son.

"His name is Erik," said Thorvard. "Erik Thorvardsson." He glanced at Freydis, hoping the name would please her. But his wife didn't seem to notice her son had her father's name.

"I am glad he is a boy," said Freydis wearily. "It is so much easier to be a boy." And then she shut her eyes and slept.

Freydis was up and in command again the next afternoon. It was not what women did, but Freydis was not like other women, and there was no one in the camp to dispute that now.

She fed her son that morning but let another of the women who had a month-old child of her own nurse him as well. Snorri was also sitting up, though Hekja would not let him move much. Snorri let her order him about. He seemed half in pain and half amused.

That first day Freydis checked the stockade and ordered the men to build another, even wider than the first, which would include some fields as well, where the cattle could be brought for safety. She spoke to each man, praising their bravery, and never mentioning that they were about to flee till strengthened by her courage.

It was time to bury the dead now. Freydis had ordered each of them a hero's funeral, with their graves marked out like ships with stones, as there were no spare ships to bury them with.

Hikki was buried on his hill as Hekja had ordered. He had no possessions to be buried with, Hekja realised. He had died before he'd found the wealth and freedom that he dreamed of. She sat by Hikki's grave after the others had left and tried to grieve for him, and for what might have been. He deserved that, at least, and so much more. But her mind was too full of worry for Snorri and Freydis. Instead of thinking of Hikki she found she was looking at the harbour to see if the Skraelings were coming back. So she went back down the hill to see if Freydis needed help.

Freydis was still everywhere, checking this and ordering that. Hekja persuaded her to lie down again, and let the women change her bloody pads and bring her baby to her, while Hekja took her orders to the men. Finally Freydis beckoned Hekja to sit beside her while her baby fed.

Freydis was silent for a while, stroking her baby's fine red hair. And then she said, "Why? Why should they attack us now?"

"Perhaps they were waiting until after harvest," suggested Hekja, "so they could take what's in our storerooms."

Freydis shook her head. "Then why trade peaceably for so many months? To go from friend to enemy in just a few weeks? No, something must have happened to turn them against us."

The baby was almost asleep now, though he still sucked at Freydis' nipple. Freydis gazed at him for a moment, then said, "Finnbogi."

Hekja shivered at Finnbogi's name. "What do you mean?" she asked.

But Freydis shook her head. "Tomorrow," she whispered, her face suddenly whiter than it had been before. "Tonight I am too tired."

Next morning Freydis ordered the women to bring her best dress, her chains of gold and brooches and bangles too. Hekja was to wear her other dress, the one that was not stained with blood.

Freydis looked her up and down, as though to make sure Hekja was dressed correctly, then smiled. Her face was still white, but the shadows beneath her eyes were not as dark as before.

"We must get you more dresses," she said. Freydis pulled the curtain aside then walked out into the main hall, with Hekja behind her. The room was full of men, swallowing their breakfasts, and women bringing them horns of ale or slabs of bread.

"Listen!" cried Freydis.

The hall fell silent.

"Now I have a son!" called Freydis, and her voice was clearer than a bird call. "His name is Erik the son of Thorvard. I call on you all to witness that I have a daughter too. Her name is Hekja."

Hekja gasped and stepped back, but Freydis grabbed

her hand and held it high. Then she released it, and instead lifted the heaviest of the gold necklaces over her head and draped it over Hekja's shoulders. "Today you are my daughter," she promised, and kissed her. "Hekja Thorvardsdöttir."[43]

Thorvard looked a bit surprised, then smiled and nodded. "Granddaughter of Erik," added Freydis, looking pointedly down at Snorri lying on his furs. "A heroine from a line of heroes."

Someone thumped their sword on the ground. Suddenly the room was cheering. Snorri was cheering too, despite his wound.

Years later Hekja would remember it as perhaps the most terrifying, happy, proud and confusing moment of her life.

As for Snarf, there was a haunch of venison by the fire and no one was paying any notice. He'd finished the lot before anybody thought to look.

Chapter 41

FINNBOGI

In all this time no one knew what had happened to Finnbogi's camp. Had they been attacked as well? Perhaps destroyed?

Finnbogi's men had stayed well clear of Freydis' camp all summer. Now Freydis decided that she and Hekja would go and see how Finnbogi's camp was faring.

"No!" Thorvard banged his drinking horn against their bedroom wall, so its end shattered and the skyr ran everywhere. "You're still too weak," he said. "I will go, with half the men. The others will stay here and protect you."

Freydis' face was white but her mouth still looked determined. "Bodily strength has nothing to do with it," she stated. "If I take men with me I admit that I need them. No, my daughter and I must go by ourselves. Our weakness is our strength."

"Woof," said Snarf, from the floor.

Freydis smiled. "And Ice Nose will accompany us," she added.

"His name is Riki Snarfari," said Hekja softly.

Freydis looked at her consideringly, then nodded.

"Riki Snarfari will escort us," she corrected. "Who could have a better guard?"

"I will not permit…" began Thorvard, then shook his head helplessly. He watched Freydis dress herself in her best jewellery, with Hekja helping, then stride out into the hall.

Hekja lingered. It would need courage of a different sort, she thought, for a husband to accept that the men would follow his wife, not him. "I'll make sure she rests," she told Thorvard gently.

Thorvard patted her hand with his big clumsy one. "Thank you, daughter," he said.

Freydis' brisk manner lasted till she and Hekja were just around the bend of the river. Then Freydis stopped. "I need to sit," she said quietly and sank onto the ground.

Hekja knelt by her in alarm. "Shall I fetch help?"

Freydis shook her head. "Back there I had to be strong. I will need to be strong for Finnbogi too. But just for a moment though, let me rest."

They waited till a bit of colour flowed back into her cheeks, then walked on, more slowly than before, resting often. Finally they came within sight of Finnbogi's camp.

"Well," said Freydis, staring.

Hekja nodded. Finnbogi's camp was smaller than theirs, with no fields of animals or grain. Instead there was a high stone wall, topped with a palisade of sharpened stakes, and a lookout high above it all.

"So," said Freydis softly. "Finnbogi has known for a while that the Skraelings were a danger."

Suddenly Freydis drew a breath. She pointed.

Two women knelt by the lake. For a moment, Hekja thought they were the thralls Finnbogi had brought from his farm. Then she saw that they were Skraelings.

Hekja gasped. "Do you think the Skraelings have taken the camp?'

"No," said Freydis softly. "Those women are captives. Thralls. Look at their faces."

Hekja bit her lip. "Yes," she whispered. "Free women never look like that."

The women hardly glanced at Hekja and Freydis. One had scars across her face, not from a sword, but as though she had been beaten many times, with no care how the blows fell.

"State your business!" someone yelled. It was the man up on the lookout.

Freydis called out, "I am here to see Finnbogi!"

Hekja could hear the sound of sliding wood as the gate was unbarred. Then it swung open and they entered.

This camp was different from the one down on the river. The long house was small, and grass was worn to dirt by many feet. Flies buzzed about a great heap of deer guts that had been dumped by the store shed.

"Look," whispered Hekja. Over by the far wall was a cross between a cage and a storehouse. There were women in it, and girls, and boys too young to have a beard. All of them were Skraelings. They were there to be taken back to Iceland, Hekja realised, and sold as slaves.

Suddenly Finnbogi was before them, tall and confident as ever. He looked Freydis up and down, then inspected Hekja, lingering on the gold chain that shone about her neck. Then he looked at Snarf, as though wondering if he was near enough to kick. And then he grinned at them like they were some kind of a joke but didn't know it. "Well?" he demanded.

"Not well, Finnbogi Throstsson," said Freydis calmly. "The Skraelings attacked us two days ago."

Finnbogi nodded, as though this was no surprise. His grin grew wider. "And you have come to beg for shelter?"

"No," said Freydis shortly. She added, "We saw two Skraeling women as we came in. I see you have more over there."

"Perhaps you did," said Finnbogi carelessly. "My men need women."

"Then you should have brought some more," said Freydis.

Finnbogi laughed at that. "Why waste good ship space on women? We needed women so we found some."

"And have made enemies of the Skraelings for us all," said Freydis.

Finnbogi laughed at that. "There speaks a woman!" he cried. "This is our land, and if we have to kill a thousand Skraelings to make it ours and have their women serve us we will!"

Freydis was silent a moment then she said, "The land is rich enough to keep us all. Can I persuade you to reconsider, and let the Skraelings live in peace?"

"Peace!" boomed Finnbogi, as though it was the most absurd thing he'd heard, but his eyes were hard. "Peace? Skraeling men and women will bring as good a price as the timber or even better, and take up less room in the boats too. Why sweat at cutting timber when you can harvest thralls?"

A woman stepped out of the long house then. She stared as Freydis stepped up to her. "Helga Mordsdöttir, will you speak to your husband? We need to…"

The woman sneered. "Do not speak to me, Freydis Ericsdöttir. I respect my husband, unlike some I know. Listen to your own man before you bother mine. We have a chance at riches here. Go away and do not bother us."

A girl child peered around her skirts. Finnbogi's baby daughter. The mother picked her up, still glaring at Freydis with contempt.

"But the Skraelings…" began Hekja.

"Who are you, thrall, to speak to a free woman?" cried Finnbogi's wife. Another Skraeling woman peered out the door, then ducked away from yet another blow.

"If your own man cannot capture thralls for you to earn you silver, do not come whining here!" added Finnbogi's wife. She turned and disappeared indoors.

Freydis watched her go, her face impassive. Then she said, "Come," to Hekja, and began to walk slowly from the compound.

Chapter 42

A DECISION

Nothing was said until they were around the edge of the lake again. Only then did Freydis sag upon a rock. There was sweat on her forehead.

"Rest," said Hekja gently. "There is nothing more we can do now."

Freydis stared at the ripples on the lake, then out at the bare winter forest. "Red leaves," she said. "There were red leaves upon the trees, as though they knew that this winter there would be blood."

"But the trees will be green again in summer," said Hekja earnestly. "Maybe no more blood will be shed?"

Freydis shook her head. "The Skraelings are warriors," she said wearily, "as we are warriors. If men came and took our women we'd fight till every one of them were slain. This is what the Skraelings will do to us. And Finnbogi will take more and more of them to serve him and to sell as thralls."

"But that is Finnbogi," cried Hekja. "Not us!"

"It makes no difference to the Skraelings. We are guilty because they are our kin and we do nothing. So," said Freydis standing up, though Hekja could see how much the effort cost her, "we must do something."

"What?" cried Hekja. But Freydis just shook her head.

Suddenly Thorvard appeared, with four men, carrying Freydis' chair. Freydis walked towards him, but Thorvard scooped her up and placed her in her chair. The men carried her back to the house, with Hekja walking on one side and Thorvard the other.

Freydis slept after that, while the wet nurse fed the baby, then after she woke she stayed on the bed and fed the baby herself again, then called for Thorvard, and had the curtain pulled.

It was night when Thorvard came out. The fire flared in the pit, as the meat dripped from its chain above. Bread was baking on the hearthstone, and porridge cooking in the iron pots.

Thorvard looked troubled. But he shook his head when someone spoke to him, and wouldn't answer, just took his meat and horn of ale and sat staring at the fire.

The women had made a small milk pudding, with eggs and dried strawberries soaked till soft. Hekja put some on a plate, with a slab of wheaten bread and a mug of skyr, and carried them in to Freydis. The other women never went behind the curtain unless ordered, but Hekja now went where she wanted.

Freydis had a blank, worn look, as though every bone and sinew was too tired to carry on and only her will still kept her moving. The baby lay asleep in a carved cradle by the bed. Hekja had seen Thorvard carving the cradle this winter, polishing it with a smooth stone.

"Well?" demanded Hekja. "What have you decided?"

Freydis took the plate. "Thank you," she said. She stared at it a moment, as though eating was a duty that had to be borne, then slowly took up her spoon and swallowed. Then she said, "I have decided that we have two choices. We can join with Finnbogi and try to wipe out the Skraelings. Or we can try to convince the Skraelings that we are not their enemies."

"But how can we do that?" cried Hekja.

"Tomorrow," said Freydis quietly. "You will know it all tomorrow. Now go." She smiled a little. "Snorri will wonder where you are."

"Snorri knows exactly where I am," said Hekja dryly. She pulled the curtain behind her as she left.

Chapter 43

THE BATTLE

The house stirred early the next morning. Everyone knew something would be happening today, but no one knew quite what.

Hekja slept next to Snorri now, though not as man and wife. Snorri was too weak for that and anyway, the wedding was still to come. Hekja wasn't sure when she had agreed to marry Snorri, if she ever had, but somehow the whole camp assumed the marriage would take place, Snorri included.

Not that it mattered. Sometimes Hekja felt her life and Snorri's were like two great ropes that finally twined together, stronger than they had been apart. And besides, if Snorri was going to get himself shot by Skraelings again – or in any other of the dangers Vikings seemed to plunge into – she was going to be there. So Freydis had given orders for a wedding feast to be prepared, and Thorvard had explained the marriage contract to Hekja, and how her new parents would give her a share in the expedition's profits, so she would come to her marriage a rich and respected woman.

And Hekja slept wrapped in her cloak and Snorri slept wrapped in his, but Hekja was there if he needed anything.

Finally the curtains parted and Freydis emerged. She wore a man's round metal helmet today and carried a man's shield and battle-axe. She waited till all were quiet then said, "Call the others here."

Someone ran to summon the other household.

Freydis looked at the faces before her without speaking. And then she said, "I ask only one thing this morning. Will you follow me?"

"Yes!" cried someone, and another man called, "To the gates of Ragnarok[44] – and further!"

Freydis didn't smile at that. She just said, "Not quite so far, perhaps. Each man must arm himself. For those who should have been our companions have betrayed us. They have turned the Skraelings into our enemies. They threaten our very lives in Vinland. And so..." Freydis gazed out at her followers. "And so we must destroy them, like the ship rats that they are."

Someone cheered then and the others caught it up. Since the Skraeling attack it seemed that every man in camp had behaved as though Freydis could get them to Greenland and back without a ship, or call the clouds to milk the cows.

But the cheers chilled her, nonetheless. Somehow it seemed wrong to cheer killing, even if, as Freydis said, they had no choice. These men cheered like their blood was up. For the first time in months, Hekja felt the horror she had felt at the destruction of her village.

The men began to straggle out, swords, axes and shields in their hands. Snorri tried to struggle to his feet but Hekja pressed his shoulder. "Don't you dare," she said.

"But…" began Snorri.

Hekja shook her head. "You will collapse before we leave the fields. And then I would have to stay with you, when Freydis needs me." She forced a smile at him. "I have my duty, and this is yours – to get well. I will tell you everything that happens later, I promise. We can make our songs together."

"Even with a Norseman?" teased Snorri.

"Even with a Norseman," said Hekja and pressed his hand. "Snarf," she whispered, "stay. You're on guard." Snarf whined, and licked her hand. He knew something was happening. But he obeyed.

Then Snorri said, "I want you to have my shield. I'd give you my sword too, but it could be taken from you, and used against you. But take the shield. I wish it could be my arms that shielded you instead."

Hekja hesitated. Then she nodded. She lifted the shield that lay beside him and followed Freydis from the hall.

It would only be half a day till she was back again. But forever after the battle it seemed to Hekja that in that one day, she had lived almost half her life.

Chapter 44

THE DEATH OF HONOUR

It was late when they returned, the shadows almost merging with the night, the owls hooting untroubled by human squabbles in this land. The women ran from the stockade to meet them, calling out. But they fell silent when they saw their faces. Freydis was in the lead, carried by two men in her chair. Her arms were bloody. The men were subdued, not cheering and victorious. And none of them would meet Freydis' eyes.

Hekja walked next to Freydis' chair. She carried a girl child on her hip, her head buried in Hekja's hair, as though she was afraid to look beyond. There was blood upon Hekja's skirt and on her arms, and on the child as well. Thorvard walked behind them. There was a great cut on one arm, and it was roughly bound up in a sling. But he made no sign that he felt the wound.

The women went from man to man, checking that all were there. A few were wounded, but it seemed that Freydis had brought all her army back.

One by one the men slipped away, to wash or think or talk among themselves. Hekja followed Freydis into the house. She handed the girl to one of the women, with instructions to bathe the child and feed her, then nodded to Snorri as he lifted his head anxiously. "What happened?" he cried. "Are you alright?"

Hekja met his eyes. "I'm not hurt. I have to help Freydis, then wash. I'll tell you about it then." Snarf ran to her, sniffing, as though looking for any wounds. But Hekja ordered him back to Snorri. Snarf returned, tail down.

Hekja went with Freydis to her curtained room and helped her take off her blood-stained dress and armour, and beckoned to a woman to bring cloths and water. Then Hekja too walked down to the river bank and knelt and washed and washed and washed.

She would never feel really clean, she thought. But finally she knew that there was no point scrubbing any more. Nor could she stay away from the long house any longer.

She walked back slowly, feeling the night wind cold on her wet skin. The women were serving food and hot ale to the men. Hekja shook her head when someone offered her a plate. She checked on the child, but she was sleeping. Then Hekja sat by Snorri and took his hand, and only then did she begin to shake and tears ran down her cheeks, till he struggled up beside her and took her in his arms.

Snarf whined and licked her face, on the side that wasn't pressed to Snorri. Finally she stopped crying. She put an arm around Snarf, while Snorri called a woman to bring her ale and fish, and made her drink and eat.

Finally, when the cup was empty, he said, "Tell me what happened?"

"So you can make a song?" whispered Hekja.

"So I can understand," said Snorri softly.

Hekja shook her head. "I don't understand. At times I think I do, but then I think…"

"Tell me," said Snorri again.

Hekja tightened her arms around Snarf. And then she said without expression, "We marched to Finnbogi's camp. Most of our men hid in the trees. Then Freydis called out to Finnbogi that we were leaving Vinland, and wanted to hire his ship to take our goods back, in return for half our furs. Finnbogi believed her. He came out, with some of his men, and came down to our ship to sail up here to inspect our storerooms."

"And then?"

"And then we killed them," said Hekja.

Snorri stared. "Without a legal challenge?"[45]

"Yes," said Hekja simply. "We just killed them. They suspected nothing, so they were easily killed. Then we went back, and killed the others. They didn't have their swords or shields, and there were many more of us."

"I see," said Snorri softly.

"Do you?" whispered Hekja. "There was so much blood. The whole place stank of blood and so did we. Sometimes I think I will smell it for the rest of my life."

"I should have been there," said Snorri. "For good or evil I wish I had been there to bear this thing with you."

"No. It is enough that one of us…" Hekja said no more. And then she said, "Then there was Finnbogi's wife too."

Snorri frowned. "What about her?"

"The Skraeling women ran off, into the forest, and so did Finnbogi's thralls. I let the people in the cage out too. I hope they keep running till they are safe. I hope they run and…" Hekja bit her lip, and continued more quietly.

"Finnbogi's wife struck one of them when she tried to run away. She broke the Skraeling's arm, I think, but the Skraeling was still able to run. When all the men were dead Finnbogi's wife waited in the house with her daughter, as though defying us to touch her. And no man would. So Freydis took Thorvard's axe," said Hekja calmly. "She killed her with two blows. And Finnbogi's baby daughter saw it all."

Snorri said nothing, just tightened his arm about Hekja's shoulders.

"Snorri?"

"Yes?"

"I never asked you before. I think I was afraid of what you might say. Have you ever gone a-Viking? Raided lands and killed?"

"I have fought," said Snorri simply. "In battle with enemies of my father. I have killed as well. But no, I have never gone a-Viking. Those I have killed have always been armed. I have never fought a man unlawfully."

"But you sing of heroes…" began Hekja.

"You've heard my songs. Have I ever sung of killing?"

Hekja shook her head. They sat in silence for a while.

"The worst is," said Hekja at last, "I don't know what I should feel. Those men had to die, so we might live in peace – and the Skraelings too. Finnbogi and his wife were evil. But then I remember what I felt this morning. It was as though Finnbogi's camp weren't people at all, just enemies to kill. And I realise that is how my village was destroyed. We were simply enemies, no longer people. I will always see the blood and hear the screams. I will see Freydis' face as it looked today forever in my dreams."

"Time," said Snorri softly, into her hair.

"What about time?" Hekja's face was buried in his shoulder now.

"Time will make it clearer. Easier. When we are far from here."

Hekja took her face from his shoulder. "Are we going far from here?"

"Yes," said Snorri. "When spring comes, when the ice clears up in the north. We will go with the trading ship, to Greenland then to Iceland then to my home."

"But your family – what will they think when you bring home a thrall?"

"I will be bringing home a wife to be proud of, Erik the Red's granddaughter, a heroine, a Valkyrie."

"Who was once a thrall," insisted Hekja.

"Who was once a thrall, as my grandmother was."

"Your grandmother?"

"An Irish thrall. Daughter of a chieftain, but still a thrall. Besides," said Snorri lightly, "You will be rich."

"Will I?"

"I imagine we all will be," said Snorri gently. "From the proceeds of this voyage."

They were silent for a moment. Then Snorri said, "I would like you to see my home. But we do not have to stay there. It is your choice. But I would like us to sing together. To the king, perhaps, and to other kings. To sing of heroes we have known, and what we've seen."

"Even of this day?" whispered Hekja.

"Perhaps," said Snorri quietly. "Perhaps one day, when we have found the words and thought how best to say them."

They sat quietly after that, perhaps hoping that the other one had dozed, while about them the men and women went quietly to their attic or sleeping closets. Finally Snorri moved his arm, as it was going to sleep. Hekja whispered, "Perhaps it will be worth it. Perhaps we will have peace, and the Skraelings will be our friends."

"Perhaps," said Snorri.

Chapter 45

LEAVING VINLAND

It was a mild winter, as Leif had said it would be. There was no snow, and the grass continued to grow almost through the season. The cows stayed in their fields and the sheep were fat. Hekja and Snorri were married, and Hekja and Snorri sang together at their wedding feast, a song of love and happiness, and Snarf joined in the chorus with his howl.

But in late winter the Skraelings came again, this time with flaming arrows, to burn the palisade. They did not break through this time – there was water enough to put out the flames. But everyone knew there would be a next time… and a next…

Snorri offered to lead a party to the Skraeling village, to try to negotiate a peace. But when they reached the place the houses had been burned, and the fields were bare. Finnbogi's men had been there long before, leaving a bitter legacy.

There would be no more trading with the Skraelings. And now the seas were open. It was time for Snorri to go home, with the trading goods that would bring the colony wealth and with his new wife.

Hekja stood with Freydis for the last time, while the final bales of furs were loaded onto the ships. They were taking Finnbogi's store boats, as well as Freydis', for as Freydis said, no one else would use them now.

Freydis had made every person swear they would never tell what had happened, that everyone would say that Finnbogi's party had decided to stay behind, and that Finnbogi had sold his ships to Freydis. But no man quite trusted that someone wouldn't let the true story slip.

Freydis was still the leader. The men obeyed her, but they didn't love her as before. The slaughter of Finnbogi's men and women had gained them nothing, except riches. Perhaps for some of them, that was enough. Others would remember a fight that had no honour, how they killed their countrymen without a legal challenge, and a free Norse woman slain as well.

Hekja could not forget either. Vinland had given her more than she had ever dreamt. But there were memories of blood and hatred now as well, and Freydis' face as she wielded the axe against Finnbogi's widow. Perhaps, as Snorri said, it was best that the songs of heroes always happened a long way away.

Over by the long house the wet nurse was feeding baby Erik, while Finnbogi's daughter looked on. Freydis had adopted the child, though the demands of defending the colony had left her little time for motherhood.

Hekja glanced at Freydis, to find her smiling at her. "You have come a long way from the little thrall from the island village," she said, "and now you are going even further."

"It's Snarf's fault," said Hekja lightly. "Did I ever tell you how the witch gave him his name, and said he'd be a Mighty Rover? I accompanied him, that's all."

"Arf," agreed Riki Snarfari, sitting to scratch a flea.

"Maybe," said Hekja tentatively, "you will come to Norway one day. To trade next year's furs, perhaps."

Freydis shook her head. "No, my dear. Wherever I go from here, it won't be back to Norway. This is goodbye." She hesitated. "Even if we never meet again, you will always be my daughter. I will never forget that when the men ran from the Skraelings you stood with me. You are a daughter to be proud of."

Freydis paused, then added, "There is a song, not one of Snorri's. It says the life of a man is only what people remember. Perhaps that is true of a woman too. If you ever sing of me…"

"It will be a good song," promised Hekja. And she thought, but didn't say: *but it may take years to find the words*. If heroes weren't careless of life – their own or other people's – would they ever be heroes? Who could understand, who wasn't there?

She embraced Freydis then. For a moment Freydis clung to her, as though she might ask her not to go. Then she stepped back and gave a laugh, almost like before.

"Good journey!" she called. "And if you see a cloud like a new land on the horizon, think of me, and all your family here!" Then she was gone, striding back to the long house, without waiting to see the ship sail.

"Hekja!" It was Snorri, striding down the path from the long house, a final bundle under his arm. He held out his hand and Hekja took it, and they climbed into the boat together while the men uncoiled the ropes from the deck.

The wind filled the big woollen sail and sent it flapping. The ship creaked, the oars splashed deep into the water, all the familiar sounds that Hekja had thought she would never hear again.

She stood with Snorri at the ship's rail and watched the land recede, the golden beaches where she and Snarf had run with Hikki, with their white-tipped waves, the long house where she had found love and family, the tall trees on the hill where Hikki lay. And slowly Vinland turned to clouds, then vanished from the horizon.

Chapter 46

A SONG FOR FREYDIS

For a long time Hekja heard little from Freydis. The distances were so great it could take years for a message to find its way from Vinland to Greenland, then to Iceland and to Norway.

They were good years for Hekja. Her home was in Norway at Snorri's family estates, but most summers she and Snorri travelled. She had even been back to her old village. The girls had survived, and Tikka, and even Bran, though the wound had left him simple. He was married to Branna and they seemed happy, in their hut by the sea.

The village was richer now, for Hekja brought them sheep and hens, glass beads from Venice for her friends, and two of Snarf's puppies, so there would still be dogs hunting across the mountains where he was born.

Snorri and Hekja sang for kings these days. It was at the king's court in Norway that she met the trader. He was an old man, with a shrivelled arm, crushed by an iceberg in a storm at sea. He listened while she sang one of her Vinland songs. Sometimes Hekja felt strange singing about running with Hikki and Snarf along the endless beach, here in her silk dress, with rubies at her wrists and neck. But she had never sung of Freydis. Even now her feelings were too complex to put into words.

After the song, and the congratulations, the trader asked Snorri if he might meet her.

"Vinland!" he said to Hekja. "I was down there, just last year."

Hekja started. "How are they all? Freydis? And the colony?" she asked eagerly.

The old man barked a laugh. "Colony? There's no colony there now. Ruins, that's all we found."

"No!" cried Hekja.

Snorri took her hand. "It doesn't mean that they're dead," he said quietly. "They may have gone back to Greenland. Or even to another place in Vinland, safe from Skraeling attacks. I'll contact my uncle, get him to send a ship to Greenland next summer. I'm sure we'll have news of them then."

"Of course," said Hekja, numbly. She walked over to the palace window, and stared out at the neat fields, trying to remember the smell of Vinland forests, the sound of Freydis' laughter or the look on her face all those years before, when she told a frightened thrall how the albatross soared across the world. Freydis, the generous, the ruthless, the visionary.

Suddenly Hekja knew that what Snorri said was true. And now at last she knew the song that she should sing for Freydis.

Somewhere, far from land, Freydis was still sailing, her eyes fixed on a great bird overhead, waiting for the clouds on the horizon that would be a new land, with jewels hanging from the trees.

AUTHOR NOTES

This story is based on real events, told in the 'Gräenlendinga Saga' and 'Eirik's (Erik) Saga', about two hundred years after they happened. When the sagas contradict each other I've chosen bits from each. In other places I have simplified events.

Perhaps no one in history has ever been described in two such different ways as Freydis Eriksdöttir. In one saga Freydis is a dutiful, courageous wife – I didn't make up the scene where she charges the Skraelings, nine months' pregnant and sword in hand. In the other saga she is a villain, killing five women with an axe. I have assumed that both stories have some grain of truth.

We shall never know what Freydis Ericsdöttir was really like. There is no doubt she was an extraordinary woman. I suspect she has been lost to history mostly because the later male writers didn't know what to make of her.

Thorvard, Leif the Lucky and Erik the Red (or Eirik Raudi) were real people too, and the places they travelled to also exist. Hikki and Hekja are mentioned in the sagas as two Scottish runners who were taken on

Leif's first voyage to Vinland, but nothing else is known about them. I have placed them on Freydis' voyage instead. Finnbogi too was a real person but there is no reason to think he was a villian. I may have done a brave adventurer a real injustice.

No one is sure where Vinland is. Viking long house remains have been found at *L'Anse aux Meadows* on the Newfoundland coast. But the coast there doesn't fit the detailed descriptions of Vinland in the saga, and wild grapes don't grow there. The grapes may have been other berries that could be made into wine – or maybe Leif Erikson was boasting about the lushness of the new land, just as his father had called his icy wastes Greenland.

But it is likely that the long house remains are from another Greenlander voyage, and Vinland is further south where wild grapes do grow and the winters are milder than in Newfoundland. Or maybe the weather was very much warmer for a brief period in the years when the Vikings travelled up and down the coast of what is now Canada and the United States, and the land was very different.

I have tried to keep the Vinland in this book close to the description in the sagas, rather than place it at any known bit of land today. The 'Skraelings' are based on descriptions in the sagas and also from accounts of 15th and 16th century European explorers. However, cultures – and areas occupied by various Native American nations – would have varied enormously between about 1000 AD, when Vinland was 'discovered', and the 15th century, and almost certainly changed even more in the next five hundred years as well.

And if I have only come within whistling distance of the truth, perhaps I have done no worse than the saga singers, all those centuries ago.

Dates No one knows exactly when Leif Eriksson and the others went to Vinland. It may have been anywhere from 987 to 1011 AD. Our only information comes from the 'sagas', which were written as entertainment rather than as an exact history (and were almost certainly rewritten for political and religious purposes too), and like the other information in them their dates can be contradictory. But very roughly:

- 982 AD: Erik and his followers are outlawed for three years in Iceland. Erik had already been outlawed in Norway.
- 986 AD: Erik leads twenty-five ships of immigrants to Greenland. Fourteen ships reach the new land, with 400 colonists. The other boats sink or turn back.
- 1000 AD: Leif 'The Lucky' Eriksson travels to Vinland, stays the winter and returns again a year later.
- About 1002 AD: Freydis Eriksdöttir leads an expedition to Vinland to trade or colonise, or is a member of another expedition with her husband Thorvard and Erik's son, Thorvald. The expedition returns a year or three years later, though in one version Freydis stays behind.

NOTES

[1] The dogs of this time were giant, long-legged dogs, the ancestors of Scottish Wolfhounds or Deerhounds.

[2] Literally Mighty Sailor, or Rover, who travels fast.

[3] Shellfish that live in the sand.

[4] A stone bowl used for grinding grain.

[5] Small stream

[6] A very low-alcohol beer, more like ginger beer than the beers we drink today.

[7] A summer hut

[8] The dried strips of calf stomach needed to turn the skimmed milk solid, so it could be chopped into tiny pieces and hung in cheesecloths from the sheiling rafters, to drain before the women took it back to press for cheese.

[9] These ships were of the kind known as knarr, or knorr, though that term may not have referred to a cargo ship until a century or so later; they were wider and deeper than a longship. Longships, or drekars, were longer and faster with oars all the way along each side, and were used for raiding along the coast of northern Europe; knarrs were used on long voyages across the Atlantic Ocean.

[10] King Harald wasn't yet called the Fair Hair, but this is the name he would be known by.

[11] By 999, when this is set, most Norse people were Christian.

[12] Vikings were great traders, and thralls were one of the most commonly traded items, captured in all the countries where Vikings fought. Thralls could be freed by their owners, in return for special service, or their freedom could be bought by others.

[13] They would have stood to row, not sat as rowers do today.

[14] The glacier at the end of the fiord ground the rocks to dust – it's called glacial flour. This is what made the water look milky, and made it sparkle in sunlight.

[15] Small branches

[16] Small birch trees (There were no big conifers in Greenland for roof beams or boats.)

[17] Hens

[18] Whale bones

[19] A loom, for weaving.

[20] Storerooms

[21] Getting the last of the milk from the cow's udder.

[22] The horses in Viking times were smaller than the horses of today.

[23] A fermented milk drink.

[24] Skalds were renowned poets, historians and singers. The stories they chanted were for entertainment, beauty and to record the past.

[25] Honey wine

[26] The heavy, flat stones that weighed down the cheese to force any moisture out. A "wet" cheese turns sour.

[27] Master of the household

[28] This was where the skins were fletched i.e. cleaned and tanned.

[29] One-legged mythical monsters believed to live in the south.

[30] This was the method the Vikings used to tell how fast their ship was going.

[31] A calf's bladder that was scraped clean, and kept soaked in water so it didn't dry out till it was needed.

[32] This was probably wild rice.

[33] Sunflowers

[34] Maize

[35] Several types of pumpkins and gourds, tobacco, beans and spinach.

[36] These wild grapes had tough skins and were pretty tasteless.

[37] Pearls

[38] Maize

[39] Sunflower kernels

[40] Pumpkin and winter squash.

[41] Oat or wheat flour set like a sweet jelly.

[42] The Greenlanders were mostly Christian now, but old beliefs and myths lingered.

[43] The ending *döttir* means daughter. Adopting teenagers or adults into your family was much more common then; it was a way to make important alliances, and ensuring loyalty. Today we take it for granted that women take their husband's names. This used to be the case only in England, where a husband legally had all his wife's property. In the rest of Europe, and Scotland too, a woman kept her father's name, and could still own property after marriage.

The English practice spread to Scotland and then with colonists to North America and Australia. By 1800 the English style was fashionable in Europe too, and it spread still further, till now the peculiar legal habits of a tiny island have affected women's names across much of the world.

[44] The battle at the end of the world according to Viking mythology.

[45] Under Icelandic law it was no crime to kill someone in a legal challenge, but if you killed them without that – or after sunset or took them by surprise – it was murder.